Off To The Next Wherever

Stories

John Michael Flynn

Fomite

Burlington, VT

ISBN-13: 978-1-942515-15-9
Library of Congress Control Number: 2015947752

Fomite
58 Peru Street
Burlington, VT 05401
www.fomitepress.com

Author photograph by Alexander Lugovskoy

Cover painting
Midnight
   2014, acrylic, graphite, dry pigment, glitter on Arches paper
   14.25" x 10.25"
Artist: Mary Tomasso, MFA
Website: tomasso.smugmug.com

For Dad

&

Angelica

*You've wandered all over and finally realized that
you never found what you were after; how to live.*
Marcus Aurelius

A stone is a better pillow than many visions.
Robinson Jeffers

Acknowledgements

These stories appeared, in some cases in slightly different forms, in the following print and online publications:

"The Four-Cent Tip" in *Quiddity*, and in *Voyages: An Eden Waters Press Anthology*;

"Heavy Up The Lines" in *The MacGuffin*;

"Blow Out All The Candles" in *Green Hills Literary Lantern*;

"Each Bumpy Spiral In Its Cone" in *Vermont Literary Review*;

"Lady Mist" in *Fat City*;

"Boss Visa" in *Istanbul Literary Review*, and in *A Small Key Opens Big Doors: An Anthology*;

"Geezerville Without A Cadillac" in *The Circle Review*;

"Albino Elephants" in *Conjectural Figments*;

"Rowing The Beach To Shore" and "All We Have" in *Blue Lake Review*;

"Jolene, Jolene" in *Dead Mule School of Southern Literature*;

"The Flora Sandwich" in *Rock Bottom Journal*;

"Wanderer Overlooking The Sea Of Fog" in *The Literary Yard*;

"You Remind Me Of A Naughty Springtime Cuckoo" in *Iconoclast*;

"Apron And Shawl And Housedress: in *Superstition Review*;

"Forge A Tomorrow" in *Paper Tape*.

Contents

Rowing The Beach To Shore

About a mile from home, Opal starts talking money. I ask her in my best diplomatic tone to change the subject. She switches to her Dad, who may be a goner before summer's end. I'm fond of the old buck and I'll miss him the way I miss my own late father, but I don't want to talk about him, either.

Then out with it, says Opal. Before you have a coronary.

There's this guy at work. He's just a kid. I asked him to do something, you know, just to help me out with some orders, and know what he said?

What?

He said he wasn't my bitch.

Opal's been listening while trying to wipe suntan oil down her calves, but there's not enough room.

So?

So I'm the assistant manager. His supervisor.

Then fire him.

I can't.

Then talk to Warren. He still in charge?

He is and I did.

And?

And what? For some reason, he likes this kid. I spelled the whole thing out for him and he said it was okay.

Opal studies me as I drive. I get the feeling she feels sorry for me, but I don't know why. I never know. The smell of lotion blooms, Opal's oily fingerprints covering the dash.

Everything is, she says.

What's that supposed to mean?

Opal shakes her head no.

But you told me to get it out.

So it's out. Let it go.

I'm sick of myself.

You like ranting, too, don't tell me you don't.

But he's gonna feel it one day.

Who? Warren?

No. That kid. Same emptiness I feel. He's gonna wonder why nobody prepared him for it.

You didn't listen, either.

But that attitude. I just don't get it.

He's not stupid.

Neither am I.

C'mon. He knows he's being lied to. Just like we do.

Right. Okay. It's all lies.

Maybe it is.

So I'll forget about it. I'll decompress.

Maybe you should.

Don't want to blow a valve.

Maybe you don't.

We're at a red light. I close my eyes and breathe through my nose, thinking there's too much tension, let it out, stop dragging Opal into a misery she doesn't deserve. She's the one with thick skin who understands this is how days and marriages go — with their checks and balances. I ask myself why I've been so touchy of late. Every little wrinkle drives a bug up my ass.

The light green, I drive not really seeing the road, letting it pull me along. When younger, dumb enough not to fear cops, I'd light up a joint during such jaunts to the beach. I long for those care-free days, but scowl at myself knowing I'm old by my drug-days standards and have no clue as to where I'd find weed. Nowadays, nothing may shock, but there's a camera at each intersection, and at least one joker on a cellphone at every public urinal. Few know how to relax. Myself included.

My 12-year-old Honda runs 20 miles faster than the limit and it's still unable to keep pace with traffic. A wasteland of sickly trees lines the road on both sides. A smokestack, black at its tip, stands like a burnt wooden matchstick. All so ugly. Better to shut down, see nothing, hear nothing. Take me under, drown me, should have used myself up when I was too young to know any better.

At the beach parking lot, I groan out of the car cranky and stiff, a more common physical state than I care to admit. I bend at the knees, pushing out my arms, stretching my legs.

Up, down. Up, down.

Will you stop!

Embarrassing you?

Opal shoves her canvas bag into my arms.

You embarrass yourself.

Right. I want to gripe about why she's packed so much stuff. I don't. I've griped enough. Her workday was as trying, if not worse, than my own. This is our chance to salvage calm, to renew ourselves. Tomorrow's another slog at the pump. She'll scrape plaque, and I'll fill delivery orders. Somebody will yell at us over a protocol indiscretion.

We gotta live for the moment.

Whatever.

I hike her canvas bag over my shoulder; ask her what's in here, anyway?

She's in sandals and remains a consoling presence at my side, her long legs pale and fine. She runs a hand over my hip and tugs on the rear pocket of my shorts.

Essentials.

I shrug, falling into a slackened beach mode. Insistent and hazy, late sunshine brings a welcomed sweat. I start feeling balmy as I imagine the ocean against my skin.

You know something. If I get frustrated on the job, it's because I care. Not because I'm impatient. But I gotta tell you I'm not paid enough to care.

No, neither am I.

I look at her. She's aged during our ten years of marriage, but she's still comely. I feel the percolations of a carnal urge to ferry her off to the dunes. It gives me no pleasure to think that there was a time when such spontaneous eruptions were never out of the question.

Give me a minute, she says.

Whatever you need.

I smile at her as she wipes lotion down her legs. I want to kiss her knees, to nibble on them. I want blissful release.

But stop staring at me like I'm fresh meat. You're making me uncomfortable.

Since when?

There are other people around.

There are?

Don't you care what they think?

I look around. There's no one in sight. I grin back, getting her sarcasm. A breeze kicks up, one of those benign seaside bursts. A soothing hand for both of us that takes us in and lets us disappear.

Boss Visa

For no apparent reason, the train stopped and soldiers began checking compartments. It was 8 a.m., August 1994. Gabriella, a Moldovan-born English professor, had joined me for a two-week vacation in Moscow and Saint Petersburg to celebrate my 34th birthday and my first train ride out of Moldova in a year.

We taught at the State University Alec Russo in Bălți, an industrial city of 250,000 known for its cognac factories. Feeling exhausted but gratified, we'd boarded the train in Saint Petersburg, destination Chisinau, Moldova's capital. This required two days of travel, with border crossings through Byelorussia, the Ukraine, and into Moldova. We'd weathered delays, track changes, long lines, and were running nearly a day behind schedule. Not bad by Soviet meltdown standards.

Perhaps the Ukrainian soldier sensed that Gabriella and I were in love because a look of anguish reddened his features. A willowy blond with watery gray-blue eyes, he studied my passport with such curiosity that I had to assume he'd never faced an American.

I'd bribed, danced the *hora*, and polluted myself with vodka and wine in consort with apparatchiks, ex-KGB operatives, train conductors, gypsies, cops, retired Ministry officials, students, teachers and soldiers alike. Though armed and in uniform, this boy reeked of virginity. He told me I'd have to get off the train because my three-day Ukrainian transit visa had expired during the night.

Gabriella protested that no one had said a word at the borders of Russia and Byelorussia. She explained that we were colleagues, and I worked through a program new to the former USSR, funded by the U.S. government. As a volunteer, I received no pay for teaching. By mid-August, we both had to return to work.

Earnest, solemn, perhaps a little drunk on power, the soldier insisted nothing could be done.

In Byelorussia, I'd bribed a conductor $15 bucks so Gabriella and I could have a bunk where we'd made love as the stars rolled past our window. I considered bribing this soldier when another one appeared, just as young. After a year of greasing palms, I'd learned it was impossible to do so once a second authority figure appeared. Gabriella began to cry, begging them to reconsider.

As she pleaded our case, both soldiers appeared to respect her fine Russian diction (she'd been raised on military bases in Siberia). This didn't stop them, however, from shoving me down the aisle and out the train's open door.

Cellphones, laptops and Internet connections existed in rare quantities, even among Moscow's elite. I'd asked Gabriella to contact the Peace Corps office in Chisinau if she didn't hear from me during the next two days. I had no idea how I'd get in touch with her, but I'd worry about that later.

Watching the train roll out of sight, I heard the echo of her tears in all their sincerity. I felt paralyzed and dizzy with anger. Not about my fate, but hers. How could those boys have done that to a woman so lovely and one of their own? It was another example of the cruelty I'd seen Soviet citizens inflict on each other, and I assumed it came out of frustration.

I inventoried what I had: some Moldovan coupons, my passport, a plastic sack that held short pants and a T-shirt, and $60 dollars' worth of crisp new greenbacks. Nobody accepted bills that were creased, torn, stained, or more than five years old.

Making my way to a small square building where a dog slept out front next to a bench, I gauged the horizon, saw no trees and wished I'd brought a hat. I dawdled near hollyhocks that stood as tall as the building and scented the air. No breezes stirred.

Behind the building, I found an adjoining room made of limestone blocks. Its two window openings without glass, its door squeaking, I entered and addressed a pair of uniformed soldiers. One remained seated, indifferent, a cigarette glued to his lower lip as he played a hand-held computer game that sounded little blips. The oldest one, fair-skinned with a mustache and an orangeade tint to his short hair, faced me across a desk and asked for my passport. Not thinking, I handed it over.

He tried to speak English, blanching when I told him in Russian (Gabriella had been my teacher and that's how we'd met) that I spoke his language.

He asked my nationality. I told him American.

"No." He scowled at me. This was his game, not mine. "Your *nationality*."

I held my ground and repeated myself.

Sounding angry, he insisted that American was a form of citizenship, a system, not a nationality. I disagreed but kept my lips sealed as I watched him take a form out of his desk, instructing I read and sign it. It stated I had no translator and lacked a correct transit visa. I could have my passport if I signed. I did so.

He didn't return my passport.

A new pair of soldiers arrived and the old pair left. The new supervisor could have doubled for the old one, except he wore no mustache. A crystalline glint hardened his hazel eyes. His wingman didn't play computer games; he held a Kalashnikov in two hands and kept it pointed at me.

Grabbing a fly swatter off the desk, slapping it against his thigh, the supervisor circled me as I pickled in my own juices. He asked if I wanted to hear a joke. Why not? He shared it in a vivid style, rife with details and I was careful to laugh even when I didn't grasp the humor. I kept a wary eye on the Kalashnikov. Twice in my life I'd had a gun pointed at me. I relied on a trick I'd used in both cases. Biting my lower lip, I breathed through my nose and imagined a smooth lake at sunrise.

He filed my passport into his shirt pocket. Trains to Kiev would pass through, but he couldn't say when, probably late at night. Nobody knew anything anymore. Only God knew. He leered at me and suggested I relax in front of the building. Eventually, I could get to Kiev and buy a transit visa there. Trying not to sulk, I told him I lacked enough money to pay for a night in Kiev, a transit visa and a train ticket to Chisinau.

He shrugged and ordered me out of his building.

I wandered down the railroad tracks for a while, found a bottle and smashed the anger out of my system. I looked around. The horizon made me feel puny. The tracks angled off into a haze of heat ripples. Much of the land had been tilled, stretching like sun-scorched rhino hide and motionless in every direction.

While I hiked back to the building, I decided to ask for permission to board a train to Odessa rather than Kiev. I'd be closer to Chisinau, about three hours away. The ticket would be cheaper, perhaps leaving me enough to afford a visa.

With the sun at its noon peak, the building an oven (nothing was air conditioned or refrigerated in this part of the world), the supervisor's face gleamed with sweat. He seemed impressed as he smoked a cigarette, pondering my suggestion. I asked if Odessa had an airport. Could I buy a transit visa there? He said maybe. I should wait out front. He'd make a call. His man with the Kalashnikov led me out.

I had the sun to measure time by. About an hour later, the Kalashnikov poking my ribs, I was ushered back and granted permission to ride to Odessa, but had to wait until 5 p.m. He asked if I'd exchange five American dollars for 150,000 Ukrainian coupons. I said I had no idea if that was a fair rate. Toying with me, he joked that as an American I surely missed toilet paper and wouldn't all those coupons come in handy? This brought sniveling laughter from his sidekick. Then he chased me out.

At the front of the building, under a sign that read KACCA, my spirits rose when I saw through the ticket window a woman seated behind her desk. She wore the customary Soviet blue. I tried to get her attention, but she ignored me.

A railroad man appeared. Paunchy, with the bulbous nose of a drinker, he wore a bright orange vest. I asked if I could buy a ticket to Odessa. He shrugged and walked away, mumbling, "It's your problem, not mine."

The dog still lay asleep. My forehead baked. I sat on the bench and napped, hour by hour more thirsty. As five o'clock neared, the sun began to cool and there arrived two skinny boys with primitive fishing gear, followed by an old man with a girl, perhaps his granddaughter. They stood in line at the window as if this were proper etiquette. The old man got the woman's attention. She shouted, "Go away."

More villagers had gathered, true peasants, looking as if they'd emerged hunched over from long hibernation in the earth. Their faces wretched with road grime and sweat, their backs bent, many no doubt had walked a great distance to meet their train. Two stout women in wool skirts and beat-up slippers, their opaque nylons and long-sleeved sweaters over legs and arms like thick beams, gripped in their red hands one corner of a burlap sack of potatoes and onions. They lugged it between them one slow step at a time. They wore bright yellow and orange kerchiefs on their heads, their faces seared a dusty crimson, their eyes a bit mean. Over their shoulders hung gym bags. As they put them down, I saw the bags were packed full of loaves of bread, jars of homemade sour cream, and tubes of kielbasa.

They dropped the big burlap sack on the platform and sat on it. Their backs to each other, hands on their knees, scars and scabs in plain view, they sighed and lolled about on their heavy bottoms. They ripped hunks from one loaf of bread, using a knife to carve kielbasa and onion. Looking annoyed by heat, flies and mosquitoes, they chewed ever so pensively with their black teeth. How they sweated, drinking now and then from an unlabeled bottle that experience assured me was full of moonshine. The Ukrainians called it *gorilka*, the Russians called it *samogon*, and the Moldovans called it *rachiu*.

I'd been treated to them all, distilled from ingredients that ranged from rotten apricots to apple cores, lengths of wood and strips of leather. In the words of poet Andrei Codrescu: "Drinking is a Russian religion with a complex metaphysic."

At quarter to five the ticket window opened, a line formed and I waited my turn. I explained everything to the woman. She refused to help me without my passport, so I ran back to the soldiers. I interrupted their session with a bottle of vodka, a loaf of bread and a raw onion. The supervisor looked annoyed. He said no ticket, no passport.

I ran back to the window. A sleek long-distance train had arrived from Russia, olive green with lots of cars and sleeper compartments and a red star fixed to the locomotive's nose. "No," said the woman. "Get your passport."

Hurrying back to the soldiers, desperate now, I begged for my passport. They scowled at me as if despising any show of weakness. Teeth clenched, I waited, watching them each down 100 grams of vodka from the same glass.

At last, bleary-eyed and looking bored, the supervisor flung my passport out a window. He laughed as I chased after it.

I ran to the ticket woman, who took my money. All other passengers had already boarded. The train had slowed but hadn't really stopped. The woman shoved the money back at me, crying, "Go, go, go."

I was too late. Doors had closed. The train rolled and I ran alongside, yelling "Stop" until sweat stung my eyes and I gave up.

* * * * * * * * * * *

Runnels of sweat snaked down my back as I stumbled on inspired by the sight of a smokestack on the horizon. Goats munched grasses along the road. I cursed myself for leaving my knife and matches with Gabriella. I smiled at the sight of a motorcycle with a sidecar, its headlight on, the woman behind her man, both hands around his waist as they bounced toward a sliver of scarlet that lit the horizon.

I kept a dogged, sputtering pace. Passing a woman with a young girl, my voice brittle and cracking, I asked if Moldova was far and whether a town was nearby. Startled by my accent, she pulled the girl close to her skirt. I asked about a bus or train, but she refused to answer.

Slapping at mosquitoes, walking on, I felt soothed by the amber twilight that settled over the earth. Dank evening air cooled my burning face. I turned right at an intersection and headed down a tree-lined dirt road fragrant with leaves. I came to limestone block walls and the rusting paint of the hammer and sickle insignia that centered an arch over a gated entrance chained up for the night. I heard dogs barking. My pace grew brisk. I kept to the road until reaching a sign for Mardarovka, 10 Kilometers.

Chickens clucked in matted chicory and fragrant onion grass. Houses appeared, their high steel fences painted green or blue, trimmed in white, gates shut, each a self-contained compound with fruit-bearing trees, a corn crib and a pungent barnyard aroma.

A trio of teenage boys, each in sandals, T-shirt and polyester sweatpants, sized me up. I hurried past them. One I would talk to, but not three.

A dog chased me, growling out of the dark. I sprinted away until nearly running over a burly peasant woman. After dodging me, she picked up a rock and heaved it at the dog, nailing it on the snout. Then she whacked it with a big stick until it scooted off.

Winded, a bit stunned, I thanked her. I asked if there was a train station nearby. She grinned with a whiff of malice tainted by alcohol, showing a jacket of gold teeth. Then she began raving in a slangy Ukrainian that I didn't understand.

Around midnight, I found a train station and a startling amount of activity. I used a dollar to buy six bottles of water and some large confections of baked dough and white cheese that the Moldovans call *placinta*. What did the Ukrainians call them?

Bread and water had never tasted better. I drank three bottles, *Arcașul* brand, which was Moldovan and meant I was getting closer. I couldn't find a public phone. I learned there used to be a bus to Chisinau, but like everything else it couldn't be relied on. Yes, I was still far from the Moldovan border. My best bet was a train coming from Moscow through to Odessa.

My spirits lifting, I sat in the grass in front of the station and listened to The Scorpions sing "Winds of Change." One of Gabriella's favorites, this was an anthem for the Perestroika generation that played from a kiosk where villagers could buy cigarettes, Snickers bars, vodka and homemade cassettes.

Ace of Base was singing "Happy Nation" when the Odessa train arrived. I bribed a female conductor with a five-dollar bill. She gasped in delight and led me to a berth I had to share with two older men who argued that it was their berth; they'd paid good money for it. The conductor ignored them.

My sneakers off, I climbed up into a bunk and passed out. Neither man looked happy when they saw my filthy socks and bleeding feet.

* * * * *   * * * * * *

I arrived at two a.m. to a bustling Odessa. Briny air cleansed by an occasional breeze off the Black Sea hugged my skin. I walked sidewalks heaved, sunken, pitted and dusty, a faint whiff of the sewer about them. In Lenin Square I found a park and under a row of plane trees slept on a bench until a flashlight beam awakened me and two uniformed cops asked for my passport. They looked it over and explained I couldn't sleep there but could join others in the train station where it was safer.

Leaving those cops, I felt grateful as I returned to the station and sat on its granite steps, joining many others, some waiting for rides, some loitering. I watched the streaming of traffic, most of it taxis circling a rotary that was home to an outdoor café called Arena, with sea-blue lights around a water fountain and a disco glitter ball that peppered nearby buildings, trees and dozens of white plastic café tables and chairs where young new Russians drank under Pepsi, Coke, and Camel cigarette umbrellas.

As the song "Lady In Red" filled the night sky, a woman approached and asked if I needed an apartment. Her eyes lit up as I explained my situation. She knew a place where for a hundred in American cash I could sleep on the floor.

A crew of sidewalk sweepers appeared, most of them large humorless old women in kerchiefs and blue smocks. Some barefoot, some in slippers, each worked stooped over short-handled brooms that looked like thorn bushes. They kicked up enough dirt to scare off a mob about thirty strong that abandoned those steps for a side entrance to the station.

Like many Soviet public buildings, the train station was massive but old enough to evoke Odessa's international past with its mix of Italian and French architecture, four polished marble staircases and a high domed ceiling. From the top of the centrally located staircase, a monolithic statue of Lenin looked down upon those who entered. In this case, a wee-hour army of drunks, homeless beggars, cripples and seasoned drifters carrying sheets of cardboard to sleep on.

I watched them quickly turn the station into a dormitory as they occupied each inch of floor space. I had to step around their bodies, some of them already snoring, until I found a spot at the base of the Lenin statue. I slept that first night shivering through vile dreams, both hands clutching my passport.

In the morning, I stumbled into the white gold of sunrise and it occurred to me that no one on the planet knew my whereabouts. I could stay here, create a new identity and start my life over. It was a Sunday. Winsome, fearless — what did I have to lose?

I wandered in awe of Odessa's diverse architecture, her lanes and boulevards and views of the Black Sea. I walked mile after mile, at times disturbed by the number and condition of beggars and amputees. I changed dollars into coupons, keeping my money hidden at all times. I learned there was no train to the airport, only one bus. A cab would cost me $100,000 coupons.

For one coupon, I bought a loaf of bread and two-dozen plums, toting them in my sack. When I bought water, I downed the whole bottle, leaving the empty for a beggar.

Blisters throbbed, bleeding through my socks, yet I liked the aimless drift in sunshine, energized by throngs of beachgoers. I worried about not having enough cash to pay for a visa and tried not to dwell on it as I slummed through outdoor markets and rode crowded buses and trolleys. I learned from a cabbie whose taxi was a converted ambulance that I could find an international phone at the airport.

It was noon when I took a bus there, a two-hour wait for a half-hour ride. I'd need to wait two days before the visa issuing office opened. I phoned Gabriella. Our connection lasted about a minute before getting cut. I'd had to shout, but at least she knew I was safe. After walking back to the train station, a three-hour hike, I decided to bathe in the Black Sea.

Though I found the beach surprisingly litter free and ascribed it to a culture that had yet to adopt ridiculous amounts of packaging, it was too crowded for my American need for personal space. Naked boys and girls peed at water's edge. Far too many dogs paddled to masters, some of them quite plump for their Speedos.

I swam in my underwear, scouring off the road grime without guilt, and no one even bothered to take a second glance. Then I napped blissfully on hot grayish sand, relieved that none of my belongings had been stolen.

On my way to the train station, I found a length of cardboard to my liking. While sleeping a second night, a cop kicked me in the ribs and asked what the hell I was doing there. Taking my cue from the other drifters, I didn't tell him. I got up and walked away. He didn't care. He just kicked another set of ribs and asked the same question.

On Tuesday, the visa office was supposed to open at 11, so I showed up around ten expecting a wait. I sat with two Syrian men, both of them striking in handsome suits. I began speaking to them in Russian and they looked stunned when they learned where I was from. Neither had ever met an American.

I chatted and they listened politely. They didn't smile, but seemed genuinely entertained as I told them my story. Three hours later, a cherubic officer in uniform arrived with a brown-bag lunch and a bottle of vodka. He happily took my $15 dollars and stamped my passport.

The next morning, I clawed my way on board a local diesel bound for Chisinau. Out of the mob of passengers, some had crawled through windows to get in. I was likely the only one who'd bothered to buy a ticket for this short-distance turtle. Those lucky enough to sit, did so on wooden benches.

When my passport was asked for, I thought twice before handing it over. It was returned without comment. I stood most of the way, squeezed between other passengers, all of us sweat-soaked, smelly and miserable. I didn't care. I amused myself by thinking of different ways to tell this story. I'd use hyperbole, an audacious style, starting with: *There I was, alone in the middle of nowhere, Gabriella's tears weighing on my heart....*

Forge a Tomorrow

That last night. That last counterpunch with a sneer toward death. And life. All so unreal and he a ghost somewhere between those that conformed and those that fought while wired on dex, meth and Jack Daniels. That night he and Terry and Neil snaked the back roads of Mecklenburg County at high speeds — was there any other way? Neil said he was just one more black man nobody cared about and it was the same for his brother, Charles, who had been killed on his Harley outside of Hampton Roads. That last night — he and Terry together. Now gone. All of it gone.

Terry, like him, was a mixed-breed, but he had Osage blood. Mason's own native lines ran Chickasaw and some Choctaw, or so he'd been told. Nobody in his family — if he could call it that — really knew.

Last he heard, Terry was living somewhere near Tulsa. Terry the skunk, who had dared him to rob that jewelry store, said he had planned it out. A sure thing. Those were Terry's words, and three of the filthiest ones Mason had ever heard anyone use in the English language.

He didn't hate Terry for it. Hated himself for giving in to Terry's pitch, screwing up, getting busted again. No, wrong. He despised Terry. When it had gone bad, Terry had disappeared. Later on, Terry hadn't spent a minute to visit him in lock-up. Nor had Terry helped him to make bail or pay a lawyer. Mason had used his one phone call to tell Starr, his sister, that he'd been printed and charged again. They'd hold him in county and that was all he knew.

Hadn't known much, had he?

We'll get you out, Honeybunch. We'll help you.

Sweet-talk from Starr. Sounded like his Mama. He couldn't hate that, either, not as much as he hated the idea that Starr and Mama had done their best to love him. Not like his old man — whoever he was.

All the others talked too much. Neil Pierre was the only quiet one. Only wise one. Neil was a thinker on a spirit quest. Hard to believe he was dead of an overdose on meth. Neil was always testing limits. Neil his brother, his father figure, the gaping hole that ached each night in Mason's side.

Starr was in California now, married a third time. Why did she bother? Her third husband was from Argentina, had a little money and must have known he had someone exotic in Starr with her African blood mixed with God knew what else.

We all suffer, that's why I refuse to bring a child into this world without a Daddy.

Starr. His only sister. Same mother but different father. Maybe. Nobody knew. Nobody cared except him, rotting in stir, with time to think about it. In the end, Starr had done nothing. Neither had

Mama. But she was gone, too, and on hopeful nights Mason liked to think that Mama and Neil were together, part of a spirit union, guiding those who needed love and wisdom. On bad nights, he thought of them both as dead too soon, their lives wasted.

Starr was the only kin he had left. Like he'd never happened. Like he shouldn't have been born. Just like Neil. And that's what they shared. A couple of lost fearless souls.

Seeing Neil in his dreams, Mason often counted the pieces of his friend's body; the little rags of flesh that the cops had found hanging from bushes and tree limbs along a fifty-foot stretch of road. Neil had survived that accident, had lost an arm, had never ridden again. Swollen on beer, running a gas station, constantly seething on meth, he'd lasted two years in a state of miserable juiced-up limbo.

All the partying together that should have brought release. But it didn't. They slept it off and kept on partying. Now he wanted those nights back when he awoke wild-eyed and ready and stayed that way, the way he was supposed to be, speeding east to the shoreline and finding girls, one for each of them. They'd get high watching the surf under moonlight, rolled into blankets, paired off. Sometimes at dawn a cop would threaten to arrest them if they didn't get moving. Mason couldn't remember a time when Terry didn't mouth off at a cop. Yet he got away with it. Had to be his high yellow tone and his good teeth.

Neil never mouthed off. He was darkest of all of them. Something smart and cunning about Neil always kept cops at ease. He and Neil went back to high school, never finished, both joined the Army and Neil made it through and served in Germany, but not him. No. They'd arrested him for possession his first week of leave after he'd finished Basic.

Back in riding days, he and Neil would devour breakfast in their jeans and then go hunting for sluts with long hair and a licorice-sweet smell to their underwear. White girls that liked whiskey and weed and knew how to hide money, shoot a rifle and change a flat tire. Under the blast of a new day, he and Neil would roll to a beachfront hideaway. They'd lie in the shade dazed, maybe even swim, not wanting to talk until they decided to wheel to the next wherever. Sometimes, it was a friend's place, or a bar, music, a garage and fixing bikes, or trouble — a dealer, some whores, a card game they'd heard about. They just kept it going somehow, sleeping in their clothes much of the time. When money ran low, they'd call Neil's old friend Jackson in Newport News and he'd hook them up with errands and drops, and pay them in cash or dope — whichever they wanted. When things ran dry, they'd get into some stealing or pimping or even day labor to keep cash-flow going in both directions.

Mason grinned as he remembered one job and how he'd lucked out and scored over twenty-grand from a safe in the back-room of a used car dealership near Virginia Beach. Lived on it and fed himself good. Met a red-head with a body that wouldn't quit, called herself Lu but that wasn't her real name, said she was from Corpus Christi and the daughter of a Navy captain — probably lies, but those had been sweet healing times with Lu and she'd kept him out of stir and in a real job in a road construction crew for nearly three years in the sun and he'd been strong and honest, for a change. As if to say: Lookit, it's me, Mason, I can do this straight thing. I'm nobody's donkey-slime.

Lu didn't want him running off with Terry, but he tried to explain that he got bored easy. God-damned dumber than a fence post is what he was. After he left her and got busted, Lu — wherever she was — wanted nothing to do with him. Nobody did. There had only been Neil and he was a prayer now.

***** ******

The time had come.

Mason ginned up a fake smile for the lawyer. The guards were there. A starchy administrator in a suit. Mason didn't like or trust these cogs, their faces as they loomed in front of him like those gone timeless years, one falling and rising after another in a foggy deranged roll. He closed his eyes a moment. At high speed on open road he was in that dream again, the one he kept having where he told everyone he was getting out, and nothing less would do than white lines under the new bike he was going to build with all the money he was going to make. In the dream, every face he saw — from Starr's to Lu's to Mama's — was big and cartoonish and asking him: But how you gonna do it?

I'll figure it out. I always do.

Starr had said she'd hold his bike for him, but she'd sold it. He owed her, so she'd taken the coin she had coming. He'd have done the same.

He'd once known so much, cared so little. Now? Nothing. A by-product of the institution. Law and order. These cog faces? They spoke of conquest and the red-clay ditches that lined the roads of gated communities, littered with the corpses of failed renegades like him.

Lu liked to say he was no failure and that it wasn't a racial thing — he needed to be more sure of himself. Oh, he was sure, all right. Sure that he looked old for his real age, had a knack for winning fights, bets and games of blackjack. If there was a party, he'd find it. He had plans. He'd speed along forever ignoring death. One trip to the next, but as Neil had told him: Nobody crossed the great spirit and got away with it for long.

Terry, too, had figured this out. He'd known when to bolt and start fresh, leaving so-called blood-brother Mason high and dry. Didn't matter now. All part of his unreal life. The life inside. It had a future and a past that tried to flow but mostly they just collided with the walls around his present state, his perpetual confinement.

Did this lawyer in front of him with the dark hair, the phone, and the thousand-dollar rock on one finger think she had a say in it? Mason scowled as he looked up at her seated across from him at the table. She was most likely Legal Aid. Clean and ambitious. A nobody trying to make her name. She was on the ample side, the way he liked his women, and she wore a dark-blue suit, filled it out nicely. She carried files, a leather bag, a laptop; she was Latina, maybe. Mason couldn't pronounce her name when she shared it. Didn't care. Who where these legalese people? Why did they bother him?

She started with questions. Mason shrugged, craving a cigarette, thinking: All the dark time stays dark.

"If you don't talk, how can we expect me to help you?" she asked.

I don't.

Didn't she know he was through, part of the system, a stone in one big boot stomping down the avenues of prosperity that powered each gear in the machine? The charges against him, his record — these were not real any longer. The real was the unreal, what lived on inside.

His first mistake was that he'd been born. Yet he was a minor infraction compared to the freaks he met on the inside and tried to avoid.

She was talking to him about the crossing of state lines — trafficking — the worst of his convictions. There'd been weapons involved in the jewelry store screw-up. There'd been earlier convictions. Shoplifting, burglaries, vagrancy, counts of B and E, drunk and disorderly, assault and battery. There'd been other cesspools where he'd served time. All of this put him in a category.

Would he get parole? She didn't say jack about that.

If he got out, he might just bring his anger back to life, find Terry, saw off his nuts with barbed wire and stuff 'em down his throat. Meat for the county lock-up, that's all he was. A burden to taxpayers. He'd taken his doses, cooled off, lost swagger, found it, lost it again. But he wouldn't get parole or a suspended sentence. They'd let him rot for at least another nickel, maybe more.

The lawyer said something about a deal in the works, about good behavior, crowded prisons, state funding. Maybe there was hope.

Big maybe.

The lawyer and the administrator talked more to each other than they did to him. It was, as always, as if he didn't understand, wasn't smart enough. He'd read books in prison. Hadn't wised up. Hadn't converted to Islam, either, and he'd grown fat on starchy food, but he'd never been what they saw him as — one more big dumb shadow in the shadows.

No point in hope. Not like he wasn't guilty. If he went to California, Starr wouldn't take him in. She had her own habits to feed. Not to mention her Argentine husband.

The lawyer sighed, remarking that her time was up. She admitted to Mason he should have been up for a hearing months ago and they were working on that. Some record-keeping issues, a computer glitch, a backlog, she wasn't sure.

She didn't sound convincing. "I'll see what I can do."

She had to leave. A busy woman, she and other paper-pushers had more walking corpses to see. He liked watching her bottom when she passed through the open doors and moved down the corridor, her heels clicking as a guard on each side acted as her escorts. Another guard led Mason back to his cell as if he didn't know the way.

No, he couldn't have a cigarette.

That night, he remembered the lawyer's ass in motion, but he couldn't summon strength to pleasure himself. He lay there and listened to his breathing and wondered why he never cried.

Heavy Up The Lines

Careers, well, most back into and out of 'em, like in that old western when Joel McCrea tells his gal he couldn't decide between being a pirate or a fireman, so he wound up in engineering.

I did the same.

See, after I got out of the Air Force, not really knowing what I wanted, I drove a hack to and from Logan Airport and figured that would get old fast, which it did. I went to school nights at Harvard and got my GED. Not *the* Harvard, of course, we were never lace curtain enough for that, but a night school on their campus which was fine with me since by that time in my life, all of 22, I'd seen some of Africa, a lot of Europe, Corsica, Alaska, Iceland, Hawaii, Greenland and about 36 of the lower 48. I had no patience for the shenanigans of undergrads. If anything, I was too serious for my own good.

Someone told me civil engineering was the right field to be in. It sounded like easy street. I started classes three nights a week at Northeastern. Quit driving a hack and nailed down a job at Foster and Wheeler on the third floor of an old building on Huntington Ave, near Symphony Hall, with a bowling alley at street level.

Walter, my cousin Penny's husband, got me in. He was an electrical engineer and I told him I could handle school full-time and a Texas-sized work week. I didn't beg old Walter. I showed him respect, and for some reason he liked me. I explained that I wanted to do the work I was studying, that I couldn't just learn it from books, so he talked to someone and then told me to go see him — I can't recall the man's name now. Walter sensed I meant business, and I think the man at Foster and Wheeler did, too.

All it takes is one meeting, one connection, and if you're prepared it may lead to opportunities. Networking is a profession for some. Looking back, time and again, those networks, one falling into the next, are what made my life. They'll make yours, too, you'll see.

Six days I rode the trackless trolley from Roslindale through Forest Hills and got off at the Symphony or the Huntington stop. All my Saturday hours meant overtime, and I needed it since I was dating your Ma at the time and helping to support my family. At Foster and Wheeler we were drawing the foundations for oil refineries in Venezuela that were owned by Caracas Oil, Standard Oil, and Esso. Caracas Oil is Citgo now, pretty much the baby of Hugo Chavez. Standard bought Gulf and became Chevron, and Esso became Exxon. They were all men working there, hard-nosed, quick-drinking sometimes foul-mouthed but dedicated to their work. At the time, few of them were concerned with the politics of oil. Least of all me, a tenderfoot, and I could hear from my drafting table the typewriters from the second floor, and bowling balls crashing into pins on the first. That place was not only noisy but thick with cigarette smoke.

As I recall, the light wasn't very good either. No wonder so many complained of migraines and had to down a shot or two at the corner tap after punching out.

* * * * *   * * * * * *

Picture these big men seated on stools, or standing over boards that were tilted up at an angle. We worked under saucers of light that hung low off a cord, like you see in old pool halls, the rays of light layered with smoke, each man puffing as he drew all day long, non-stop, slurping on coffee, taking a half hour for lunch. We went through scores of pencils and markers, and when you didn't hear graphite scratching against paper, you heard a manual sharpener getting cranked, and I was often the guilty party. I'd sharpen fifty pencils at a time and distribute them into cans next to each board.

Today, CAD software does all that work. Maybe it's leading to a better product and more efficiency, I don't know. Computers are faster, but like all machines they put a percentage of the able-bodied out of commission, and I doubt they make for finer looking buildings. You've seen the housing developments and strip malls they throw up. No soul. No love. No inspired design. Just a bottom-line approach.

Sad, really. I remember a while back how Prince Charles of England complained about this, but nobody listened.

* * * * *   * * * * * *

After work, I'd ride the green line with my big black case, what they called a flat. It had two snaps at the top, and I kept my pencils in there, my sheets of vellum, tracing paper, rulers, compass, templates, erasers, and my T-square. I'd bury the T-square's rounded edge in the bottom corner and still it would be too long, so I'd run its end out of the top at a diagonal, and no matter how careful I was its sharp edges would always nick a commuter. Embarrassed, I'd have to apologize. I'd find my way to a seat hoping I wouldn't tear an eye out with that thing. My board was heavy, too, not to mention my book bag, because three nights a week I headed straight from work into classes.

When I was drawing these foundations for oil rigs, I had a supervisor, can't remember his name, he smoked one of those small cigars, always had it in his mouth. Heavyset, he wore blue suspenders and black shoes, what they called Brogans, same outfit every day. He'd mosey between us hunched over our boards and have himself a look-see. If he hated what you were doing, he'd flick ashes from his little stogie onto your drawing and say not a word. I came to learn what that meant. If he did it often enough, you were kindly asked to not come back. Nothing was negotiable.

Me, I was pretty good. But my super, when he did speak, was always barking, "Heavy up the lines, Shea. Heavy up the lines."

At first, I didn't know what the B-Jesus he meant, but one night after work, unwinding in the bowling alley downstairs, I asked one of the fellows. The company sponsored a team in a league, and I'd joined up and bowled a few strings every night when I didn't have classes. I shot some pool, too. I was a streetwise kid, not really book smart and with plenty to learn, and that night I got a lecture about how the phrase heavy up the lines meant I had to draw them darker, which in that era meant going over the lines at least ten times with a pencil. I had to keep that pencil sharp and the line steady. No easy task. I'd blow a blizzard of graphite and eraser dust off the page. Like the others, I was always grimy with graphite, sweat and pencil shavings, my butt sore from hours on a hard stool, my back stiff, my throat parched from two packs a day.

We all craved our nicotine, it kept us going, and nobody thought much about it.

* * * * *   * * * * * *

A fellow they called Thirty Long — don't know where the name came from, suit size maybe — had eyes like ice cubes in a glass of gin. He was my favorite. He'd sit with an elbow on his raised board, a fist against his cheek, leaving a red imprint there. He kept a lit non-filtered cigarette, a Chesterfield as I recall, in his ashtray, and sat as if he were doodling like DaVinci on a celestial mission, when in reality he was sound asleep.

Thirty Long could doze through a hurricane. He wouldn't stir; he'd just sit there, no words, pencil in hand, not moving. Eventually, he'd come to and get back to work. Not one super ever bothered him and this always puzzled me until I learned Thirty Long had drawn all the foundations for the Empire State Building. He was, I guess, both half-baked and a genius. The more I live, the more I think those qualities come packaged together.

Seated over a sheet of checkered paper — you know the cross-hatched kind that looks like an unfilled crossword puzzle — Thirty Long would fly though stats, writing them out as if guided by a divine inner force. Tensile strength equations, depth of immersion, densities, any kind of formula for a stat that needed to be worked out and Thirty Long would blow through it, his pencil flying across the page like it was a baton and he was conducting an orchestra. He'd solve problems in a few hours that normally would take others no less than a week. Nobody dared interrupt him. Four, five hours at a clip with his pencils and then he'd stop, rub out his cigarette, rest his elbow on his board, fist against his cheek, and sleep.

Hunchbacked, skinny, he stood all of five feet four in his elevator shoes, his face gnarled up and brownish like a dried apple, his teeth yellow from smoking, his thin white hair flying off his head to make him look like he'd just electrocuted himself. I never saw him eat, and though I wanted to I never talked to him. I was afraid. I'd only been there a short time, a night-school kid, not someone who'd been a key part of the team that had built one of the classiest skyscrapers on the planet.

Early on, it made me nervous, but I was flattered when Thirty Long would stop by my table on his way to the can. He'd pop up on his toes and look over my shoulder and mutter to himself. As I took my super's advice and learned how to heavy up the lines, I got better and Thirty Long's attitude changed. He stopped muttering. He'd walk by, pause a moment, and he'd sigh, but then he'd pound the desk next to my board and shout in his weak crotchety voice, "Shea, get the hell out of here." Boom. He'd punch that desk again. "What are you doing here?" Boom. "You don't belong here, Shea."

Why the heck was he singling me out? This went on for about a month until I'd had enough. What had I ever done to him? I stood up, at six-six and in the best shape of my life, ready for him, and still that old pipsqueak pounded my desk with his fist, crying in his two bit voice, "Go home, Shea. You don't belong here."

I could have creamed him with one hand behind my back, but I kept my cool and maybe he respected me for that, because one day he didn't pound my desk but motioned for me to follow him into the can. We each had a smoke there as he answered my question about why he insisted on bugging me and making my work more difficult.

You know what he said?

"Shea," he said. "Ten cents."

That's it. Then he walked away.

Ten cents. What did he mean? I took pains to find out, and I learned that talented men like him had worked their whole lives hunched over a board going from one company to the next for a salary increase of ten cents a day. From Foster and Wheeler, to Stone and Bend, and from there to somewhere else, all their days on a stool bent over so that by the time they got to Thirty Long's age they couldn't stand up straight because their spines were curved like fish hooks.

For what? Ten cents.

So I got up some moxie and went back to Thirty Long. We had another smoke together in the can and I told him I could live with ten cents. And he told me, flat-out, "No, Shea, this ain't the place for you. I can see that. Mark my words. You've got other, better things to accomplish in this life."

That was the end of it. He never bugged me again.

* * * * * * * * * * *

I took home with me what he'd said, and thought about how much I disliked the math, the dim light and the long hours of sitting. Still, I didn't come to the conclusion that Thirty Long had me pegged. I quit and found a higher-paying job at Eastern Steel Rack in Dorchester, which was a stupid move because they didn't pay overtime, and half of the day I wasn't even done with a drawing when an engineer would hurry in and rip the thing off my board, crying, "We gotta get it out, we gotta get it out."

At Eastern Steel Rack there were no worries about making sure

I'd heavy up the lines. No, they were mass-producing racks for commercial kitchens and it got so crazy I was doing ten drawings a day, 50 hours a week, school three nights, dating your Ma, and bowling all the others. I kept it up for a year until I was dizzy, could hardly move my neck and dreaming in my sleep about kitchen racks with wings.

I switched to a job drawing for Eastern Aerial, mostly subdivision layouts for the town of Holbrook, and I thought maybe working for an aerial company I'd have the chance to fly again, but after a week I knew that would never happen. My grades weren't exactly stellar, and around the same time I learned that your Ma was expecting.

I came to the grave and humbling realization that Thirty Long had been right. I'd become one heck of a bowler, but that was about it. I dropped my career in engineering like it had never happened, and decided on the same day to get married, to quit Northeastern, to be a good father and husband and to find another line of work.

I landed a new riskier job in advertising sales, but I really liked it, and I went back to Foster and Wheeler to tell Thirty Long what I'd done, and to thank him for being honest. I wanted him to know that I'd caught on and his advice had been right.

I never got the chance. I learned from fellows at the corner tap that he'd had a heart attack one night at home, at his drafting table. He lived alone and worked 'round the clock, apparently, which explained his napping on the job and, I think, the edge to his genius.

By the time they found his body, rigor mortis had set in, and they had one hell of a time getting that pencil out of his hand.

The Surface

Freshly shaven and sweet with Aramis cologne, Hugh beamed at Esteban who thought his gringo roommate's face shined as pink as ham. Still, Hugh was handsome, thought Esteban. Light caught his green eyes and for a moment made them kittenish.

Esteban didn't smile back at Hugh. Much was wrong everywhere and he couldn't fake it. He'd never pretended with Hugh and that's why they got along.

Hugh ran fingers over his copper-colored mustache. He rubbed his forehead. He'd just gotten off the phone with Mom. He called her every day, sometimes twice, and they talked while he ironed shirts in his bedroom. At 35, Hugh was no longer a boyish actor and his career clock was ticking louder. Though Esteban had never seen Hugh exercise or lift weights, he looked athletic, if not too thin for his own good.

Billie had been right. Hugh had lost weight, but he still looked sophisticated. Esteban liked that about him. The man left an impression. Sometimes he wondered if Hugh didn't practice this. Billie had developed a similar front, just as enigmatic and challenging to

Esteban. Actors, as Esteban was learning, were never what they appeared to be. He'd begun to think each of them was a product of imagined portrayals of themselves.

Hugh had once assured Esteban he stayed trim because it allowed him to audition for movies. He needed stage and screen. Flexibility. He'd always be a student. An actor dies a student. An actor must work, he'd said, and take any role available.

Hugh had recently completed a production of *A Streetcar Named Desire*. When he'd started to play Mitch, he'd begun adding gel to his russet hair, combing it back in waves. Since that performance, Hugh hadn't changed his hair. Esteban wouldn't ask why. He felt uncomfortable getting too personal. They shared gaps in age and sexual preference. Not that Hugh saw them as gaps. Esteban did. He sometimes saw them as canyons.

Standing close to his iron, Hugh didn't look up from the board when Esteban asked him why he'd behaved so prickly toward Billie. Esteban hadn't been able to think of a more suitable word. He'd never thought of men as openly haughty or temperamental until he'd started spending time with homosexuals.

Hugh smiled at Esteban as if to smile was to answer any question. Esteban thought him arrogant, but no worse than other actors he'd met, including Billie, regardless of her generosity in bed.

Hugh stood taller than Esteban, who was stocky with a low center of gravity. Hugh was a fairer presence. A gold cross fell out of his sleeveless T-shirt. Hugh ignored it and continued to iron a blue shirt, the kind that prep-school boys wore, with button-down collars. The cross swung on its chain, tapping against the side of the iron.

Esteban liked this cross. He wore one just like it. Leaning against the lintel in Hugh's doorway, he tapped his feet and waited. He wondered why Hugh wore so much cologne. He felt hurt that Hugh had treated Billie so rudely at the party last night. What Esteban wanted from Hugh was not an apology and not an excuse that it was a gay thing, but an admission he'd behaved like a spoiled child.

Esteban nudged the toe of his boot against the edge of a crack in the kitchen linoleum. It never paid to expect much from people. He'd wanted their landlord to pay him to repair this crack. It was an easy job. He could use the money. He'd asked countless times, but the Asian landlord had refused to consent.

That's why he was leaving. They were all so stingy here in San Francisco.

Hugh refused to glance Esteban's way. Esteban thought Hugh looked smug. They were snobbish in San Francisco. It might be different in New York.

At least Hugh had stopped with his coughing fits and color had returned to his face. These were good signs. Ever since Hugh had learned his lover, Kevin, had contracted the AIDS virus, he'd confessed his own body was a ticking bomb, a fault line ready to shift underfoot and suck them in.

Esteban had to admit he felt pity for Hugh and Kevin. He felt confusion. Maybe this explained why Hugh had been so snippy with Billie at the party. But Billie had been good to them both, had even loaned them money. She'd shown Esteban around when he'd first moved up to the city from his native Oxnard. She'd become his lover, of sorts, though Billie was a type who had many lovers.

Okay, so he was leaving. Heading East. Had three cousins and a Yankee uncle in New York. They would help him. Didn't Hugh see he was trying to make his American dream?

Hugh would have to look for a roommate. Kevin had AIDS. Didn't Hugh see none of this was Billie's fault?

Esteban reminded himself that Hugh had been snippy with everyone of late. Kevin was looking terrible. Even with medications and his fighting bravely, it was too late. A lethal illness was hard to accept, but it still didn't justify Hugh's rudeness.

Maybe it did. The bigger question was if Hugh carried the virus. It was a time of panic and such unpredictable emotions. Esteban wanted Hugh to know he understood this, that he forgave him. For what? Being gay?

Man, was he confused. Hugh must have smelled it on him because he flinched when Esteban said, "Don't take your unhappiness out on others who don't deserve it."

Hugh mumbled as he kept ironing. Esteban often thought his roommate treated him with a condescending attitude. This time was no different. When Hugh turned to Esteban, it was as if he was delivering lines from a play. His diction was too perfect.

"I may," said Hugh. "I may not. I'll judge by how I feel. If I'm fine, I won't. If not, I will. Nobody needs to know about my panic attacks. I'm sorry about being so catty with Billie. You can tell her that. Maybe I'll tell her."

"You embarrassed her in front of a lot of people. She's not a slut, you know."

"Of course I know. I introduced you two, remember. I'm sorry. Okay? I'm *sorry.*"

It wasn't very good, but good enough for Esteban. He worked up a smile. "I didn't expect you to apologize," he said. "You know how I feel. I appreciate it."

"Trust me. I know."

For Esteban, they were the same friends they'd been when Kevin and Hugh had first interviewed him to share the apartment. Esteban had met Kevin's bright face head on. He'd felt challenged by Hugh, but believed he'd be accepted by him, with time. During the past two years, the three of them had grown close. Hugh, especially. He'd been the big brother Esteban never had.

Hugh tucked the crucifix under his T-shirt. His chest hairs were tiny reddish scratches, darker than the hair on his head.

"Wanna go out?" Hugh asked. "Why don't we? You and me, we'll be lovers."

Esteban flinched. Then he laughed at his skittishness. They were all so cocky and sophisticated and sometimes mean in San Francisco. He'd survived it, but he didn't fit in. Billie had said maybe he'd like Okland better. No, Oakland might be too much like what he'd left behind. He wanted it all to be new. His uncle had promised him it would be. Just the idea of being on the the road thrilled him.

Hugh said, "I bet you're a lousy lay. But I like shaking you up, just a little."

"Not so much that it hurts," said Esteban. "Okay?"

"Really? As if anyone could hurt a person as closed off as you are."

Esteban didn't know what Hugh meant by this. Why did he always feel as if he were being insulted? He wasn't a terrible person. He meant well. They were all stuck-up in this city. He wasn't leaving for nothing. He had a boatload of reasons.

Like his sinuous arms, Hugh's face was pale and freckled. His collarbone reddened at the high points of his shoulders as he laughed at the way his comment had cut Esteban down to size.

Cruel, thought Esteban. Shadowy, muscular, like flexible wire and he cut deeply.

Hugh raked a hand up his forehead over his widow's peaks. He moistened his shirt with a mist of spray starch. He resumed ironing. "Don't worry. I'm okay. You're okay. We're all so fucking okay."

Hugh was too sarcastic. Esteban wouldn't criticize him, but he couldn't look at Hugh any longer. Nor could he move or get his hands out of his pockets. This forgiving of Hugh, this understanding, it had frozen Esteban. Didn't they both have every right to anger and frustration?

"What did the doctor say?"

Hugh paused before replying. "No results yet."

"You look better," said Esteban.

Hugh, chuckling, peeled his shirt from the ironing board. He shook it, fluffing out long sleeves, raising it toward the light to check for stains. He started humming as he slipped his arms into the shirt. Esteban knew that feeling. Any man liked it.

Hugh glanced around his room. Cracked walls received poor light from a window that heightened the colors in a postcard of Dorothy and her friends from the *Wizard Of Oz*. There was a caption about not being in Kansas anymore. Esteban knew Billie had the same postcard.

He began to feel as if he were prying. He liked Hugh so much. They'd shared at times philosophical discussions, breezy nights of food and music from Castro Street to North Beach to the Mission District. Before Hugh, Esteban hadn't known any gay men. Hadn't known many straight ones either. He'd always been a lone wolf, close to his Yankee mother and his Honduran-born father who'd worked in agriculture, mostly with strawberry growers before dying in his late forties of cancer. Esteban liked knowing that differences in his background and Hugh's — not only sexual orientation — had seldom got in the way of their rich times together.

When Esteban thought of the other actors he'd gotten to know through Hugh and how he'd often been surprised by the way they'd treated him, he felt a warm glow toward his roommate. He would miss him. Hugh had often talked about his mother, his job as a restaurant supply salesman, what he learned in his part-time acting class, his auditions, and how he thought his career was going. He'd showed Esteban each new 8 by 10 headshot and asked what he thought of them. Esteban had confessed to fearing that Hugh came across as vain in his photos. He'd liked when Hugh had told him he was pursuing a career that epitomized vanity and not to worry about the photos, that he'd use the look to his advantage.

The look. *Superficie.* They were all obsessed with this.

Hugh moved away from his ironing board toward his bedroom window, drawing back a curtain to view tree branches still green in front of their building. Esteban heard him sigh as if struck by a terrible epiphany. Hugh turned to Esteban, a wretched look on his face, one that begged for pity. Esteban's throat went dry. It was as if Hugh had just melted. He watched Hugh lift the iron and study its holes. They were shaped like teardrops. Was he crying?

Hugh put down the iron and stared at Esteban. His eyes were red with tears. "What do you think?"

Esteban, blushing, lacked a ready answer. He stepped away from Hugh, backing into the kitchen.

"Go ahead. Run off."

"I'm not running."

"You are. You're lucky I'm in a good mood. And stop kicking at the linoleum. You'll just make it looser."

Esteban felt a twinge of courage. "Don't tell me about floors."

"I should call Billie," said Hugh. "Apologize. Would that make you feel better?"

"I'll miss her. I'll miss you, too."

Hugh nodded as if to say he knew only too well. He stopped buttoning his shirt. Stared at Esteban, blinked twice and seemed to undergo a transformation.

Hugh slapped at the air and let out an overdone sigh. "Is Billie really doing a show called *Eight Benches*? Is Max directing? Most of the time, I can't stand that little queen."

"She said to me it's called *Eight Inches*."

Hugh chuckled. He looked more relaxed. "I like *Eight Benches* better. Built like you. From stud lumber, right? The key word is stud, my friend."

Esteban relaxed with him, thinking: Why not relax, since they were both drowning. "You know, I don't know how to talk about this. It feels weird."

"You writing a report?" asked Hugh, joking.

But Kevin's going to die, thought Esteban.

He watched Hugh pout over his iron. Hugh then looked at his watch. He hurried to tuck in his shirt.

"Esteban, please, if you don't mind, I've gotta go to work. I really don't want to talk about it."

Things have a way of getting better, thought Esteban.

"I'm leaving very soon," he said.

"*Not* on a jet plane," said Hugh. He sighed, patting down his shirt. "I look okay?"

Esteban shot him a thumbs-up.

Hugh said, "Just don't forget what Stanley Kowalski says. Luck is just *believing* you're lucky."

The way Esteban saw it, the ironing board divided them. It was a border between friendly countries. As allies they had to cross it now and then because the most important thing was to show tolerance and to accept each other without conditions. Friendships evolved. Forgiveness acted as mortar that held them together.

He'd learned a thing or two. He shouldn't worry so much. He should relax while on the road. Still, he had to act. This was the time and it felt good to move around the ironing board and squeeze Hugh with a fraternal hug. An older gay man and his younger straight roommate could find and maintain common ground. If they could do it, so could the whole world.

After the hug, Esteban felt a high. He didn't know what to say. He hoped he hadn't crossed a line. Borders were always a challenge. Even with a Yankee mother, he never knew with gringos when he'd gone too far.

He stared at the ironing board like a boy hoping to cross a river without a bridge.

Hugh said, "That was nice, Esteban. But just go now, please. I need to be alone."

* * * * *   * * * * * *

It was his last hour in this beautiful city on the bay where he hadn't really fit in and Esteban thought it a shame he hadn't said goodbye to Billie. That was how it went sometimes. He'd decided to take a silent leave. No *adios*, Billie. No regrets.

Seated at his kitchen table and sipping coffee, Esteban smelled aerosol spray-starch coming from Hugh's room. Hugh's door was closed. They hadn't seen much of each other these past few days. Hugh had often been at the hospital or at work. Esteban had been packing, preparing his car, wrapping up last days on a lucrative flooring job.

Esteban felt ready for the long drive ahead, imagining how he'd roll each morning into the sun, day after day. He'd bought a new pair of mirrored sunglasses. He'd phoned his mother one final time. He'd told her he'd know where he was going once he got there. She'd liked this, laughing through her tears, insisting he phone her once he arrived.

He wouldn't attend Kevin's funeral. Maybe Kevin wouldn't die. No. Not a miracle. Not in this case.

He'd never see Billie again. Maybe he'd never be back. Life was about moving forward.

He needed to hug Hugh before he left. He felt such sadness and this one hug was an act he needed for himself, for closure. It would represent a meaningful parting to mull over while the miles between them rolled away.

Hugh and Kevin deserved better. The whole thing was a tragedy.

Esteban took one last long look around the kitchen. He stood and ran his hands over the wood of Hugh's dry sink, a gift from Hugh's mother. Paint had been stripped off; the wood had started to dry out. It needed refinishing.

So do I, thought Esteban. That's what the road was for.

Each shelf of the dry sink was littered with Hugh's paperwork and memorabilia. On the top shelf, close to a low ceiling, a ceramic Madonna stood amidst Hugh's framed photo of Judy Garland, his Elvis bust, and his lewd Betty Boop figurine.

The Madonna was a sign, thought Esteban. He'd never seen it there before.

Another friend of Judy's. This was how Hugh had put it one night when they'd got drunk together — as they often had — in that kitchen. What Esteban had told Hugh was that in a time of change came questions of faith in forces greater than darkness. His faith wouldn't discriminate. It recognized all people as bearers of light. He yearned to tell this once more to Hugh.

When Esteban heard Hugh arguing, he knew Hugh was in there ironing while on the phone. He heard Hugh say, "But it's okay to sell out. Everybody does it."

Again, Esteban looked at the Madonna. Had Hugh put it there?

Music began to play in Hugh's room. It was a song Hugh listened to often enough that Esteban knew its name: "Symphony" by The Supremes. Hugh played their music as often as he played Michael Jackson's.

How could Hugh iron, talk and listen to music at the same time? He was a classic multi-tasker. So different from me, thought Esteban, who needed to do things slowly, thoroughly, with care, one at a time. Like his father assessing strawberries. How he missed his father. Dreamed of him. But he knew his father would approve.

He couldn't wait forever. Sighing, Esteban lifted from the table a stack of books he'd wrapped in brown paper. He nudged open Hugh's door and stepped inside.

Hugh didn't even look up from his ironing. Nor did Billie look up from her book.

Billie? What was *she* doing there?

She sat in Hugh's bed, knees up under covers, a box of chocolates at her side. She was holding a hardcover book and Esteban read the words *Lost Illusions* on its cover.

"Esteban! My sweet *muchacho*. Surprised to see me, Baby?"

His mouth dry, Esteban choked trying to find words.

"Well now you know," said Billie. "Hugh sometimes likes to play both sides of the fence." She put down her book. "Don't you, Darling?"

Hugh had said goodbye and put down his phone. He shrugged. He looked irritable, gaunt, with that pinched gringo look that reminded Esteban of his own mother and that he sometimes could not stand.

At first, Esteban felt confusion. He felt envy. Then rage.

"Esteban, Baby," said Billie. "Don't be upset. Remember what I told you. You were *never* the only one. Besides, you're leaving. Zooming off. After all I've done for you. So I think I have the right to a little fun, since Hugh here at least knows how to appreciate me."

Esteban seemed at that moment to have been dropped like a stone into a liquid nightmare. Was he sinking? Was he hearing Billie talk to him underwater? What kind of sick crude joke was this? Screw it. He was leaving. He'd be free of feeling so much confusion, of suffering their cruelty.

Hugh's iron, he thought, removed wrinkles but not a virus. The man was a tiny boat on big waves, and if Billie had been sleeping with him they both could come down with the virus. Such a murky sea. Such ugliness.

Esteban strained to find words. He held up the wrapped package for Hugh and Billie to see. "I brought a present. They're plays. I bought them at City Lights. Some Tennessee Williams, and Joe Orton. I know you like those two."

Hugh said nothing.

"They're good playwrights, don't you think?" asked Esteban. He really didn't know. Thing was, he wanted to know. He liked learning.

Hugh put the iron down. "Why? Because they're *gay*?"

"No," shouted Esteban. This pissed him off. Was such a friendship worth it? No. He blew a sigh. "That's not what I meant."

"Of course you didn't," said Hugh. "I'm sorry. I'm just tired and grouchy."

Billie laughed. A chocolate rolled around in her mouth. "You both are."

Esteban wanted to call her a pig. A whore. A cunt. How many times had he made love to her and really meant it? Yet at the same time he wanted to hold her one more time, get into the bed and make love to her. Take with him a strong memory of her warmth and her scent.

But this was all wrong! Esteban's voice leaped, "You know, I don't get it, man. I mean, I try. I do. But I don't, I can't, figure any of you people out."

"You people?" asked Billie.

"Neither can we," said Hugh, shrugging, nonplussed. "And don't listen to her. It's not what you think."

Billie grinned at Esteban. "So why bother, Baby? Just be yourself."

"She means we're all gonna live for a long time," said Hugh. "I got my test results back yesterday."

So that's it, thought Esteban. The difference maker.

Hugh said, "I'm beating this virus thing while I'm watching it kill Kevin. Jesus. Talk about guilt."

Hugh began to weep.

"But it's not your fault," said Billie.

"Who said it was?" said Hugh, sniffling.

"Really, look at you Esteban," said Billie. "My lost puppy is finding his way."

He should say something. These people were a mess. "I just want both of you to know I care." The words wobbled out of Esteban's mouth. They sounded weaker than he'd hoped for. "I just wish we'd spent more time talking about it."

"What good would that make?" asked Hugh.

"People need to know how they feel about each other," said Esteban.

"You mean straight people," Billie remarked.

"You're straight," he said.

"Am I?" said Billie.

"Stop it," said Hugh. He glared at Billie, silencing her. He turned to Esteban. "I'm safe. You're safe. Billie's safe. It's none of your business, anyway. You're off to the Big Apple. Go have a good life."

"He's right," said Billie. "And I love him for it. Just like I love you, Baby."

"But you know I care about you," Esteban told Hugh. "You said you'd come visit me. Did you mean it?"

"I even said we'd go to a show on Broadway," said Hugh.

"He will," said Billie. "I'll come, too. Just you wait and see."

Hugh leaned against the ironing board with two hands and almost tipped it over. "Of course, I care. Of course it means everything. But what the hell can I do about it?"

"Nothing," said Billie. She wiped chocolate off her lips. "Love sometimes means nothing at all. It's an existential dilemma. We gotta live with it."

Hugh lifted the iron, held it a moment. As if flinging a discus, he launched it across the room. It struck sounding a dull thud, leaving a dent in the wall. A framed photo of his mother slid down the wall, its pane cracking when it hit the wooden floor.

The three of them stared at the picture. The silence lingered. Esteban handed Hugh the wrapped books. "So you don't have it. You're not infected."

Hugh took the books. "Healthy as a horse," he said.

"That's good news. Even if you were screwing my girlfriend."

Billie laughed. "I am not your property, Baby. And I'm *nobody's* girlfriend."

Esteban waved one arm as if shooing her off. Sometimes restraint said everything. He watched Hugh drop to his bed, the books in his hands. Hugh sat staring off into space. Billie moved toward him to rub small circles against his back. Hugh kept the books in his hands. He saw the note Esteban had taped to the package. He tore it off.

"Read it to me," urged Billie.

Hugh opened the note and read aloud, "It's like this, Hugh. I believe in unconditional love. That's what lasts forever. Esteban."

"Oh, Baby, that is so sweet and kind and real."

"Shut the fuck up," shouted Hugh. "And leave him alone."

Again, silence.

It was broken when Hugh, sounding a low mournful sigh, rose from his bed. Esteban thought Hugh was going to hug him. Instead, Hugh took the note to his mirror. He taped it next to his postcard of Dorothy and friends waltzing the yellow brick road.

Where We Gonna Put Her

Seated on the living room floor, my big brother wasn't faking it when he looked up at Nona and told her he liked Mario Lanza singing "Como Prima."

I liked it, too. I loved it.

My brother waited for a reply. None came. I sat next to him on the floor and we listened together. I was the only girl, the youngest.

Nona didn't say anything. She just kept sewing.

Poor Nona. Our Italian wasn't good enough. There was so much we couldn't say and our mother insisted we speak English.

All day long Nona listened to music and sewed linen doilies by hand and she would ride the train from Boston to Manhattan where she'd try to sell them. Made from scratch, the doilies showed a sturdy elegance and I adored them. They had a special gravity, the smell of the old world. There was something in the thread Nona used — it was like her food — silky and lasting.

Even I knew that Nona's lack of English made it hard for her to make sales on Madison Avenue, but she got help from a friend of a distant relative from a place near Napoli. He was a lawyer named Victor who lived in a town called Pelham and he'd meet Nona at Penn Station and they'd ride the subway together uptown to where the richer people worked and didn't mind seeing a heavy old woman dressed in black selling her handmade doilies. Victor would return to his office and work a full day. He'd pick up Nona in the evening and bring her to Pelham for dinner and to stay the night. He'd put her on the train back to Boston in the morning. With Victor's help, Nona seldom returned with any doilies

I felt a young girl's mix of puzzled awe and pity for my grandmother. She was short, heavy-legged, bosomy. Would I end up the same way? I hoped not, though even at that age I knew I'd have children. I'd just keep it to three rather than fourteen.

Nona looked so tired and old in her apron and blue cardigan. Always a set of rosary beads nearby or in her hands. Her silver hair in a bun. She sewed in a vinyl chair she kept coated in plastic, her stubby fingers working non-stop by window light. Watching her, I had begun to have thoughts about her I'd never experienced before. I couldn't say why or how, but I'd started to realize Nona had never owned a car or a house and she never would. I realized she might die soon, that her body had suffered after so many childbirths. According to Mom, when Nona died she would go to heaven to be with her husband and the two children she had that died stillborn. This concept — stillborn — had terrified me when I'd learned of it.

You mean, Mama, they didn't come out of Nona's belly, at all?

No, they came out, but they were already dead.

So they died *inside* of Nona?

That's right.

Are they still inside of her?

In spirit, yes.

* * * * *   * * * * * *

Nona's apartments were always small. In the bathroom, they smelled of Lysol and menthol. The kitchen always smelled of tomato sauce, what all my uncles called gravy. Nona owned two books, one of them a bible, the other a collection of psalms, both in Italian. According to Mom, Nona had read a great deal as a young girl in Italy and she had been proud to learn that her grandchildren liked to read. I enjoyed my Pippi Longstocking books and had placed third in my school's spelling bee.

Next year, I told Nona, I'm gonna come in first.

She didn't understand me. My mother didn't bother translating it into Italian. She just said to me, Of course you will Sweetheart.

There were rosary beads that hung from the post on the bed where I slept as a guest. My brothers seldom slept there. In that room there was also a framed black and white photograph of one uncle, Enzo, who was the oldest of the sons and had fought in the Battle of the Bulge when he was a soldier. Of course I didn't know this at that time. I only knew that Enzo was Nona's favorite. With a high school education, he had become an engineer for Sylvania in Buffalo. Nona was proud of him.

Enzo looked so serious in the picture, skinny and even a little afraid. I had only met him twice and I remembered how he hugged and kissed me, how warm he was and strong. I suspected Enzo didn't look like that handsome man in the picture any longer. Still, I felt proud of him, as I was proud of all my uncles and brothers.

What about sisters and aunts? Always the boys, the boys. I was getting used to this; I knew better to complain. You could say correctly that I was outnumbered, but I sided with my mother when she lamented we didn't see her family often enough.

A large ceramic Christ hung on the wall above the sofa. The drops of blood painted on Christ's bony ribcage haunted my sleep and gave me nightmares. Sometimes that Christ pulled the nails out of his wrist, got down off the cross and visited me in my guest bed. Once, I showed Christ the little psalm book in Italian that Nona kept on the end table and I explained that I couldn't read it because the print was so small and it was in Italian. Christ had told me it was okay that I couldn't read it. That if I read it in English this would make Nona and my mother happy.

Nona had a big black and white television, an Emerson, but it didn't work. Her 8-track tape player worked: the one my father had bought for her. He'd also bought her the Mario Lanza tapes.

Sometimes, one of my aunts would call and talk to Nona in Italian. I would stand in the kitchen and wait for my turn to say hello. I would stare at Nona as she stirred tomato sauce with a wooden spoon while cradling the yellow phone under her ear, stretching a coiled wire from one end of the kitchen to the other. I pretended I knew what Nona and my aunt were discussing. I'd smile whenever Nona would stare back at me. I never got to say hello. She'd shoo me off into the other room.

I'd sit there alone on the hard plastic sofa that matched Nona's vinyl chair — it, too, covered in plastic. I'd mumble some of the Italian words and I'd think of them as olives and grapes in my mouth and I'd elongate the vowel sounds that ended so many words. One day, I was going to be a singer. I'd look up at Christ on the cross and

I'd say to him: I can do this. I understand. And he'd say: yes, you can. You have a wonderful singing voice.

I was too young to know the belittling humiliation of being old and in the way, but I was also old enough to understand that this was, in many ways, Nona's state. My brothers seemed oblivious to this. Each time they visited, they'd play too loudly and physically in her little apartment and sometimes break something. Maybe they looked at Nona, but did they ever really see her?

I liked to think I was the one who did. I thought often of poor, poor Nona. She was the immigrant mother of 14, two of them dead inside her. Did my boisterous older brothers even know this? I doubted it.

I looked up at Christ on the wall. I asked: How could you let this happen?

Regarding uncles, aunts and all cousins, I could remember only a few by name but not exactly where they lived. Nor could I remember where Nona lived or had been living the last time I'd seen her. She moved constantly, often disliking a place so much that she bickered until one of my uncles found her a new one.

My mother often said to Dad: She could come live with us.

Dad would say: Where we gonna put her? We don't have enough room.

True. Two of my brothers had grown tired of sharing the same bed, and Dad had started saying they were old enough for the same kind of bunk bed system that my oldest two brothers used. My youngest brother was long out of his crib. So was I.

This particular Nona apartment — and it was my second visit there but my first overnight stay — was on the third floor of a three-family in a row of three-families, each of them standing like stacked sandwiches. They had porches in front that faced a busy city street and another row of three-families with porches where some neighbors, like Nona, hung their laundry out to dry.

Inside, it was dark as a cave. Nona had candles everywhere in small short red glasses, not unlike the ones I saw in church around the Virgin Mary where people dropped coins though a slot in a metal box after they prayed. In many ways, the quiet in Nona's apartment reminded me of church and I liked that about it.

What I liked most was that the back of the apartment overlooked train tracks. There was no backyard. Nona was right on top of the train line.

I was eight years old and my parents had wanted me to stay the night with Nona, far from home. I knew something was wrong, but I didn't ask. Years later, I learned my mother had to be hospitalized due to complications that started after my birth.

My parents always said I was the youngest because they'd stopped once they'd had their first girl. Over time, I learned there had been other reasons. My mother was the one who told me. She'd wanted me to have a sister, but after my birth she had required various surgeries. Not only hemorrhoids but uterine damage.

My father had come home from work one day and found Mom passed out in a pool of blood in her bed. Scar tissue had healed, but her hemorrhoids were prone to swelling and they tended to burst. It was awful, just awful and I felt so badly for my mother and so guilty that my birth had created such misery.

My mother suffered this and other physical complications her whole life. Though I felt it was my fault, I never knew how to apologize. Apparently, I'd been a difficult birth. Poor Mom. Just like poor Nona.

Like poor me. In my worst moments, I blamed myself for my

mother's pain. Sounds over the top, I know, but I insisted on it. It was as if I, too, wanted pain.

So while Mother was hospitalized, my father planned to separate his five boys, having them stay with relatives and neighbors. He had to keep going to work. Mom had lost dangerous amounts of blood. He didn't know how long she'd be away from home.

I recall longing for my mother as I smelled the fumes from Nona's food coming from the kitchen. Nona must have felt this from me, because she cooked her tomato sauce with the softest portions of beef and sausage I'd ever eaten. I loved the smell of Nona's sauce, its earthy green pepper and garlic essence, but it was too heavy for my constitution. To Nona's credit, she wasn't insulted by my endless moans from behind the bathroom door.

Nona forbid me to do anything or go anywhere. I was to stay in my dark cavern that smelled like mothballs. The high bed in its center featured a massive pineapple headboard. How hard that bed was and how tightly Nona tucked in the sheets! They were so tight I didn't bother to peel them back. I slept in my underwear on the blanket. Nona didn't mind. Nor did she complain when I stood on a chair to boost myself up to the room's only window so I could look out and watch the top of a train as it roared by, shaking the walls.

The sound of that train filled Nona's apartment, consumed it, and for what seemed a long time in a wind tunnel that train rattled her building, weakened me at the knees. It whistled and shrieked and thundered along. The silence in its wake expanded second by second, growing so large that I thought I'd lost my hearing.

Then I heard Nona speak. She muttered in Italian something I didn't understand. I nodded and smiled, letting her know I was okay and that I'd liked that train.

No, I'd loved it. How close and real it had been. Just like Nona as she hugged me.

* * * * *   * * * * * *

She didn't know how to work her eight-track player. She asked me to play music for her. I picked up Jim Nabors, but she shook her head no. She wanted "Moon River" by Andy Williams.

She never showed me pictures. She never smiled. She seemed genuinely unimpressed with the doodles and drawings I shared with her. After a solicitous pat on the head, she'd mumble off to her darkness and lie down to rest. I'd climb on to the bed in my cavern, thrilled to have space without having to fear my brothers barging in.

The train came. It woke me. I lay there as if pinned to the sheet, unable to move. I felt the power of an engine lumbering, surging along, devouring me. When it whistled, it gave me goosebumps. I watched its lights flicker erratically across the ceiling. I lay there charged, enchanted, thundering along with its clacking wheels.

All was still again. Time slowed down. Nothing stirred. I prayed my mother would get well soon.

I'd sleep, little knowing that the soft yet heavy slipcover I lay on with its floral pattern, with its sturdy heavy weave and its holes in places — holes I learned in the daylight that were supposed to be there and were part of the pattern — had been sewn by Nona by hand. That she'd sat for months, night after night, making a thing so fine and useful out of mere thread.

* * * * *   * * * * * *

My brothers were collecting baseball cards with their friends on the street, trading them and flipping them against walls. What mattered to them was how to build a fire and pitch a tent and tie a knot for a merit badge while camping with their Boy Scout troop.

I felt left out. They never talked to me about my interests. My favorite songs. My Nancy Drew books. My white figure skates.

Mother was well again and what mattered to the boys and all I ever heard about were their models built from kits bought with shared paper route money. They called me Little Sister. They looked after me, but they were always talking about Chevy *Chevelles*, and *Barracudas* they'd painted by hand, adding each decal and assembling the parts until the cars were not only perfect reproductions, but they could roll across a floor.

They never talked about Nona.

I had my own room by this time and there were no models in it. There were no dolls either, but there were photographs of Nona, some of them of her seated with me. Many were black and white snapshots with perforated edges and in one of them she's holding a tiny purse and wearing a hat that looked like a piece of pastry on her head, with little fake pearls hanging in a piece of false lace netting. My mother had told me this had been the style at the time. That the picture was of Nona at my father's college graduation.

I thought it so sad that Nona had had so little. It wasn't fair. It hurt me that my brothers never asked or talked about her.

I still knew so little about Nona and what it must have been like working long hours in a shoe factory, her husband an unemployable alcoholic. Her native land was far away, a place according to my mother where she'd once supported Mussolini and read books by Victor Hugo in Italian, and studied under nuns in a village called Castel Baronia in the low-lying hills of the Abruzzi.

The nuns had taught Nona how to sew. My mother kept promising she'd teach me, as well, but she was busy working full-time and I was busy going to school and helping with the cooking and the washing of clothes. Yes, my brothers helped. We all did our share, but it seemed I was always in the kitchen washing dishes by hand while one more brother trooped out the door to play baseball or visit with friends.

My mother would scold them whenever they made wisecracks about Nona. No gift they bought her for Christmas was good enough because they never knew what to buy or what she liked. My mother was impatient and irritable in those days and she would eventually throw up her hands and say, "Just you boys get her anything. It's the thought that counts."

But I had to make her something by hand. I made her a Christmas card with an angel on the cover. I sewed her initials into a little face-cloth. I baked cookies. Were they good enough? Did she love them? I never felt I knew. She said so little. She'd hug me and thank me, of course, but there was never that moment when I sat on her lap and she told me a story.

This I realize now, all these years later, was all I wanted. Such a short amount of time: enough to allow me to feel closer to her. To let her know I loved her. It seemed to me nobody loved her enough. I wanted her to know I felt this way. I wanted to tell her.

I never did.

***** ******

One year, I was desperate. I hadn't been able to make something for Nona. I was in the Brownie scouts. I wore a dress now and then. My mother made it appear that she was granting me a special privilege by leaving me alone in a pharmacy while she and some of my brothers did last-minute grocery shopping. I didn't feel special. She let my brothers shop alone in stores all the time, as long as they weren't gift shops with lots of ceramic items in them.

Christmas, the big day, was fast approaching and the pressure was getting to me. My mother had gone a little berserk with the strain of work and buying and wrapping gifts. I was starting to feel that Christmas wasn't exactly the mumbo-jumbo it was cracked up to be. I'd even said this in CCD class. This had sent my teacher into a conniption. She had made me go to confession and admit this to Father Andy. After I'd said my five Our Fathers, my teacher and my mother (whom the teacher had called) assured all would be okay. Jesus, after all, was there to forgive me.

But there was one more catch. I could make up for this sacrilege by finding the right gift for Nona. It had to be special because it was the first one I'd ever buy for her. I couldn't get her a comb or a hair dryer or a box of Sucrets, so I grabbed something colorful, some round shining candies, about a dozen of them each the size of a gumball in a round plastic case with a satin crimson bow on it. I thought they looked pretty and Nona would love them.

I kept my gift a secret from my mother, because I didn't want her criticizing me and forcing me to take it back at the last minute. Not that she cared. With one day to go until our visit to Nona, Mom was out of her mind. This came to be a regular occurrence as each of us got older. To say my brothers drove my mother insane would be an understatement. It didn't help that Mom was an aggressive over-achiever in all things, especially when it came to having the house fixed up nice for Christmas and all the other holidays.

Mom never did anything half-way and we were her work crew, so to speak, each of us assigned tasks that had to be accomplished to a certain standard and by a certain time. I'm not talking about simply taking out trash. I'm talking about boiling the lasagna noodles and mixing up the ricotta and separating the whites from the colors and making sure my father's shirts got put into the pile for the dry cleaners, and making sure my older brothers vacuumed Dad's car and made their beds and scrubbed the toilet so it shined. I didn't have to scrub the toilet, but I had to make sure the work got done.

Why me, I'll never know. My brothers never listened. The amazing thing was we got all this work done, although the house stayed clean for about fifteen minutes, which was usually long enough time to impress the priest Mom always invited over for holiday dinner, along with just about everyone else in the neighborhood, including all of Mom's immediate family, out of which usually only my Uncle Bettino and Aunt Denise would come with my four cousins, all of whom were boys, loved sports and spent no time whatsoever with me.

There were dinners when so many people filled the house we had to borrow card tables and metal folding chairs from the church so that some adults could sit together in the tiny corridor between the living room, kitchen and dining room. Each of those rooms was noisy with people seated on the arms of sofas, a paper plate on one knee, or in any chair they could find, or standing and eating in corners. All of us kids huddled on the floor in the basement, or else outside in the dirt in our cleanest of clothes, even if it was snowing. It just got so hot in that little house when so many people came by.

As far as food went, Christmas was usually a two-lasagna, one-ham, one-turkey affair. The same for Easter and add in a few ricotta pies. Add one more turkey with squash and lots of pies if it was

Thanksgiving. My mother complained all the time that there was never any food in the house, yet we never went hungry and my father often lamented, "You kids are eating me out of house and home."

Not that Mom spent much time watching Graham Kerr or Julia Childs on television. Not that our television ever worked, either. Our milk came from a box, in powder form, usually Carnation brand. One of my daily chores was to help one brother mix it by the gallon. When it wasn't a holiday, I could be sure Friday meant fish sticks and baked beans, Saturday meant tuna fish casserole, and Sunday some kind of roasted meat or stuffed shells dinner for Daddy. Monday through Thursday usually meant hot dogs, brown bread, cans of Franco American brand spaghetti (which I detested), more tuna fish casserole, or a huge pot of what we called American goulash, which was elbow macaroni mixed with what Mom in her Boston argot called *hamburg* and two cans of whole tomatoes.

Breakfast was never taken seriously. We drank our milk and ran off to school and stayed hungry until lunch time when we paid three cents for a little box of milk. If there was cereal, it was Shredded Wheat, a big box that lasted one day. It was a rare treat to bust open a box of Captain Crunch, or Wheaties with the likes of Bruce Jenner on the cover. Mom disliked sweet cereals that held a toy inside because they were expensive and led to a fight between my brothers. The toy was stepped on by someone with bare feet — usually me — or else broken within minutes of getting freed from its wrapper.

Being ungainly, bloodthirsty and vulgar, my five brothers were neither timid nor careful when it came to making fun of others, family or not. They could be cruel. So violent. They took after Mom.

She seldom talked to them. She slapped and shouted. She cursed like a sailor. She roared. It didn't matter. They still didn't listen.

Regarding Nona, for example, one of her favorite shouted rapid-fire lines was, "You have no idea what that woman went through. It makes me ache all over just to think of how she suffered."

I ached for her, as well, and that was why I wrapped her Christmas present in some fine silver and crimson paper that I'd hidden away. You had to hide everything in that house if you wanted it to be there when needed.

During our Sunday visit, I gave it to Nona and waited, smiling and playing it bashful as I watched her open it. Nona's response, hardly what I expected, was a sour questioning look. It puzzled me. It hurt, as well. I'd really wanted to please her. I'd begun to remember that apartment and train — two apartments ago and I was a little older now. I really wanted to see her smile.

I never got it. Just as Nona never got the gift she expected.

The following day in one of those rare moments alone with my mother when I knew she was serious and angry because she wasn't yelling at me, she asked, "Why did you get that gift for Nona?"

"I thought she'd love it."

"Did you know what they were?"

"Hard candies. Can't Nona eat them?"

My mother's face reddened, but it wasn't the scarlet I was accustomed to when she was about to unload on me in a fit of suppressed rage. It was more of a blush, embarrassment, a mixture of emotions that were far too complex for me to grasp.

"You thought they were candies?"

"They're not?" I asked, innocently.

"They're bath oil beads."

"Oh." This seemed okay to me. "But they're still pretty."

My mother shook her head, sounding one of her heavy sighs as if blaming herself for my indiscretion. "They're for taking a bath."

"Doesn't Nona take a bath?"

Mom looked at me closely, studying my face. "Honey, do you understand what I mean when I say that's a personal gift?"

I started to whine. "But I didn't have time to make anything. You sent me alone to the pharmacy. It was pretty. I even wrapped it pretty. You said you didn't want me to bother you with it and that I was a big girl and I could take care of it myself."

"But big girls don't give such things to their grandmothers."

"But why not?"

"Do you think Nona smells funny?"

"No."

"No, of course you don't. But you really hurt her feelings."

I wanted to cry. "But I thought they were candy. Like big gum drops. My teachers in school eat them all the time."

To this day, I don't know if my mother believed me, but it was the truth. She made me promise that I'd apologize.

I planned to, but Nona died before I got to it. She became ill shortly after Christmas. Her health was all that mattered to my mother, even though during the next six months one of my brothers was making his first communion, another one was caught smoking in school, another already had girlfriend problems, another broke his arm, and they were all getting lower than expected grades.

What terrified me most was hearing from Mom that doctors had sawed off both of Nona's legs. She called it the sugar disease.

This was life? No husband for Nona, no house and getting her legs sawed off?

Poor, poor Nona. I cried alone in the dark of my little room. I'd given her bath soap instead of candies. I hadn't really loved her. No one had. Not enough anyway.

I promised myself I'd never forget her, but even Little Sister knew it wouldn't change anything.

Lady Mist

Tor Baptista read the Braille of the emerging sun. It said five a.m. Peewee Coyle's words haunted him.

Time. Once that boat steams out, there's no place to hide. You're gonna get this sinking feeling in your gut because you know there's nothing else, just you and the boat and a crew of diehards that you better hope to hell you get along with.

He'd leave it to the sea to help him tune out Peewee's voice, and all the radio noise whirling between his ears. Help him tune out the mood.

Even if you're good, you'll be lucky to last ten years before your body starts falling apart. Look at me. Got ganglia in my hands the size of elephant turds.

Peewee had been in port. His message had been to slow down and stick to a plan.

And forget about skippering your own boat. You ain't got the knowledge or the money. The insurance alone wipes most of these guys out their first year.

A plan spelled out the possible. Helped define change as ac-
ceptable risk.

Takes an effort to become somebody else.

He could bury himself under work. Discard who he'd been.

* * * * *   * * * * * *

Bonito were running. Mackerel, too. Always too much squid.

At fifteen years old and seventy-two feet long, the *Iron Jane* rode
low in the water with bald tires sagging like a bracelet of black wash-
ers down both sides of her enameled green hull. She chortled through
a harbor crowded with moored sailboats and yachts with sleek bright
keels. Exhaust from her muffler left ragged stains on the air.

Trap fishing's one of the oldest most honest types of fishing left.
But don't count on it for a living. Use it to earn your reputation.

A glazed light, the last of dawn's purity brought a silver tint to lacey
cirrus that had begun to lose their suggestions of pink. Tor squinted
into that silver and felt he'd already lived a full day. That's how it went
sometimes. Like a half-sleep. Like he was a secret in waiting.

Most landlubbers were still snoring.

* * * * *   * * * * * *

Looking astern, Tor saw Goat Island, where a hotel of brick and
tinted glass rose out of the harbor like an office building that had
been dropped there. He thought of Zeno, a retired schoolteacher
who'd grown up in Newport. In his drinking days, he'd seen Zeno
often at Three's Company. They'd eat breakfast at The Satellite.
Zeno had tagged Peewee with the nickname, Dumptruck. According
to Zeno, there'd been a time when Goat Island was deserted. As a
boy, he'd walk there in the morning with his father. Pants rolled

up, they'd dig with bare hands for quahogs in cold shallow water. Fill a bushel basket, and once home Zeno's father would make red chowder, using tomatoes from his garden.

There was a time when I could drop my line into the harbor and pull up a dozen flounder in a few hours. Harbor's fished out. And lots of luck digging clams on Goat Island without getting busted for trespassing.

For sixty years, Zeno had lived in Newport. Goat Island had been his wild place, not a tourist compound, every inch of it fenced-off and patrolled.

The old-timers, they'd known the America of clean open land, lakes and oceans. They'd seen it vanish.

***** ******

Fight the mood, the lunatic hungers. Keep it level like the horizon.

Tor lingered at the starboard rail as *Iron Jane's* deck vibrated up his legs. He'd chug along as she did —leaving a rippling V of froth under the three silver dories that bounced in her wake.

He studied the harbor's shoreline. Clustered rooftops stretched out at nearly the same height, with a church steeple like a lance — like a needle — up the sky's throat.

Like a needle. In his world that made perverse sense.

He looked back to Goat Island, and beyond it to tiny Rose Island, and then the Newport Bridge, which connected Aquidneck to Conanicut Island and the town of Jamestown, Fort Wetherill Park and the lighthouse at Beavertail. They were approaching a channel sometimes referred to as the East Passage, where Narragansett Bay met the open Atlantic.

To the south, Tor saw the walls of Fort Adams, the white mansion of the Ida Lewis Yacht Club, and the lawns of seaside mansions with wrap-around porches, widow's walks and Victorian-era turrets. One was owned by the sculptor who'd created the Iwo Jima monument. Tor couldn't remember his name.

He saw the mansion owned by the Kennedy clan. As far as he knew, JFK had married Jackie O in the stone cathedral up the hill along America's Cup Ave, not far from the waterfront at Lower Thames where Peewee had told him there was once a grist mill and a brawler's paradise called Blood Alley.

He watched Fort Adams approach; its cannons poking out of brown stones where they once protected the promontory beyond Brenton Cove at the southern reach of the harbor. He saw fiberglass sailboats and yachts bob on their moorings. Marveled at the size and design of a cabin cruiser. How did people afford such luxurious toys? For starters, they didn't blow their earnings on trips to oblivion.

He should take stock in what he had.

Or else it fades away or it's taken.

Decay and loss were not provinces. They defined a natural state of being. Learning this seldom made any loss easier to accept. With the ease of a gull veering toward horizons, anything could slip away.

Then why not bring new life into this world?

* * * * * * * * * * *

An old dragger, a survivor, steamed toward them, its bow cleaving the water. Tor read *Lady Mist* scripted in gold against black. Her name was romantic, better suited for a sailboat. Tor blinked and the dragger was gone. Maybe she'd been a mirage. It was possible on the sea.

What day was it? He couldn't remember. He liked knowing that he didn't have to.

At port side, having passed the Newport Country Club, they were near the rocky shoreline of Brenton Point State Park. Wanting one last glimpse of where he'd been, Tor looked to starboard. Flashes of sunlight bounced off cars crossing east on the Newport Bridge. With vertical cables, green iron trusses and riveted I-beams, the bridge was a masterpiece of engineering. No sunlight heated the water beneath it. A few yachts floated there, their wet hulls shining like dull pearls. Strands of fog twisted off the water like cold flames, touching down and skimming whitecaps that clashed as they unrolled in explosions of suds.

Round beacons topped the bridge at its two highest peaks. They flashed red with each rotation. Tor never tired of admiring the bridge. Its sense of completion and purpose helped soothe the ache he felt throughout his body. He worried he couldn't stay sharp, that he'd need a nap before the work began.

He let his chin drop and he closed his eyes. He heard the murmur of the engine, gulls shrieking, waves lapping, a bell clanging from a buoy. All like a soothing poetry that told him it was okay to be tired. Perhaps when he awoke, he'd be another person. He'd have no thoughts, no memories, no conscience. He hoped so.

"How about a light?"

Tor opened his eyes. He rubbed them. There stood Manny Fraction. Arms folded, Manny was sturdy, pudgy and hairy. His breath smelled of beer. His teeth were filmed yellow. He looked old before his time. They all did.

Tor remarked sarcastically, "Let me guess. Manny's Zippo shit the bed."

Manny cackled. Cape Verdean, with fine amber skin, he looked boyishly dumpy. He wore his kinky hair in a wayward Afro that wiggled as a breeze caught it full-force.

Wearily, lips dry, Tor handed over his lighter and offered Manny a cigarette from his pack. This was the best time to smoke, before they started pulling nets.

"Good day for plugging," remarked Manny. "I like going off Ledge Road. Blackies, mostly. You ever go there?"

"Yeah," said Tor. "Real quiet."

"Gonna be good for trapping, too."

Tor shrugged. The three nets would be bulging with fish. They'd likely get to only one of them. They'd man the three dories tied to *Iron Jane's* stern, and they'd pull as three separate crews until their shoulders roasted in their sockets. Once *Iron Jane* was loaded, they'd tie up the dories, steam back in and sort fish at the end of Bowen's Wharf. From 4:30 a.m. until dark for $50 bucks, cash. The average guy lasted a day or two. They weren't average: they were hard-ons, rat bastards, ex-cons, and dope fiends on the mend in a diurnal struggle against the mood. Weapons-grade inner circle members of a bad attitude club.

None could say for certain what the catch would be like. Tor wouldn't dare spout off like one of the veterans. "How long you been doing this, anyway?" he asked.

"Off and on."

"But how long is that?"

"Longer than my dick," said Manny.

Tor flinched and looked away. He stared at the water, seeing nothing, seeing it all.

Manny said, "I gotta get on a swordfish boat. Make some real swag."

"Not much out there now, is there?"

"That's why Chucky and Mayes and them other guys are around. Slow season for sword. Trapping kind of sucks, but at least I'm working."

Kill the mood before it kills you.

"Georges," said Manny. "Grand Banks, too. That's where all the fish are."

Compared to the tenures of some veterans, especially the foremen, Manny's three years on swordfish boats were nothing. To Tor, they meant a great deal. He respected Manny, who hadn't finished high school. Few of them had.

"Swordfish boats come up from North Carolina to Maine. Long trips," said Manny. "Especially when they ain't catching."

"So trapping's easy for you, then?"

Manny scratched soft black swirls of hair on his neck. He offered another shrug. "Guess so. Spend time riding out. Pull the traps, everybody working together. Ride in. Worst part's the sorting, though. And the money sucks, but what can you do?"

"It's fun," said Tor, strong on sarcasm, "looking at the different fish."

"I was gonna work yesterday," said Manny. "Got loaded the night before. Slept in."

"She a piece?"

Manny studied Tor's face. Scowled at him. "So what if she was? So what if she wasn't?"

That meant Manny hadn't gotten any. Tor left it alone. The rising sun forced him to squint. He rubbed his chin. Hadn't shaved in a few days.

"I got shit-faced again last night," said Manny. "Don't remember nothing."

Tor dragged on his cigarette. "That I believe."

"But I'm changing my ways."

"Yeah right."

"When I got home my old lady was all mad," said Manny. "I said give me a break or else I'd split, she'd never see me again. She blew up at me, started throwing shoes."

Tor's face darkened. He didn't want to hear about Manny beating a woman.

"She acts like we're married, but we ain't married," said Manny.

"I thought you had kids."

"I got two. But with my other old lady. She lives down in Florida. Knocked her up twice, but she wanted them kids, but she didn't want me, so now I'm just paying and I never see them."

"You're shacked up with somebody else," said Tor, sourly. "Maybe that's why."

"No, my kids live in Florida with their mother's parents. They hate me, so I stay away."

"Even your kids hate you? That ain't right."

Manny shook his head no. "They don't hate me. Their mother hates me."

"Because you beat her ass," said Tor.

"Fuck you, man. That cunt hates everybody. Look, I tell you straight. I knocked her up, but I did the right thing. I been there."

Lines deepened in Tor's forehead. He'd just walked a mile in another man's shoes. He watched Manny flick his cigarette out over the water.

"I didn't want to work this morning, but I got up and here I am," said Manny. "I send money to Florida for my kids. Not because I want to. Because they're my kids. Ain't no other reason. It's just what you do, man."

A worker named Geno approached them. Shirtless, not a hair marked his oiled tanned chest. Tor thought he looked like a bar of cocoa-butter soap. Like all the crewmen, he wore black rubber boots, and a fillet knife in a leather sheath attached to his belt. A black bandanna knotted at the back of his head kept his long hair covered.

Manny said to him, "Hey, what's up?"

"Screw this guy." Geno grabbed Manny's arm and shoved him along toward the bow.

Manny stood his ground, turned to face Tor. "You coming or not?"

"Where you going?" A fume of marijuana smoke sweetened the air. Tor paused a moment, getting the picture as Manny motioned toward the bow where others stood huddled and passed a joint.

"C'mon, we'll burn one."

Tor blew a sigh. Another day, another temptation. Skipper Sonny Lombardi didn't like it, but he allowed it sometimes, and looked the other way.

Weed, whiskey, or heroin — each fed the mood, and Tor didn't draw distinctions. Swear off one, swear off them all. It was easy to lapse. As much as he liked Manny, any explanation would be a waste of breath.

Tor took his knife from his sheath and studied the blade. He ran it softly across his wrist, testing his flesh, his will.

He could do it. One swipe. Change would be everywhere.

"Do what you gotta do," he muttered. "I'd rather slit my wrists."

Had he really said that?

Manny offered a puzzled shrug. Tor didn't see him. His eyes were set on his knife blade as he cut a slice in his left forearm. He held the blade there until the slice started to burn. He knew they were watching him. He didn't care. He dug the blade in deeper and formed a groove.

That Portughee's crazy. He's half Portughee. Half German. Out of his gourd.

Tor sheathed his knife. He sucked the blood out of his forearm. The cut was deep, but salt water would burn it clean. It was a victory in line with the others, forming a seam of slices up his left forearm. They were his walking papers. His new set of tracks. They told him how he'd arrived to where he was. Proved he was taking steps.

Manny said to Geno. "Freaked-out, man. I don't get that dude."

"Junky shit," said Geno. "Nothing to get."

Tor snickered. They knew so little about him. Nor did they care, not really. This was fine. Every busted-up soul trying to make good knew the mood that fit, created, and heated diabolical need. Once the mouth of need opened, it had to be filled. It was a need to obliterate shame. The likes of Manny and Geno didn't study it. With their eyes on fire, they worked, they ate, and the sun set on their earning enough swag to get wasted by midnight.

He didn't look at them. He had his seam to study. His new slice, his new stair tread. For too long he'd lived hand-to-mouth with a fuck you like a pistol on his hip ready to blow away the first landlubber that crossed him.

He had changed. No surprise Manny thought him a freak.

The money don't matter.

It was commitment, and the balls it took to have focus. That's what mattered. Anybody could be a screw-up. *Iron Jane* was full of them.

Tor kept his thumb against the slice to stanch blood flow that stung. This pain — now this was honest. This he trusted.

He looked astern and watched Newport's horizon line. It was

one more serrated edge. As he watched it recede, he thought — not today, nope, the mood doesn't win.

JOLENE, JOLENE

I'd stood up too quickly, machete in hand, dizzied by a head rush, sweat raining down my sides. This dream woman, I tell you, she wore a long skirt and floated like a ghost between the rows, her blond tresses shimmering as she danced over wide green fronds.

There hadn't been a message from her. She was the message and made of the windswept ashy light that I'd sometimes see misting the late dawn across hollows in Cullowhee Mountain. That silver patina of allure gleaming out of pines so frail and translucent, and ever so temporal — like the past, like any moment of certainty. Here one minute, gone the next.

I stood in that field and I gasped at my dream woman. She'd locked me within the pearly shine of her lips. I embraced her, and the two of us gleamed like smooth pebbles under a creek's surface. She was water for my thirst, shaping damp beads of speech I couldn't shake off my lips.

Wiping my brow, sucking in deep breaths, I resumed bending over to swing my machete again. I struck the tobacco stalk two inches off the black earth, perfect swipe, one clean gash into a stalk that snapped like green bamboo crackling as I tilted it, the whole of the plant, breaking it free at the gash, lifting, wrestling with it, dodging all leaves as they swiped across my face, tar burning in my eyes, sweat stinging as I turned and twisted until I'd mastered the plant. They were six feet tall in some cases, no small bit of vegetation. Tangle on, I told myself. No end to this *'backer* until Harlan's field is cleared. Harlan and his brother, based in Franklin, handled more allotments than anyone else in Macon County. I took it as an honor to be in their employ. Jolene saw things differently, but there was more to her leaving me. There just had to be.

Impossible, I thought, but my dream woman had come. I'd seen her happening. I felt a kind of thrill, but I was so tired it hurt just to keep arms at my sides.

I drove the plant sideways over a conical steel tip fixed to a wooden stake, watching that green stalk splinter but not break completely. That is the trick. Get it on the stake but do not destroy its stalk. Then push the stalk down all the way, and think repeatedly of the word: impaled.

I tilted the plant in the same direction as the others, already impaled, four of them on each tall wooden stake. Four was enough. They'd be left one after another, each like a little pup tent to dry in the field for a few days until their leaves started to yellow, or else it looked like rain. Then we'd hang 'em in the trucks and spend longs days moving them to Harlan's barns to cure.

I removed the conical steel tip and dropped it like a tin-man's cap on to the next stake. Harlan got a rise out of seeing a field done, and so did I, with all that staked tobacco tilted like leafy tents stretched row after row as far as the eye could see. All the little nubby cut stalks like busted teeth in the loam. All the money Harlan was due to make once his harvest was cured, baled, sold at Winston-Salem, and stored for three years in Kentucky warehouses.

The trick was to establish a rhythm, economical use of the body, control of breathing, slow air singing a humid opera in my nostrils, a tarry tobacco reek, so heavy, so piquant at times. I took that conical tip off one stake and fit it on to another, row after row: plants, stalks, leaves and wooden stakes. Nothing soft, easy, or slick about it.

Hot heathen labor in the restless sun. What early settlers bought slaves for, shipping them over, whipping them into the earth, making their fortunes on a leaf that couldn't be eaten.

All kinds of rabbit-crazy thinking went on in my head. I sucked in another breath, kept my rhythm, and when I needed a jolt, I looked for that woman again. I didn't always see her. Sometimes, I saw stray mist — or was it smoke? I saw it rising and falling from breezes that pushed the verdant fronds; lifting them so high that for a moment they'd whiten with the horizon in front of me, the whole field buzzing like a white-hot insect. Yellow winds shifting gently, syrupy, sweat boiling from my forehead, and the leaves, those fronds so lovely to watch, white, yellow, silverfish at times — and such a lovely word: fronds. I kept mumbling it. Frond, fronds, fronds...

Sharp yellows and greens. That taut tobacco aroma lacing hot heavy winds that lay like bath waters in a sea of soft green, bottle-green, and then turning on a dime into limeade green and flashing brilliant velveteen green peppered with high occasional golden yellows.

My head, my head — full of purple prose for my laborer's brain, nothing edited about it. Jolene, Jolene, why'd you leave me? I'm coming to you, Jolene. I'm having visions. Once this is done, once I'm free and paid, we'll be together. I'll be riding a Greyhound due north to Manhattan to be with you. I miss you like I'm a character out of an old song.

Dang. This heathen work. Gonna kill me by the time I'm thirty.

But my vision wasn't of Jolene. She was a blonde. What did that mean? Not now, I thought. Not on this day when I had finally made up my mind.

I saw the two of us thirty years on. Nope. She wasn't Jolene. She was someone else, the next woman I was destined to meet. I knew this, somehow, just as I knew my days of heathen work were not over.

At least, I wouldn't realize my fear of dying as a lonely bachelor. Was I insane? I knew nothing. I was driven by hope, delusions, wishful thinking. Just shut up, I told myself, and keep chopping 'backer.

Once sure that conical steel tip was secure on the next stake, I bent again and swung back my arm like old John Henry with hammer. I brought down my machete with aim and purpose true. *Thwack*. Nothing more satisfying than learning to use an effective tool well. *Thwack*. A machete, if anything, can be effective, and that ain't no lie. *Thwack*.

All this work, I told myself, the way I hold this long heavy blade, the way I grip its handle — it's all making a man of me. All my fathers — and I had many — would be proud.

After so much time in tobacco fields, I never took a cigarette for granted, no matter how harmful they were to one's lungs. I needed one and so I lit up and damn near lost my lighter in my slippery tar-black sweaty hands. If I ran north to Jolene, none of those urban sophisticates in Manhattan would want to hear about this kind of work, this life here, and how beautiful it was to take a smoke break and look around. To smell the soil. To feel the cutting breeze as it swept in to carve away the settled heavier winds and heat. To see over the tops of all those fronds how the distant hills remained still. My eyes followed them. They rose and dipped and moment by moment changed their soft benign colors.

Better I kept my mouth shut once I got up there. Let Jolene do the talking.

Nothing was impossible. I could handle Manhattan. A smile glowed across my face as I thought of how Jolene was going to pleasure me once I got there.

I heard someone yelling. I couldn't see him. He was yelling at me to hurry up, to keep moving, to get it done. It was Harlan's nephew, all right, no surprise there.

I put out my cigarette and looked around for my blonde. She wasn't there. She'd left me.

I saw a snake move toward my boot. Startled, panting, I jerked away. Eyeballed that skinny thing, gripped my machete and raised it. I let it sing down through the air, sounding a chink when it hit soft dirt, cleaving that snake in half.

Wasn't no copperhead or eastern rattler, that's all I knew. I watched its cleaved rope of a corpse as it twitched. Maybe wasn't no snake, at all. Maybe it was some part of my soul. In the fields, the mind turns to gruel. Jungle instinct takes over. More than once I'd started babbling.

Jolene, Jolene, what's a poor boy like me gonna do in that big city?

Running on fumes, I resumed getting my rows done. I ignored Harlan's bellowing nephew. I knew I had to change myself. Nothing was gonna stop me.

BLOW OUT ALL THE CANDLES

Mike Shea in bliss, sunburned arm out the open window of his '53 candy-red Buick 48D *Special Tourback Sedan* as he drove Route 20, a black eel that dipped through the folds of rural New York. Loved the way she floated cresting a hill, got her for $800 cash and had steered her north from Florida to Niagara Falls. After a day at Howe Caverns, where he and Connie had shivered after two weeks of grapefruit and tanning oil, they were headed to his folks' place. Be there by midnight, where over a whiskey he'd tell his Pa that Ike's interstate still wasn't completed.

He stretched his right arm over Connie's shoulders and pulled her closer. Eventually, they'd have to agree on the boy's name. It would be 1960, a new decade by the time he arrived. If a girl? No different, but a son would come first. This one intuition Mike trusted. With only a sister, he'd known a lonely childhood in a Roxbury apartment; he wanted eight, ten, twelve, an even number of Sheas. Connie thought six a perfect amount; half as many as her mother had brought up in a North End brownstone, where the Spino sisters had slept four to a bed.

She nestled against his ribcage and ran her hand across his chest, lamenting that their honeymoon would soon end. He told her the fun had just started. After his folks, they'd head to Cape Cod for a few days. She smiled at him, saying she loved Cape Cod, but it couldn't match the peach twilight of Florida at dusk, the sand so white, the ocean so tepid and soothing.

Tepid. A nice word. For a working girl, Connie showed a rich vocabulary. Nona Spino spoke very little English, but had kindled in her daughters a love for reading; she believed education remained the only way to get ahead. Mike had agreed with her from the start.

Adoring the sweep of Connie's raven-black hair and the gentle caress in her smile, he reminded her they were one lucky couple. He'd chosen the Casablanca Hotel on a whim, knowing she liked that movie with Bogart. At $300 a week, including a pool and a trip to Parrot Jungle, they'd scored a bargain. He'd like to visit again, but it would be years before they could afford it. Family must come first, and that meant money. Not a job, but a career with a future. Gasoline had already climbed to 16 cents a gallon.

Lurching, the Buick threw them forward. Mike's foot hit the clutch, and jerking the wheel to his right he downshifted as the car bounced over a narrow shoulder, gravel flying into the chassis, the wheel vibrating in his hands.

"Mike, what's wrong?"

The wheel tugged whether he braked or not, and he fought it, downshifting again as he saw steam rise from the Buick's grille.

"Some kind of fluid," he shouted. "Not a flat."

"I smell it," she cried.

He saw a moon-colored glow close to the road, topping a rise ahead of them. He sped up, pushing the big engine, had to, until he reached that glow.

"Mike, are you sure?"

He wasn't, but he remembered drill sergeants and forced marches on bases in muggy Biloxi, in the dry heat of west Texas, the cold of Thule, Greenland. A piece of cake.

"Mike, I don't like this."

Neither did he. The engine's dry chortle worried him. She might blow if he forced her. He slowed the car, stopped and shut her off, slamming his palm against the wheel. "Overheated."

"Can you fix it?"

Wanting to curse but holding his tongue, he got out. The night felt vast, and cool air smelled of pinesap. It took him longer than expected to find the latch that opened the hood. He saw the problem and felt vindicated, having correctly diagnosed it. He searched a cross brace inside of the hood, finding a rag he'd tucked there.

He pushed down on the rag and turned the radiator cap. It blew off, spraying hot fluid. Cursing, he pulled at his shirt, keeping it off his skin. He heard fluid hiss like oil in a skillet.

How stupid of him; this wasn't the way to handle an emergency. He chucked the rag aside.

Lighting a Pall Mall, he leaned on the Buick's fender. The road and travel, the living through it—first the startling news of the pregnancy, then his marriage and honeymoon—had filled and emptied him of so many useless fears. Nothing wrong with that. Life, after all, got serious for everyone. Apply timeless rules: be patient and keep a level head.

He patted the Buick's rear tail fin. In the same affectionate way, he'd once patted the nose of a C-14 that had sputtered over the Mediterranean. A radio operator, he and a crew of four had landed the C-14 in Corsica, in a pasture, with minimal damage. He, not the car, had let Connie down. Machines weren't evil. They were tools. The evil lived in misuse, and in those who didn't blame malfunctions on human error.

Mike opened the trunk, impressed by its size. Everything about this car loomed bigger than big, like America, like his dreams. He removed his suitcase with ease, found another loose checkered shirt and slipped into it. He wanted to toss his wet shirt into the woods, but remembered that Connie had bought it in Daytona as a gift. He flattened it to dry atop the wheel well. His mother would scrub it with Borax. Lucky for him, Connie shared a similar knack for the domestic.

Back inside the Buick, he told her to cover herself with the blanket on the back seat. "And keep all the doors locked."

Firing out of the darkness, a car passed, reminding Mike of how dangerously narrow the road was. "Play the radio. Make yourself comfortable."

"But we're in the middle of nowhere."

"Don't sweat it, honey. There's a flashlight in the trunk. See that glow way up ahead? Got a hunch it's a filling station. I'll be back in a jiff."

After walking what seemed like a mile, Mike started to think he'd made a mistake. His flashlight beam had weakened, so he kept it turned off. He wouldn't let Connie sleep in the car until morning, but this was no guess, this was instinct, and would prove him right.

He reached the yellow glow, happy to see that it lit a swinging oval Sinclair filling station sign, with its familiar green dinosaur logo. Out front, a drive-under roof covered two pumps with rounded edges. Made of fieldstone boulders, the garage building looked closed.

A voice cried out of the darkness. "Who's that there?"

Mike swatted away gnats and moths, looking around until he saw an old-timer on a bench in front of a plate glass window with stickers advertising Penn Valvoline motor oil at 5 cents a can.

Guard up, he approached the man. "Hello, Sir. Don't mean any harm. Got car trouble."

The old man, a pipe in his mouth, eyed him. He looked perturbed.

"She's overheated. A '53 Buick." Mike offered his hand. "The name's Mike Shea."

The old man didn't shake. With a hard sneer, he studied this handsome young devil of a stranger, tall, trim, clean-cut and tanned. He rose, leaning back as he yanked up his orange suspenders. Scratched at whiskers on his chin. Lifted one leg and planted a greasy boot on the bench. His pipe stem clicked as he rolled it around in his mouth. Taking his time, he removed his pipe, hawked up a gob of phlegm and sent it sailing into the dark. As if satisfied with the way he'd spit, he removed his soft flat cap and studied it a moment. With big hands hardened by labor, he scratched a thinning tangle of white hair.

Keeping his distance, Mike reminded himself to stay calm. To be young, honest and serious wasn't a crime, and the old man could see this, couldn't he? Perhaps not. He reeked of country ways, and his gas prices were a nickel higher than average.

With a frown that contorted his face, the old man snapped, "I'm Hazzard Baggs. What of it? I'm closed."

"But I drove north all the way from Florida, and now I'm heading back from Niagara Falls."

Hazzard Baggs shook his head with disdain. His voice jumped, hectoring Mike. "Damn fool thing taking off a radiator cap while the engine's hot. I can smell it on you."

"My wife's waiting there, alone. We're on our honeymoon."

Hazzard Baggs softened, muttering, "I see. A '53 Buick, you say?"

"That's right."

"Tell the truth," said Hazzard, softening, "ain't even sure I got a screwdriver around here. I'm all locked up, the missus got the keys, and she's gone to town."

Mike didn't believe this sly codger with the queer name. He seemed cagey and mean. Then again, marooned roadside in the sticks he'd been lucky to find anything.

"Should've taken your wife wit' you."

"She's expecting."

Hazzard Baggs blinked once. "That so?"

Mike nodded solemnly. "Why would I lie about such a thing?"

"You tell me."

"Plus my flashlight's about crapped out."

Hazzard fingered his nose, pulling out a hair. "Then I reckon we can find a screwdriver and some wrenches. Them Buicks, you know, you can run 'em without a thermostat. When you get back to where you're going, you have one put in. Until then, we'll let it cool. Maybe we can scratch the old one out. They swell a bit and stick to the housing, and if it was put in with gasket cement, we might have a hell of a time."

Groaning, Hazzard bent over and started to rummage under the bench. He scared off a cat as he pulled out a yellow wooden box with the words Royal Crown Cola in faint red letters on both sides. The smell of a skunk began to swell as he clinked and clanked, sorting through wrenches, mumbling, "Five-eighths, half-inch, three-eighths and a crescent. Them'll work. And here's a screw-driver that'll do us."

He held it up and admired it. "Ain't my best, since all them is at the house or in the garage. You're lucky. I was out getting time away from the Missus. You ain't been married long enough to know how good that feels."

"Sir, I really appreciate your help."

Hazzard waved off the remark. "Quit calling me Sir. It's a flat-head, too. Hate to go at it with a Phillips. Where'd you say you was from?"

"Boston. Roslindale, for now."

"Nope. Never been."

As they walked back to the car, the skunk smell dissipated behind them. They listened to the steady plangency of crickets. Evergreens swayed in soft breezes. Not one car rolled by. With no guardrail between the asphalt and its thin gravel margin, Mike thought the road sounded its own quiet black pulse.

Hazzard remarked, "Your wife is brave to be out here alone. She must be a keeper. I reckon the coons, skunks, possum and deer are enough to scare anybody. Not to mention Democrats and out-of-towners like yourself passing through. You just never know these days."

"Guess not."

"You was in the service, wasn't you?"

"Air Force." After so many hours at the wheel with Connie, Mike enjoyed male company. "Got big plans. Working days now. Going to college at night. On the GI bill."

"Ain't that a fine thing? At first, I thought you was one of them highbrows." Hazzard paused, smacking his lips together. "We'll see what we can do. This ain't no way to spend no honeymoon."

At the car, Mike stood over its engine like a mourner at a funeral. Hazzard went to work matching one of his wrenches to fit a pair of bolt heads.

"She's got a straight eight," he explained. "I think the V-8 is better, but you pay for it."

Mike shrugged. "Got her cheap because she doesn't have power steering."

"I can see that. Got whitewalls, though."

"And plenty of legroom," said Mike.

"You know how many horsepower?"

As if guilty of shameful ignorance, Mike shook his head no.

Hazzard said, "Between you and me, I reckon the *Roadmaster* and the *Super* are the better models. They got what they call fireball combustion. And the *Roadmaster's* got a 12-volt battery. Howard Hughes drove a *Roadmaster*. You're an Air Force man, didn't they teach you that?"

Mike stopped fumbling for a reply when he saw Connie's head pop up behind the windshield. Blanket around her shoulders, she adjusted the rear view mirror, flounced her hive of hair and covered it with an orange kerchief that she tied under her chin. She looked flush with sleep, confused, shifting about on the seat as if to compensate for the growing life inside her. Her limpid eyes bloomed at the sight of the grizzled man Mike had found to help them. She kept a hand to her throat, touching the crucifix there.

Stunned for a moment by her comely radiance, Hazzard removed his cap and nodded with overstated reverence. Connie blinked, girlishly so.

Etched lines weakened above Hazzard's pocked nose. He

sounded a small note of pleasure that darkened into grim resignation. Poking his pipe between yellow teeth, he took another look at the engine. He looked a long time, his neck ribbed with veins as he mumbled, "Fifty-three they brought out the *Skylark*. You ask me, nothing beats a Buick. Pure American know-how. Got this new Twin-Turbine Dynaflow engine and I reckon she goes like a rocket."

Mike sounded eager. "Anything I can do?"

"Nope." The pipe stem clicked against Hazzard's teeth. He took a rag from his back pocket and touched the radiator with it. "She's hotter than a pistol, but I kin get her."

As Hazzard removed the two bolts that held the housing in place, Mike flashed a grin at Connie in the front seat. Thinking how the pregnancy and Florida sunshine had brought a nascent creaminess to her features, his grin widened. Eight children, he thought. No less. He'd be Dad of the Year for a decade.

Meanwhile, Hazzard had dropped the bolts into his pocket and started to scratch at the manifold with his screwdriver. "Just gotta get under the lip. Ha! There it is. Should pop her now."

Mike stepped closer. "It's out?"

"You stay back. Still hot under here."

With a small sucking noise, the housing and thermostat came free of the manifold. Hazzard used his rag to remove them.

"Damnation." He yanked his hand back and dropped the thermostat. Wiped it against the sides of his trousers. "Sticky, too. We'll let it cool." Leaning over the manifold again, he poked around with his screwdriver. "Might be sealer. Hard to tell it's so dark. Don't see none. Guess it ain't got a gasket. Some do, and scraping that sealer ain't exactly a cakewalk."

Mike asked, "Can I see it?"

"Right over there. Like I said, you can run this Bessie without it, at least 'til you're home."

Mike picked up the thermostat, surprised by how hot it was. "I've never seen one before. This is only my second car. My first was a Nash."

Hazzard grunted and bent over the engine. He turned each bolt until he'd fitted the housing back into the manifold. "Now I got to clamp the hose back on." As he did so, he remarked to Mike, "Nash, you say? *Rambler?*"

"Nope. A '48 *Ambassador. A Brougham.*"

"I reckon if you're Air Force, you know more about B-52s than Buicks."

"I flew on B-29s, mostly. And C-models, for transport."

Hearing such talk, Hazzard looked impressed. He wiped with a rag his spatulated fingers, grit packed under each nail. "Me, I'll stick to cars. Keep both feet planted."

"The rate we're going," said Mike, "we'll be on the moon before long."

Hazzard hawked up another gob and let it fly. "Who's we?"

Mike glanced at Connie in the car. He shot her an OK signal. "Maybe my first child. You never know."

"Got water?" asked Hazzard. "She's parched."

Mike thought he'd meant Connie, and then realized he'd meant the car. "No, afraid I don't. Just my spare and some luggage in the trunk."

Hazzard, smirking, slid his pipe into a shirt pocket. He sighed as he appeared to think about his next step. He lit a *Lark* cigarette with a stick match that he struck against his thigh. Sounding annoyed, he told Mike, "I got a watering can. We'll go and fill it. By then, she'll be cool enough so when we pour it in we won't crack the block."

Mike, nodding, held up his hand toward Connie as if to say five minutes.

Hazzard said, "No, that ain't right neither. You stay with your bride. I won't be long. Can't hurry no ways, since the engine's still piping."

"Right," said Mike. "Don't want to crack the block."

"You're catching on, at least."

After adjusting his hat, Hazzard dropped loose hands and his wrenches into the rear pockets of his trousers. He kept his cigarette between his lips as he cantered along, looking up at the night sky, muttering to himself. "Ain't got a decent flashlight and he's talking about the moon."

Connie gestured for Mike to open the door. She asked him, "Could you get my windbreaker out of my suitcase? It's right on top."

"I think we can, Mrs. Shea."

"Wait." Connie grabbed his arms, pulling him into an embrace. They kissed for a long time.

Mike spoke first, his voice breathy and gentle. "We went such a long way, and this is our first time with problems. That's pretty good, I think."

"There are always problems, Mike. But you can fix them."

"The old-timer thinks so. Says we can't hurry."

"What a nice man."

"I wouldn't say nice," said Mike. "More like country friendly. Knows a bunch about cars."

"I'm still trying to figure out how we're going to pay him."

Mike made a sour face. "You would have to bring that up."

"But what if he asks?"

Ignoring the question, he rested his hand against Connie's stomach. "Okay in there?"

Connie removed his hand. "Don't change the subject. We have to give him something. It's the right thing to do."

"I'm thinking." He sighed. "Look, honey, I'm sorry about all this. I'm pretty new to cars. I should have known."

"It's not your fault. You did all the driving. It really has been wonderful, you know. The orange groves. The beaches. The Carolinas. Niagara Falls. It's been everything we dreamed it would be. So what's a little car trouble?"

"Just remind me next time to put tools, a funnel, and a watering can in the trunk."

"I'll get you them for Christmas. But please, my jacket. I'm cold."

Mike hurried to the trunk, still open, finding Connie's suitcase and her windbreaker. Lodged next to the suitcase, he found the dozen eggs he'd bought earlier that day. After Connie stepped out of the car to put on her windbreaker, he showed them to her.

"Day's been so long, I forgot. Good thing you packed them tight."

"But they're eggs," she said.

"They're all we got."

Connie shot him a frosty glance, but he ignored it. As he watched her get back into the car, he told her she should nap. He didn't say she looked pasty and numb with fatigue. For the time being, he didn't care to cuddle or talk a blue streak about the baby, their future, how they'd make ends meet. He wanted this waiting time to himself, so he could enjoy a smoke alone under the night sky, confront the misgivings that stirred his conscience. Was he doing the right thing? Of course, he was. Then why did he feel glad his honeymoon was nearing its end? Perhaps because he wanted to get on with it. He was a man of action, after all.

He blew smoke rings. He thought of the stars and rockets that would actually circle the moon. Perhaps he'd have a son who'd become an astronaut. What a dream. What a sweetheart he had in Connie.

Mike continued to check his watch. More than an hour had passed. Hazzard sure moved like a turtle. Then again, a hot engine was impossible to work on. The scruffy old mechanic had every right to take his time alone in the dark.

A flashlight beam hit Mike in the face. It was Hazzard. He lifted a galvanized tin watering can. Mike smiled, but Hazzard didn't smile back. His cigarette hung off his lower lip. "Found my flashlight, too." He clicked it off. "I'll pour it in slow, and make sure the hose don't leak. She should run fine with just water, but get her flushed and put in coolant and a new thermostat. For now, she'll run."

Hazzard tossed aside his cigarette. He leaned over the radiator. He put down the watering can. Sniffed a little. Listened. Touched the radiator as if testing. Touched it again. "I'll leave my light and can. Wait a half-hour and she'll be dandy. Then pour the water in and come fetch me."

Mike looked around. It amazed him that not a car had passed. "Got it."

"You know," said Hazzard, "for a service man, you ain't rightly prepared for such a trip."

Hazzard, having said his piece, wiped his hands together in a chopping motion and walked back to his station. Mike, wilting, watched him go. He returned to Connie. "See what I mean."

"Don't take it to heart. He's helping us. Besides, it's true. Live and learn."

Mike scowled and folded his arms. "Come on. We'll listen to the radio."

Cozy together, Connie dropped her head on his shoulder, napping while he turned the radio dial. He found The Crests singing: "Blow out the candles, make your wish come true…"

He shut it off, and then closed his eyes. When a car zoomed by, shaking the Buick, he looked at the lighted clock dial in his dashboard. Then he looked at the eggs on the back seat. Turning, he rose to his knees and drove his hand down between the seats, waking Connie.

"See if you can find some change," he said. "Some quarters if we're lucky."

"Please just give him the eggs. I want to go. Please. "

"So now they're okay?"

"We can always mail him money."

Mike lifted the eggs off the back seat, stepped out of the Buick, and shut its heavy door with his hip. Walking to the front of the car, he put the eggs on the ground. He picked up the watering can and poured until it was empty. He waited a moment, watching the water form a bubble in the radiator's mouth, sounding a bloop-bloop as it drained into the engine. He squeezed the hose and fingered the clamps. No leakage. He looked around for the cap, needing the flashlight to find it. He screwed the cap on, and then picked up the eggs and the emptied can.

Hazzard sat as before, chewing on his pipe. Mike put the can and flashlight on the bench. "All done. Clamped down. No leaks."

He held out the carton of eggs.

Hazzard smirked, looking at them. "What's this?"

"Connie thought you'd like these for payment. They're farm fresh. Bought them this morning from a roadside stand. You've been really generous. I don't know what we'd have done without your help."

Hazzard brushed away gnats. He stared into the night as if Mike wasn't there.

"Honest truth," said Mike. "I got maybe five dollars to my name, and I'll need it for gas. If you want, we can mail you a payment."

Sounding a slow groan, Hazzard shut his eyes and rubbed his eyebrows, mumbling, "Eggs from a honeymoon bride. If that don't beat all."

Mike leaned forward, wanting to shove the eggs on Hazzard's lap.

Hazzard opened his eyes. He took the eggs and rested them on the bench. He squinted as if in sudden pain. "But eggs mean the start of something, don't they?"

Mike, groping for words, knew he was better than this feeble show of gratitude. He couldn't face Hazzard, so instead watched the cat return to its place under the bench.

The high shine in Hazzard's face crimsoned as he frowned, looking away from the eggs, sounding a soft note of surprise that gradually darkened to resentment. He gazed off, a distant and pre-occupied look in his eyes, as if he were holding back a need to curse all the rotten luck he'd ever had. After about a minute, he let the curse fly, wearily so in a lower register while covering his mouth. He looked for a moment up to the stars. Crickets filled the silence. When he lowered his head and turned and glared at Mike, he appeared stunned to see him still there. Waving his hands, shooing him off, he shouted, "Don't lollygag there like a lost pup. You're fixed to go. So get. Go on. Back to your bride. Get."

Mike started to reply, wanting to explain as sweat ran cold in his scalp, but he stuttered and then gave up, driving his fists into his pockets. He turned away and started walking. He felt a slowing of time. The crickets sounded softer now. He thought of Hazzard's big hands wrenching down bolts one turn at a time. He thought of the road's black pulse. Blow out all the candles, but bring a flashlight just in case. With each step toward the Buick, he felt as if the breezes and the smells of skunk, pinesap, asphalt and radiator fluid, and the night itself like a cavernous mouth had expanded to swallow him.

False World, Goodnight

In her butch haircut and ebony leather jacket, Tamara stomped in from the back deck reeking of cigarette smoke, her nose ruddy with cold. After hugging our host Meg and shaking my husband Blake's hand, she took off her coat. While she sat, I hurried to hang her coat on a nearby wall peg.

Tamara asked so what's new. Meg said hold on a minute. She opened the oven door and in a moment of soft ecstasy I marinated in the aroma of her veggie and cheddar casserole as it filled the kitchen. This was a treat she baked often for Blake and me, knowing how much our daughter Lilly, a picky nine-year-old playing alone in another room, loved it.

With a yellow apron over her Greenpeace sweatshirt and jeans, Meg was hardly a slender woman and the opposite in build to her former roommate and collegiate champion track star, Tamara. There was no stopping Meg. We all knew she adored Tamara and she hurried to pour her hot herbal tea from a white glazed pot with a repeated motif of a black Cheshire cat's face.

Meg sat at the head of the table, closest to the oven. Blake, who was her brother, sat to her right. Meg silenced Tamara by saying "He's fine" when Tamara asked about her husband, Simon.

Simon had been arrested for punching a policeman in Zuccotti Park during early days of Occupy Wall Street. His bail had been set high. He had what Meg described as an adequate lawyer, and he was in prison waiting for a loan to come through, and a trial date. Simon had prior convictions that dated back to his early days of political acitivism, when he'd befriended the folksinger Utah Philips and joined a group who had jumped on Trident submarines while Reagan was president.

Meg looked wrinkled, exhausted. She said to Blake, "It wasn't the first time for Simon and me and it won't be the last. We can't just sit back and let someone else do it."

"They put us to sleep with statistics," said Tamara. She was practically chirping. "Anything to assure us we're okay. But we're not. They just keep making more weapons. Stealing more."

"I have to participate," said Meg. "I couldn't live with myself, otherwise."

Feeling a little left out, I piped in, "Neither can I. We can't just let it happen. Somebody has to keep them in check."

"Them?" asked Tamara. "Who do you mean? Obama? The most liberal president we've ever had?"

Blake grabbed my wrist, squeezed it and told me to stop.

"Go on, Caprice," Meg said to me. "I knew you wouldn't sit quiet for long."

"Don't encourage her," said Blake.

Meg brightened. She had seven years on Blake, and fourteen on me. "Caprice, speak up. I want to hear what the youth of America have to say."

I started out tepidly. "I really want to grasp your perspective, I do," I told Meg. "But I don't quite grasp your anger. I don't know how to say this, really, but what do you have to complain about?"

"Plenty," said Tamara. She looked disgusted with me.

"Yeah, how is that?" Blake asked, taking my side. "Meg you rent this little old house and don't even work for a living. All with a radical husband behind bars."

"Blake will you please," I said, scolding him. At home, he constantly ragged on his sister and her foggy notions of changing the world. "That's not what I meant."

Meg laughed. "Now here's a loving couple."

I apologized to Meg.

She smiled at me, putting me at ease. "Caprice, is that what you really think?"

I shrugged. I didn't know what I thought. I was a Mom working full-time. I didn't follow the political stuff the way these women did. I relied on Blake — perhaps too much — to more or less keep me informed about such things. I really disliked watching the news. It wasn't as if I had time for it. Besides, give me a hot cup of tea and a Jane Austen novel and I'm happy.

Meg then turned to her brother, asking him. "Blake, you think I don't *work* here?"

"I didn't say that. I mean — not a nine-to-five gig."

"It's called organizing," said Tamra. "The Internet." Her sarcasm felt nasty.

"Yeah, like a giant department store and porno palace rolled into one," I said.

Tamara sneered at me. "You just had to start, didn't you?"

"I don't like The Internet. All those pop-ups. It's so distracting for Lilly."

"Leave Caprice be," said Meg to Tamara. "I love her passion. She's entitled to her point of view. The Internet is a tool, that's all. We can agree on that."

"You're right, Meg," said Blake. "Well put."

I said, "Thanks, Meg." I leaned over the table to touch her arm. I was careful as I kept talking. "Look, I can let go of obsessions. What I planned and worked for, where I failed and where I dreamed my life might go with Blake. But I don't believe I can solve the world's hatreds and lies. I have my own problems to figure out."

"Shouldn't we be drinking wine?" asked Blake.

"Not until dinner," said Tamara. "Right now, it'll just add fuel to the fire."

"So?" said Blake. "I'm the one outnumbered. What are you worried about?"

Meg faced me over her warped shingle of a varnished kitchen table. The kitchen exuded her cozy voluptuous warmth. "Well, Caprice, honestly, I've never understood the rationale behind The Us Versus Them paranoia, as if chucking rocks at a bank window ferries along productive discussions. Such shows of anarchy do strike me as self-serving."

Blake slapped the table. "I couldn't agree more."

Meg kept going. "I was being sarcastic, Blake. What people hunger for is vision, new ideas. Sometimes reactionary violence is necessary to get them to notice."

"Right," I said. "But, Meg, nobody wants fear. I know I don't."

Blake asked his sister, "Do they want Port-O-Potties camped in their local park for weeks at a time? World government, world peace — what do these things mean?"

"Blake," said Tamara, looking at him. "Really? Are you that dense?"

"Yes, really, I am," he said. "I have no clue, never have."

"Stop it you two," said Meg. "You both know that participation at ground zero is where it's at. Not apathy."

"That's not exactly what I'm saying," said Blake.

Tamara rolled her eyes. "As usual, you're not saying anything."

Blake blew a huge sigh. He hadn't wanted to come. I'd insisted on it. I felt a little guilty.

"Go on, out with it," Meg told me. She had been studying the way I'd followed the conversation.

"Meg, please, you know Blake and I don't like confrontation."

"I can speak for myself," said Blake.

"But don't you ever ask yourself what you can do to make a difference?" said Meg.

Tamara said, "They just don't care enough. Neither of them."

"Why do I come here?" asked Blake. He was red in the face. "Why?"

"Because I'm your sister," said Meg. "And you love me."

"I do." Blake then faced Tamara. "Why should I end up in jail?"

Meg said, "You're already in a kind of jail."

"Touché," said Tamara. "It's called ignorance."

They all smirked at Blake and I had to, as well. Yes, he was my husband, but these women were my new best friends, the only real intellectual conversation I experienced regularly, and a part of me knew they were right. I didn't *prefer* ignorance and I knew I could complain if wanted to. Of what value was free speech if we didn't use it constructively? What I needed and hoped to find were solutions. We all did, including Blake, even if he didn't care to admit it.

I didn't know why, but Blake felt a need to get on his soap box. Maybe he felt insecure. He was certainly outnumbered. "Let me just say this. If I may. I think that men are imprisoned by desires and a resistance to change. This is not a political problem. It's a question of being. Our identity. The human condition."

"Women don't have desires?" asked Meg.

"It's not a political issue," said Blake. "That's my point."

"Got it," said Tamara. She was surly. "Listen to Blake the philosopher here. That's just it. All *men*."

"While women do the work," I added. "And get paid less."

"That's not true in all circles, you know that," said Blake. His face had grown even redder. "How many of us have to worry about the glass ceiling?"

"Blake, Sweetheart, calm down," I said. I touched his shoulder. We were seated next to each other. I liked feeling close to him when with friends. "It's just talk."

"But there are good men," said Meg. "Like my Simon."

Blake wouldn't give it a rest. "So you're saying I'm not worth saving from nuclear annihilation?"

Tamara sounded a cluck. "Now there's a question."

I said to Meg. "I respect that you want to save the world, but it seems to me only if the act of salvation meets your conditions."

Silence. My comment had been a dud.

"C'mon, Blake," I said. "Enough of this. Let's talk about real estate. Something harmless." I faced Meg. "You know we've started looking for a house, at last."

"Connecticut's full of houses," said Tamara. "I'm sure you'll find one."

"No," said Blake, too loudly I thought. "Meg here wants to fill the world with people who think, act and believe the same way she does."

"Right," said Tamara. "And everybody else can just go screw themselves while you look for your colonial with a two-car garage and in-ground septic."

Blake turned to Tamara and shouted, "Especially if they pee standing up."

I punched him in the shoulder. Hard. "Stop it. Now. Just stop!"

"Don't forget Lilly," said Meg.

He apologized. Meg faced him, looking concerned. "Blake, I think Simon and I fight because we care about the human race."

Tamara was really rubbing it in, her eyes squinting as she needled Blake, "But Bartleby here would prefer not to."

As a lit major before I went into public relations, I was probably the only one in the room who got Tamara's Bartleby reference. She was, at times, such a hammy intellectual snob that I wanted to kick her in the shins. She didn't know that Blake had experienced a terrible week at his job. Day by day he wasn't even sure if his job would still exist. The corporation that owned the health center had sold it to another corporation, firing a third of the workers overnight, without warning. They were all on tenterhooks. We'd come to see Meg because Blake, for all his skepticism toward political activism, admired and respected his older sister. Meg was all he had left of family. He wanted Lilly to know her Aunt Meg, to know her well, to love her. Tamara, I supposed, wasn't seeing any of this, mostly because she was still single and unapologetically self-centered.

Blake said, "I'm just posing this question." He faced Tamara. "Since I don't agree with Meg's politics, am I worth saving on the day she rescues the world from itself?"

"Our government, liberal or otherwise," said Tamara "is pumping out massive supplies of weapons all over the globe. We're financing the rich at the cost of the poor. We're always in a war of some kind. Families are getting torn apart by layoffs. Young men and women are coming home with limbs blown off. Obama extended an olive branch, but how many countries still hate us? Why is that?"

"You tell me," said Blake.

"Because we stand for annihilation, not freedom," said Meg. "Think about it, Blake. How many nuclear warheads are needed to blow up the earth? Don't we have enough already?"

"We're reducing our arsenal. Leading the way on that."

"Are we?" said Tamara.

Meg asked, "What does the word radioactive mean to you? And let's not forget all the lies about our exposure to it, and about weapons of mass destruction and all these wars where we don't really defend ourselves, but we just march in and take over as if we've got the answer. We don't have the only way of life anyone should live."

"Not to mention the warmongers," said Tamara. "What they do or *don't* do with the hazardous waste from our nuclear arms."

I sighed, saying, "It's too much for me."

"Is it, really?" asked Meg. "Or are you just lazy?"

"Stop it, Meg," said Blake, defending me.

"No, it's okay," I said.

"I'm talking about our planet. Our garden," said Meg. "Lilly's garden. And you don't seem to think it's very important, do you?"

Again, Blake defended me. "She does. Of course she does."

Part of me wanted to tell my sister-in-law that I didn't care at all, but I'd have been lying. Of course I cared, but so often of late I had felt tired, wanting, powerless to change anything. I didn't tell Meg that my concerns were smaller and more selfish. As a mother and wife, I had to ask how we would pay for the food and shelter we needed. How to make sure Lilly got the best out of school. How to afford a night out with Blake now and then. How shuffle our schedules so we could get Lilly back and forth. As it was, our apartment was small for any couple, let alone a family of three. The price of a new home in a town that would suit us was so much higher than we'd expected. Everything we'd seen of late had been dumpy and overvalued.

I looked to Blake. Didn't he see how much I cared about him?

Blake said to his sister, "You get what I'm saying, don't you?"

Meg offered a gentle nod. "You're not saying anything, Blake. I know you. You're just venting. I think you're jealous of Simon and his commitment."

"So do I," said Tamara.

Meg put her hand on Blake's shoulder, calming him, saying, "There are worse things than learning how little they really know about all this so-called terrorism. They don't even talk about it like it's been around forever."

"Even though it has been and they know plenty," said Tamara. "If you ask me, it's something they created. A military police state."

"It's what they won't tell us," I said. "That's what scares me."

"Don't encourage them," said Blake.

"But it's true," I said. "You said that yourself, just the other night."

"I did," said Blake. "I know. I'm just riled, that's all."

"Not just terrorism," said Meg. "But nuclear holocaust,

torture, the drug wars, CIA renditions and all the innocent citizens they've killed."

"But to risk going to jail?" Blake asked. "I mean, 9-11, I don't care how you spin it. It was an attack."

"So what's your point, Bartleby?" asked Tamara.

Blake said, "Twenty blocks uptown from Ground Zero, people were back at work in less than two weeks."

"They kept pursuing what they believe in," said Meg.

I said, "Blake, don't you see? From Meg's point of view, we're the government. We have to stop things when we don't like them."

"Not just my perspective," said Meg. "Jefferson's, too. And a few others."

Blake popped out of his chair. "Stop *what?* Jesus, the three of you. Like three witches. Anybody with common sense knows the government does what it wants when it wants to."

Meg eased him down. "Easy, big feller, your Caprice is right. You've got to believe in something larger than yourself."

"Okay," said Blake. "But we have a daughter. We'd like a house with a yard in a good school district. Is that asking so much? There's no way I'm slugging cops and ending up behind bars to create a perfect world."

Silence. A clock ticked from the wall. The casserole smelled divine.

Meg had our attention. "I respect what you're saying, Blake, but I think you have to risk everything. It's very hard these days to get anyone to listen. You can't tell me that my husband isn't brave."

"But that doesn't make me a coward because my choices are different."

Tamara said, "It's our right, privilege and responsibility to keep our government honest. And that includes you, Bartleby."

I squeezed Blake's arm. I wanted a truce. I said to Tamara, "I don't believe Bartleby thinks he's above it all. He simply has other interests. Let's be fair."

"No I don't," said Blake. "We have the same interests. It's just my priorities are different. There's a difference."

"Semantics," said Meg.

"There's a difference," repeated Blake.

"No, Caprice is right," said Tamara. "Let's be fair. Blake, it's obvious you'll never win an argument with us. Besides, you've already made up your mind. You think liberals are the most close-minded people you've ever met, but you keep that thought to yourself because you like to think of yourself as a liberal."

"Not true," said Blake. "I happen to think the Tea Party was a good idea initially. I liked how they began. I just hated where it ended up going."

"Maybe they brought some good ideas out into the open," I said.

"The Tea Party?" Tamara laughed at me. "Oh Caprice, that's priceless."

"We all have our choices," said Meg. "Simon and I won't let anything destroy what we share, even if we think that, overall, Obama is okay. I mean compared to Bush. But just because we like a president's intelligence doesn't mean he always stands for what we believe in. The beautiful thing about America is that we, as citizens, can and should always do this kind of work, regardless of what friends and family think."

Tamara said, "Oh Meg, you're beautiful."

Meg frowned. "But I wish Simon was here."

I added a soothing note. "You're doing the right thing. Even Blake thinks so."

"No I don't," said Blake, fuming a little. "I think — "

Blake stopped mid-sentence. Lilly had entered the kitchen. She looked pale and gloomy as she held a glass toward me. She'd been sleeping. I quickly placed the glass in the sink and then sat down.

Lilly leaned against Blake where he sat at the table. She said, "Daddy, can we go to the zoo tomorrow?"

"Sweetie Pie, Daddy's working tomorrow," I said.

Here was my baby, my everything. What kind of political hash had I been arguing? Had Meg been right? Was my husband jealous of Simon? Shouldn't Blake get more involved? No, ridiculous. Of what value would he serve if rotting in prison?

Meg would say it was for the greater good. What did that mean? As in all my political thinking, I had come to another abstraction that stood like a hurdle I didn't understand and couldn't jump over.

"Goodnight to all of it," said Blake out of nowhere.

Lilly looked surprised. "Don't be mad, Daddy," she said. "It's just Auntie Meg."

Lilly smiled at Meg, who crimsoned all over as she smiled back and asked Lilly if she was hungry and if she'd had a good nap. Lilly nodded yes on both counts.

All the redness and tension had drained from Blake's face. He reached his arms out to Lilly, eased her toward him. She in her sleepy way and with a small hop slid atop his lap and squirmed until comfortable there.

Blake wrapped one long slow arm around her waist. They both looked at me. Lilly said, "Hi, Mommy. Are you okay?"

Such warmth I felt from her at that moment, from them both, but it didn't stop the chills of fear that rippled throughout my body.

The Four-Cent Tip

Sure, sure, you shrimps go out there and get dirty with work. Best education there is. Learn the value of a buck. Least you got choices. We didn't have that luxury. Your Aunt Fay started at eleven as a maid. I started at the same age. It was wartime. I held two jobs and gave your Nana every cent of take-home. Fay did the same.

On Saturdays, I humped it as a box boy at Shreve Crump and Low. Got my first glimpse of world-class travelers. They strolled in through Park Square after shopping at Bonwit Teller next door, staying in suites at the Park Plaza Hotel.

I boxed up bone china from England, Hummel figurines, and all types of gold and silver. Shreve's didn't deal in cosmetic jewelry or junk, no, they had a first-floor watch department, a diamond department, and a glass counter that sparkled from a mile away. Up on the second floor, you could buy lamps, fifty-six pieces of dinnerware boxed, Beleek or Waterford crystal, creamers, candy dishes, silver or gold on crystal. A teacup would set you back $7.50, which at that time was a day's salary for some.

They had a ship made of crystal that sold for hundreds of dollars, and I used to stare at that thing and let it take me away. It was all fantastic. Jewelers and watchmakers on staff, and a department of artists that designed window displays. On the fourth floor, they fixed and polished merchandise with buffers and grinders and vats of cleaning acid.

Me, I worked for Frankie Stockinger on the third floor where the boxing operation took place. A whole floor of shelved boxes, spools of twine, string, tape, all sorts of fine labels, and a crew of boys zipping around with razors and big shears.

As much as I loved Shreve's, I cut my dogteeth as a newsboy hawking for corner men: Baker Baker, Red Golman, and Eugee Cohen. Those tough old birds all boasted they owned a corner of Boston. Took me a little sweat to learn what that really meant.

I'd finish at Dearborn School at two p.m. and Red Golman would pick me up with other tenement boys, allowing us to save a nickel by not riding the T. Red lived in Brookline, and he'd bring us all home afterwards. I'd get my papers from him at a stand near Pray's, and the C. Crawford Holidge store on West Street.

Baker Baker, a smarmy cigar-chewing pug with thick glasses, controlled the corner near the Brigham's Ice Cream just up the hill from the Arlington T stop. All these corner men knew each other. Baker Baker and Eugee shared racks and stacks of magazines and kept their trunks loaded with them as they rode around in sedans. To me, this seemed extra special, having your own ride in the big city.

My pal Cott Delahunt worked for them, too. Cott was a giant, one of five boys and four Delahunt girls. That Delahunt clan was like family to me, since my Ma and Pa worked all the time and Fay wasn't home much. I spent as much time in Cott's room as I did in my own.

As newsies, Cott and I met the Beantown commute and its working folk head-on. They craved headlines so they could keep up with the war. People pulled together, it seemed, in a way I haven't seen since. They worried together, too, and they mourned, so don't let anyone tell those war years were a picnic. Far from it.

I laugh thinking about Eugee Cohen, always a sad look on his face as if he'd been beaten up too many times and was burdened by doubt and history. Coarse and shrewd, Eugee taught me up to his level. It was from him that I first heard words like anti-Semitism, Fascism, and what he called the Jewish question.

He'd bark at me in his gruff voice, "Mikey Shea, you're alright for a small fry. I know you think I'm just another Jew, just like I think you're a Mick runt, but neither of us don't need to make a big deal about it. I'm your boss, but we can get along. We're Americans, right? Together, right? "

He'd go on and on like this as if he needed my innocent approval. Of course, he was right. I needed work. He needed runts like me. If the war kept going, it wouldn't be long before I'd be shipped off. I dreamed about fighting evil as I read *Mandrake the Magician* each day in the funny pages.

I shadowed Eugee and soaked up what he told me. He'd take me with him to Locke-Ober's Cafe for lunch with the suits. He'd sidle up to the bar, apron on, his hands covered in newspaper ink. In the summer, he'd wipe his forehead, just like I did, and his sweat would blend with the ink and leave a big smear. He wouldn't let it bug him. He'd hobnob with those suits, wanting them to know Eugee Cohen got dirty for a living. He'd down a few but never paid. A suit was always willing to spot sly old Eugee a scotch and soda.

That apron was his uniform, made of heavy material like canvas, and he stashed everything in there—change, counting pad, pliers, a knife, and always a handful of root beer candies that he'd give to his newsboys.

At four a.m., which was cold as hell five months out of the year, Eugee loaded delivery trucks for *The Herald* and *The Traveler*. In the afternoon, I'd help him sell *The Globe, The Herald, The American, The Monitor, The Traveler, Life, Look, Collier's, Time,* and *The Saturday Evening Post*. Those were the standard ten each day. There were others, but never less than these ten.

Three years, I took my lumps as a newsy and wore that apron with pride. It always bulged with change. Papers cost three cents each. If I sold three different papers to the same customer I'd make a penny tip on a dime. I'd sell one for a nickel, usually *The Globe*, and I'd make a two-cent tip. It was best to sell two different papers for six cents because the dime usually wasn't asked to be changed. I lived for my four-cent tips.

Baker Baker introduced me to a coin merchant in one of the buildings on Tremont where I delivered. The merchant asked me to dump my apron on his counter. This became routine. He'd sort through my take and weed out the collectible coins. It was warm up there on the fourth floor in his shop that overlooked the green grass of the Public Gardens. In summer, I'd sit and watch the swan boats and sometimes he'd give me a tonic to drink. If he found something rare, he'd pay me a little for it. I was company for him, but I didn't hang around long. I had my papers to get out.

Like Eugee, Baker Baker was a squat and hairy old bull, and he had the gift of gab. He had family in Europe and he'd interpret the headlines and teach me about the issues over there and how we had to support our allies. He, too, would mingle with suits and scrape up tips on the stock market and the horses at Suffolk Downs. He'd pull the rolled papers out of his apron and make change just as quickly as he made small talk with Beacon Hill lawyers and politicians as they filed out of the T.

"Mikey," he'd say, "it's all about flow when you're hawking the standard ten."

On mornings when Red or Eugee didn't pick me up, I'd get off the trolley near High Street at the bottom near South Station. Thousands of people would come down that street going to and from work. There was an island there and a Nedick's that sold an orange drink I could usually cadge as a freebie in exchange for one paper.

I'd start at four a.m. and pick up wire-wrapped bundles of fifty papers each. A newsy had to keep wire cutters handy. The truck would roar by, slow down, never really stop, and a thug would dump the bundles of papers on the island. I'd run across High Street, pick up the bundles, cut that wire and start shouting. These were morning editions. There were evening ones, too. While I picked up my bundles, commuters streamed out of South Station. I kept my papers rolled and organized, screamed those headlines, and in the winter made change with gloves on.

Boston had four dailies: *The Globe, Traveler, Herald,* and *American*. Some bought all four each day. I learned who they were. I worked left hand and right, pulled from one stack, kept another under my arm. I made change, barked headlines, and knew my customers. I saw them coming, and I'd have my bundle of four ready, wouldn't miss a beat as they bustled past me to work, got their rolled news, paid me in coin and left a tip. Without income tax, it was a decent wage for a shrimp like me. I'm not exaggerating when

I say that including the evening editions, I sold close to a thousand copies each day.

I kept boxing at Shreve's on Saturdays. Nobody worked on Sunday. Weeknights, if Pa was home when I'd get there, he'd call me Moneybags. He didn't care that I missed school and homework. We needed the bread, all of which Ma managed with care. After supper, I'd lie on the living room floor and lose myself in front of our upright Emerson. I can still smell that wood and those hot tubes behind the lighted dial. I'd drift off, eyes closed to *The Fat Man* and then *The Whistler.*

The radio stayed on, and Ma tuned into Walter Winchell, Amos n' Andy, and Burns and Allen. I'd park at the kitchen table and separate my coins. We had no pre-made rolls. I'd lay a stack of fifty pennies crosswise over a sheet of brown paper and roll 'em up. I'd stack a hundred dimes and two hundred nickels the same way. Since we couldn't afford tape, I'd fold the paper at the ends.

I knew it was getting late when "Opus One" came on and Pa hummed and danced a little as he came out of his bedroom in a silk smoking jacket. He'd sit in his wicker chair and listen to Sherm Feller, the deejay, doing his Club Midnight show. "Opus One" was Feller's theme song. By this time, Ma and Fay were asleep, and neither liked that I stayed up so late. It was a miracle I didn't flunk out of school. I hardly showed up there, and when I did I was too tired to stay alert. Your Nana chided Pa about this, but he shrugged it off.

Three-thirty always came early. Skinny and gawky in my tweed hat and apron, I'd ride the trackless trolley with a bundle of rolled coins on my lap, all wrapped together with twine. I'd pretend it was a cake. I'd switch to the T. Riding alone from Roxbury to downtown, I would have been an easy mark, but no one ever bothered me.

Red Golman had bought a new car, a Graham, and stopped picking us up at the tenements. On days when Ma demanded I attend school, I'd meet Red in the afternoon in front of the Park Street Church. Even without morning deliveries, I worked every weekday because Red, like Eugee and Baker Baker, complained about being short-handed as more boys shipped off to France and the Pacific theatre. Three of Cott's brothers had been gone a year. Only one came back.

I convinced your Nana to let me work Saturday nights. Between ten and eleven, I'd ride the T to Newspaper Row in front of what we called the Boston Post building on Washington Street. Written in chalk on blackboards nailed to the building, the Sunday headlines, known as teasers, urged people to buy. They'd walk down Washington after seeing a show, maybe on their way to the Parker House or Chinatown for a meal, and they'd get their Sunday paper on Saturday night.

The Sunday paper was a huge deal. Remember, no TV yet, only radio, and it didn't give the detailed info the paper was known for. I'd hawk it on Washington where Winter meets Summer Street. This area always bustled. I'd finish at three on Sunday morning and then bolt to the Newspaperman's Mass at Saint James Church in the South End. A long walk, but I got there on time if I took Washington all the way. The T didn't run at that hour, still doesn't, so I had to hustle. That Mass was always crowded. The Catholics who worked for the paper, and they were legion, went to communion grateful that the Sunday, at last, had been put to bed.

Wiped out, I'd stagger home around six. By one in the afternoon, I'd jaunt back out again, joining Pa at a matinee. My grades at Dearborn dropped below passing, so your Nana yanked me and sent me to Saint Patrick's where I studied under Sister Superior. Those nuns were beastly and strict, but whatever I learned from books came from them.

When your Nana broke her leg, she phoned Saint Pat's asking that I be excused. I worked like a dog while she stayed laid-up, until one frigid day I collapsed on the corner of Park and Tremont. Not only dehydrated, I had scarlet fever to boot. Admitted to City Hospital on Northampton, my apron bulged full of coins, as always. They took it away, and I forgot about it once the injection kicked in.

A day later, Red Golman called Pa and offered to pick him up, along with Ma, and drive them in his Graham to visit me. I'll never forget Red's teeth, crummy after a lifetime of unfiltered Old Golds. How he smelled of pickled eggs when he bore down on me with a sneering grin. "Mikey Shea, how's my best newsboy doing? Eugee and Baker Baker send their regards. We need you back, Kid."

I moaned, still weak and partly sedated. "Is that Red? Hi, Red. Where am I?"

"Where are you?" Red winked at Pa. He sucked his teeth, leaned over and keened his eyes at me. "Where's my money?"

This marked the end of my newsboy days. From that point on, when Red's name came up, Ma would tsk-tsk and shake her head. Pa would smolder, mumbling, "That no good s.o.b. You weren't even awake yet."

Just as well. The price had jumped to a nickel for each of the four dailies. It meant no gravy, no tip advantage for a newsy. The nickel, dime, and fifteen cents would go straight to the corner man. Today, they'd call it cost cutting.

In a way, I'm grateful to Red. He schooled me in what it meant to own a corner.

A Question For The Devil's Rope

Silver Thorny

Garrett and I talked for months and our answer was to drive west. He had a college friend in Taos with an extra room. We'd start there and take it one day at a time.

As with any upheaval, doubts uprooted inner voices that melted like Dali clocks. I gripped my question, itself a form of prison: *Is Freedom Possible?*

It was at a group show in a mill turned gallery where we'd first met. He'd bought my acrylic *Is Love An Ostrich?* In those days, I named all my paintings after questions with a bird in them.

I'd packed light: pencils, sketchpads, simple clothes. My freedom question would abide until it found its image. My completed — no, my *abandoned* works would remain stored with Mother in my old work-room that reeked of linseed oil.

My jobs had never been much — spray booth at a furniture recycler, clerk at JoAnn's Fabrics. Any place where I could get discounts on supplies. It's the artist's life. Even if brilliant and maybe even lucky, you're usually broke.

Garrett in his beta male dulcet way liked to explain that I hadn't lost; the philistines had taken from me. They always would. At least we had each other, my mother was healthy and still had a job, and Garrett felt like we'd made the right choice. Me, I wasn't sure, but that was okay. I'd never been sure.

He said to me, affecting a French accent while driving. "In France, it is not crime to be *peintre*."

"But I have to find *zee* job," I said, joking. "So do you?"

"That's fear-driven thinking," he said. "It just won't cut it."

"Ah, *cheri*, but you have talent."

"And you have your mother's blessings. *Eez eet* not enough?" he asked.

Maybe. Uskerton was where I'd started my misfit American life. North of north, it was where brick mills met waterfalls and flannel. Adultery was a hobby and as rampant as alcoholism. It already felt thousands of miles behind me.

"Nothing's enough in America. You know that, Garrett."

"Spoken like my Sylvie. And that's why I love her so."

We were in central Virginia. My mother's flesh came to me in flashes and glints of orange-coppery pools in combed soil with vermillion and bronze edges. Each disc harrow was a line in her ribcage. The word Kiana, and her name, Kiana Neng Neng means moon goddess. Could I paint her out of these burgundy vellum fields that reminded me that she was the garden from which I'd sprung?

She'd taught me French. She'd taught me how to go around the inevitable before it arrived. I was two in 1970 when she and so-called brother Keoki and sister Ulani arrived from Xieng Khoung province, refugees sponsored by St. Roch's church, my father dead in the Ban Vinai camp.

Keoki, already old at age ten, hating cold Uskerton, left at sixteen when Mother told him that he and Ulani weren't related by blood. Keoki traveled west and found cousins in Fresno, wound up in prison there. Ulani didn't stay either. She learned she was Taidam, from another region, and found an aunt in Iowa. She promised to write, but we never heard from her.

I wasn't born in America, but I'd arrived before I'd learned how to walk and talk. Why didn't it feel like home? In the early days, Mother spoke only French to me, but she learned English from Sister LaBonte while working as housekeeper at St. Roch's rectory. She cleaned and cooked there twenty years, leaving shortly after Sister LaBonte retired and the diocese made St. Roch's function with two priests instead of one.

Work remained unsteady. Factories in and around Uskerton continued to shut down. All the work my mother could do was being shipped to China. When the school district hired her as a cafeteria server, I began to hope she was set for life. She still worked there.

Childhood nights were frigid. I spent many hours alone drawing the percolations of insight that seeped into my half-baffled wandering Hmong-American soul.

The wisest choice Mother made was sending me off to the town library on Saturday mornings for an art class with cherubic Mr. Fontaine, who wore a beret and never took the dollar Mother insisted I give him. I'd spend four hours with a handful of other kids using all the paper, watercolors and paints Mother couldn't afford.

Best thing I had was imagination. And Garrett. Together, we

boasted no debts or material wealth and a reliable used car with new tires and radiator. We'd been married two years, living with Mother under lumpy eaves.

I kept painting in my mind. *Virginia, Shenandoah, blue-ridge.* I'd never stop. Such valleys and rivers led to change and the freedom that light possessed, palpable, sensuous, mincing. Vermeer freed my lips against a decanter. Hals whitened my cheeks to snow. Peeled melons of Matisse spilled juice down my boyish Winslow Homer chin. I'd become more American than Hmong, glad to enrich this with my husband who liked to cook and had spoken French at home with his Quebec-born step-father.

I asked Garrett if we were sprinting toward freedom. He said no. That much we already had. Better still, we had love.

"But how do we know they exist?"

He batted his eyes, toying with me. "Nice question, Sylvie. Let me think about it."

Slate riffs of cooling shadow crossed a mud-freckled road that dipped into manure fumes and a hill where I thought I saw other Lao Soung — Mother's people, not really mine, never really free — lugging their mountains of red dust.

Lao Soung. All a dream of course, but what isn't? I would become a woman tested, revised, still willing to dream. I already was. I had Garrett's sense of humor and soulful perseverance to help erase doubts.

He startled me, saying, "You know what I think? I think that when we have nothing that we're absolutely free."

"But you have me. You said so. We have each other."

"Then you have your answer to your burning question," he said. "You exist. I exist. We're free. Therefore freedom exists."

I wasn't convinced. I told him to keep his eyes on the road.

Round Single Strand

Land unfurled plush and benign, soft of bone, for the feeble of will. Families had bloomed and died here for generations, bonded to ideals such as slavery. Silver-furred vales stole scuttling tents of winnowing dusk. All hovering light dispersed, hemmed in by nut-brown wooden rail fences, not wire, to delineate estates of Virginia planters.

I had worked as an au pair and I had clerked doughnuts part-time. I'd waited tables. I had a bachelor's degree in art. Worthless on the job market. But I hadn't paid for it, so I wasn't in debt. For a while, I'd been happy working in a bookstore, but bookstores seemed to be disappearing.

My nights of clerking doughnuts ended when an armed goon in a ski mask held me up. I emptied the cash drawer and phoned my boss in tears. He phoned my boyfriend at the time. I'm what moronic males call put-together, so I've never been without a boy friend. I enjoy sex and all the eroticism shifting the sands inside my soul.

That old boyfriend came to get me. His name was Lawrence, a muscular black man who was scrumptious in the sack but had serious commitment issues. I told Lawrence if he adored his Sylvie so much he wouldn't let me work nights alone and maybe he'd get some of his friends to teach the doughnut shop manager a lesson or two. It was the first time Lawrence heard me curse publicly in French and I'd let it rip.

Enough of odd memories, though I often wonder where Lawrence is today. There's no shortage of them, just as for the longest time there was no shortage of men, but I wanted a rock to build my church on and now I have Garrett and I just love him like he's my own plush teddy bear and big brother.

We talked each night of our plans, falling into an embrace that felt gentle and steamy and electric with the promise of sex night after night. When I heard him sing to me while he strummed his guitar and we listened to Piaf recordings, I said take me. Later, I said yes when he asked me one night over dinner at a sushi restaurant if we could make the leap as a couple.

To call him my husband made me feel old at first, but I had been 28 and two years later, into my third decade, I feel ready to get older. I'd die for him now. Seated hands on thighs, spine stiff beside me, beaming and imperious one moment, looking cat-like and worried the next, his russet tresses bounce as wind shrieks in through an open window.

I was driving. I loved that he let me take control. A pile of maps across his knees. His hand slipping over the lap of my cotton skirt and I knew he wanted to flip it over my head — to rise into me and burst. To sleep until well again, sure of nothing and satisfied.

Not now. We had miles to cover. I was so wet with anticipation. He should have known this by now. Should have smelled it on me.

Just he and I in our rolling womb, windows down to syrupy air that smelled like mashed onions, he asking in his unaccented English, so relaxed and thrilled to learn of a new geographical tidbit, "Did you know that even Oklahoma has its own Miami?"

To find less than what the fractured void-dwellers call home and security. To find nothing. To just be. To keep to my question about freedom. I was still not convinced it existed. Why else all these fences?

It had snowed on Easter Sunday when I'd told Mother our plans. Snowed twice in May. Most thought nothing of it, but in our mouse hole, having removed plastic from drafty windows, we caught colds. Garrett had explained to me, "We got four thousand saved and nothing due on credit cards. First warm Saturday we'll have a yard sale."

"But Kiana Neng?" I asked.

"Doesn't your mother want us to be happy?"

"Hot, dry, with flowers?" I asked in French.

"You've been looking at that Georgia O'Keefe book I bought, haven't you?"

When I started beaming at him, he knew it was settled. We netted $350 from the yard sale and treated Mother to dinner.

The move felt neither practical nor desperate. It had felt necessary. Like freedom. At that time, there wasn't a fence in sight.

Hodge Spur Rowel

We dipped through Tennessee's conical hills and I locked on thoughts of blue-eyed grinning ginger-haired Vance Hall who had taken me to the senior prom at Uskerton High. Vance had never got past first base with me. He was just too hungry and sure of himself, but we'd had a sweet time of it that night. He'd moved on to study at Sewanee, and was now with a bicycle somewhere in Europe. Vance had become a history teacher. I hope when he falls in love, he'll invite Garrett and me to his wedding. I know this will never happen. I know I'll never see him again. But dreams motivate and mix the colors.

Smoky mountain edges in dust-blue soft indigo-inspired velvety greens were rising against a cerulean azure more pronounced than the napping lengths of cerebral hazy Virginia. More straight-backed, or was it me? The occasional saw-tooth jaw line of a sleeping ox. Billboards for Dollywood, Hank Jr., Loretta Lynn's Dude Ranch, and Graceland. Tennessee on the map felt like three separate republics: Knoxville, Nashville and Memphis.

I thought of Delta Means, another older-brother-anchor to adolescent befuddlement. After the Army, Delta had moved to Gulfport, became certified as a fire inspector on oil rigs, out there weeks at a time, riding a helicopter into and out of Biloxi. He'd yet to meet my Garrett, having moved to Indiana to be closer to his daughter.

I remembered Delta telling me about a trip he once took from Biloxi, wheeling up through Jackson and he was the nerdy one (long before that was cool) and I liked that about him even if he was a man's man at heart. We had in common a passion for Elvis to honor. And blues, Clarksville, Sonny Boy Williamson, and teenaged hours wasted over beers and poker games while Etta James crackled on record albums. Delta always made me feel like one of the guys.

Good old Delta, love you, man, wherever you are.

Garrett pulled off the freeway and we drove a while down narrow tree-lined roads through decrepit depot towns, bumping over rails and ties at crossroads under gloom of endless sawed-off lawns and ranch houses. I started telling Garrett I'd been to Graceland once and to Memphis, and I'd missed by one day seeing Rufus Thomas get his star on Beale Street, but I'd seen Graceland in the rain and I'd prayed in Elvis's memorial garden.

"I never assumed anyone will see my art work and like it. But I bet if Elvis saw it, he'd like it."

"He'd like *you*," said Garrett, smiling. "What do you say we get off this road and get something to eat?"

"You're talking like a Southern hillbilly now."

"Why not?"

"You know, one day your Sylvie's going to meet Elvis and he's going to tell me that you better treat me nice."

"But I do."

"Well, not like treated sluttish girls I had a knack for finding."

"I have no idea what you just said to me."

I grinned at Garrett. He should know better. I just love being capricious and I was starting to feel the South. It was making me loose and giddy and the last thing I wanted to be was uptight and serious and logical.

Freedom again. Nothing is what it seems.

Scutt Single Clip H Plate

If Virginia boasted eight presidential natives, Tennessee's volunteers claimed two, perhaps more. I didn't know; I never studied history as well as Vance Hall. It took me seven years while working full-time to finish as an art major at rinky-dink Uskerton State. Acrylics, oils, watercolor, pencil, sepia, charcoal, wash, ink, I studied it all. Wasn't exactly L'Académie Julian, but Mother and I, burning with pride, had given blood to the American dream. Mother thought me brilliant and harbored fantasies of me achieving an advanced degree. No art for Garrett. Business, medicine, or law. He chose business. Then he chose me and I tended to screw him all up, but for the present he was still smiling.

Garrett loved talking history, so he told me about Old Hickory, claiming that if I asked a Cherokee what he thought of Andrew Jackson I'd get a fair picture of a man hated for good reasons. He told me of the other Andrew, the tailor from Greeneville named Johnson, son of a town named after the English General turned settler Nathaniel Greene who mopped up redcoats for George

Washington to keep the Southeast clean of invading armies. Garrett once lived across the street from a school named after him. He doubted those kids in their gangster apparel knew or cared who he was. His friend Graham, an actor, portrayed Greene in history plays designed for such kids.

Garrett rambled on about how if A. Johnson was president by default, some even say conspiracy, then from what he gathered A. Lincoln was less popular in his day than politically-correct historians would have us believe. Henry Ford may have been right about history being bunk, but as a lover of trains Garrett would take history over the automobile-Frankenstein he created. I loved that Garrett preferred the past, spurred on by flowers that remained. The manses, gardens, museums and portraits — not the statues.

History staked me into a drowning map where I lapped up brine as I sank in deeper.

Knickerbocker Applied Three Point

More trucks on the road in Tennessee. Faster speed limit, nervier hustle in each crowded lane. The NASCAR mania perhaps, with bleachers of cicadas screeching in chorus from trees that thickened after Knoxville.

In West Memphis we couldn't breathe fetid air that stewed riper than any broth we were used to.

June's ascending heat basted us into a grim lassitude as we rolled across the Mississippi at sunset; heading west like so many before us — drained, cramped, hungry for a promise undefined. I felt better that night after phoning Mother from a hotel, and Garrett loved the way I struggled to spell Mississippi three times fast.

Brinkerhoff Face Clamp

Fewer people. Smokier aromas. Hand-painted sign *Peaches* cock-eyed against tree trunk. Pecan log rolls. Confederate flag on shot glass for those at gas pump who craved Dixie souvenirs. Not me. Something creepy and too dangerous about that old slice of history, despite how much some still revere it.

The Boston Baptist Church, a corrugated aluminum-sided warehouse tilting out of a bank of packed mud off a snaking road without margin for error. Wow. Not exactly a cathedral.

Bathed in sun-licks blazing, I found shade near an off-road pasture and sketched. Garrett wandered off with his camera. I got back to my question about freedom. I needed a visual corollary, defined it dissolving like a lozenge in rose water, its light a smeared marzipan. Freedom felt angry and sweet simultaneously as I watched banners of mercury steep in haze, the land like a wobble of fire.

I sketched Garrett alone in the rippled grass of a field. I sketched a beached tractor, a house on wheels, a stovepipe mailbox, a propane tank, and a monster truck.

Feeling piquant, I approved of them all. Garrett liked the stovepipe mailbox. He thought the others were just so-so. He never minced words appraising my attempts. Nothing is art, after all. Just one protracted attempt. I loved him for his honesty.

He shot pictures of me he planned to e-mail to Mother and friends, maybe start a blog. He said I looked delectably slender in my sleeveless white blouse, long batik-tourqoise and lime patterned skirt and wide-brimmed straw hat, gripping a cluster of wild daisies and dandelions. I dreamed that I was a girl out of a Flaubert novel. My parents were dead and I wasn't close to an older sister in Rheims. Made me sad to think I was really all that Mother had and for a few hairy moments I really missed her.

All wild game and critters, I supposed, were in hiding within cool hollows. As we rolled along, we saw swooping hawks and before we knew it we were in Arkansas, where in Wheatley with nothing but truckers around and a franchise restaurant and gas station (seen one seen 'em all) Garrett led me to an insect corpse blasted like a casserole against our left headlight with a blizzard of bug flesh Jackson-Pollock-style across the grille. Took Garrett a long time to gas up, check oil and scrub away that insect carrion that reeked like fish.

Another night in a cheap room, no pool, but we were grateful for a buzzing AC unit, cable TV, free coffee, and bed springs that didn't squeak beneath our exertions.

It was 5:30 a.m. when we left Wheatley headed west on 40 and I noted an Arkansas sign with a bee symbol warning to *Bee Careful*. Corny but I liked it. Garrett pegged a vintage Krispy Kreme sign, but I reminded him of my vow I'd never again eat doughnuts. Not after that hold-up. I disliked cereal, too, and the way Americans called sparkling wine champagne, and their passion for junk food. "Too much sweet," I said. I didn't mind that he was soft in the middle, but I didn't want him to get too fat. "And they eat, eat, eat. At any time. Just when they want."

He pinched my side while he drove and we laughed together. "Then do your own thing," he said. "You'll keep your figure that way."

We noted billboards advertising the town of Krystal and this led to talk of home-cooked *petit déjeuner* and I indulged in waxing nostalgically for Mother's native cuisine. I talked Garrett out of a visit to Krystal, promising him that any diner that served croissants most likely stuffed them with peanut butter and possum meat.

I then drove a while to spell Garrett's aching neck. He couldn't keep his hands off me, reveling in my smile, he said, our nights together, nights to come, the children we'd raise. Children? News to me. But I wouldn't mind when the time was right.

Early sunrise honeyed a county line, a cop in a speed trap who ignored us, and franchise hotels in clusters. We'd wheeled into a hilly fertilizer-fumed realm. The Native State. It felt haunted. Which Indian tribes once lived here? Did Confederate ghosts roam these slopes? I asked Garrett about lynchings, the KKK. He assured me that didn't happen any longer, but you never know, do you?

Land continued to school my color palette. We talked about my question. About freedom's colors. I didn't think all my paintings derivative. Just some. I said a vision needed time. A lifetime. There was much we didn't know.

Little on the radio beyond preachers and the usual piped-in soulless format music that's heard everywhere. Garrett said we should have invested in Satellite radio. I preferred the quiet. Plus we had a CD player, some CDs, and Garrett had his Ipod.

"Give me quiet," I said. "And nutty logic and heated cornpone delivery."

"You're in Arkansas," he said. "You got it."

Hot Springs first, we strolled Health Spa Row where Al Capone, Babe Ruth and Jack Dempsey — who Garret's father had met when a boy visiting Dempsey's New York restaurant — once took the waters at 143 degrees Fahrenheit.

"Did you know Dempsey was a Jew? Wasn't even his real name."

"Who was he again?" I asked.

"A boxer. One of the best of his time. Or so they say."

And then Hope, be it ever so paltry, the childhood digs of W.J. Clinton. He, like me, from a one-parent home. A man I thought attractive, the first American commander in chief I could actually imagine having sex with his wife. I was grateful for his intelligence, the path to a green card he'd provided to Mother. We'd come from nothing. So had Clinton. I liked this about him. Always would.

Merrill Four Point Twirl

On 240, minutes from the Arkansas-Oklahoma state line a bear broke through a gash in the woods of Grand Fork Mountain. His fur muddy in places, otherwise chestnut-brown, he rose on hind legs along the road's edge. I had to slow down, slack-jawed, and gawk. This prompted a horn to blare behind us, but I didn't care; I'd never seen a bear in its own habitat, so massive, pawing the air of a wild stretch of Ozark hill country. With so few cars on the road, I had every reason to stop. I wasn't going to speed up to appease an impatient redneck who was probably late for work and wished he'd had his shotgun so he could blast that bear and my out-of-state ride into oblivion.

Garrett just laughed and gawked and kept failing to photograph the bear in action.

Cady Link Double Wrap

In Oklahoma a sign read: Keep Our Highways Grand. This was followed by: Keep Our Land Grand! Loved this name: Winding Stair, Oklahoma. Kountry Bargains, country with a K. It fit in a place named Hevener. Lake Wister overlooked Damb-Muddy Water. We ate breakfast at Hillbilly's Junk'shin where they had a petting zoo out back and a cougar caged up. The cougar's name was Ben Johnson. Olympic sprinter or poet?

It was too early to partake of Wings N' Things on the menu, so I ate pancakes with lakes of syrup. It was a huge portion and I ate all of it until so full it hurt to think about moving. Garrett didn't eat much, nibbled on toast and two eggs. We both loved the aquarium, the ten-gallon hats that hung from wooden pegs in timber posts, and the parrot named Julio that whistled like a lecher every time a woman passed his cage. What a place. It tickled me to no end; I could have died there happy while listening to a lady seated in a corner with her Oklahoma accent and her bright bursts of laughter.

Some places are so perfect. They're like accidents of simple good fortune never to be experienced more than once.

Dodge Six Point Star

For a while we basked in the liberating peacefulness of not being there yet. I forgot about destinations and tomorrows, but I didn't forget about my question.

Chambray bulls and heifers for sale. Charolais and Angus cattle. Word Of Life church. Boot Store. Main Street with two red lights at each end of a Nutrena feed store. The opened gates of a ranch with a driveway to its central house that stretched unpaved like a dropped length of string — on and on into a salmon-pink blur.

Cattle behind fences on each side. The amount of fence repair work alone staggered my imagination.

Mowed hay, pasture after pasture, and dusty. So many runny shades of red and brown. The smells of feed and molasses.

Single-story ranch houses and a slight fume of oil as if refineries not too far away were perpetually burning.

McAlistar. Home of Cowboys And Italians.

A feeling as if the town had been deserted and people were still leaving. As if the buildings had been shipped in as a Hollywood set for a western, and after the western had been filmed, the set had been abandoned to bake and blister. As if that's what should rightfully happen (God's will and all) in the rouge unrelenting sun-blare of Sooner State.

Kelly Thorny Common

Scarlet veins in reddish asphalt. A sodden, cloying mugginess that accompanied my splitting of freedom into two damp ideas. My first was that freedom is an accumulation of residue at the bottom of a well. The second was that freedom acts as an illusion on which another larger, collective illusion perpetually races, never arriving anywhere. I used this to explain to myself the human need for barbed wire by the mile. I began to wonder how many varieties this kiss-of-death fencing came in. I asked Garrett. He had no idea, but he liked the question.

Glidden Hanging

The hotel had a tiny outdoor pool and Jacuzzi and after poaching in chlorine and feeling really skinny compared to the other vacationing Americans, I took my bloodshot eyes to the lobby's brochure stand and made like Indiana Jones after the lost temple of what religious zealots once called Devil's Rope. I found a brochure for a museum in McLean, Texas that told the story of Joseph F. Glidden's invention.

An Illinois native, Glidden died as a millionaire, having outdueled 530 patent holders and over 2,000 variations of barbed wire.

Why this fascination? It had to do with my freedom question, perhaps the father I never knew and accepting my American-Hmong-American identity, since barbed wire was first used at Vicksburg in 1864 as a tool of war.

If freedom was both well-bottom and wheel, it needed constraints because it ran at speeds that demanded limits. Freedom absorbed, fused, concocted and moved on.

Freedom also waddle-thumped a little wearily, herky-jerky and in spasms through the surprisingly heavy traffic of Oklahoma City. Wanting to pay respects to those murdered at the bombed federal building, we were thwarted by gridlock and a feeble AC unit. It was 105 degrees at four in the afternoon.

Garrett, wilting, had turned putty-colored. Our water jug was empty. I knew he wanted to see the memorial, but I couldn't wheel from left lane to far right at downtown exits. Traffic had halted. It was rush hour in a heat wave. Thunderheads darkened the horizon. I felt heavy, sagging, and the pressure behind my eyes was a warning that a larger headache was coming on. There were weird yellows forming in the air. A tornado?

Sweat stinging my eyes, I exited right down the first ramp I could get to and with Garrett's regretful consent surrendered downtown OK City.

We puttered along Route 3 West in a line of other cars happy to be off Route 40. Following Garrett's directions I got to Route 4 and then to Route 66 West into Yukon. He navigated well. I felt relieved. We'd avoided a meltdown. My headache started to pass. It felt as if we'd been released from a pressurized zone. We toured suburban OK City with its grain mills, ranch houses, silos and flat cinnamon-soil expanses.

The grain mill in Yukon leaned like a sturdy ode to a Walker Evans photo of dustbowl fortitude against time's ravages. As we stocked up on water and food, I found among average Yukon folk a listless amiability in their xenophobia. Not too many Hmong in these parts, but less of that unspoken northern threat to tear off my head just because I was different. Though I wasn't sure I could trust them, I liked the guileless open faces I saw, the slower speech, and a deliberate counting of change from clerks.

Pod-mall storefronts. Plenty of churches. Modern, austere, with high jutting lines. Not Catholic, Garrett told me.

I shrugged, remarking, "As long as they don't try to convert me."

Garrett photographed our first ceramic doe with fawns, a Payless Cashway's, and a bowling alley. In time, I would sketch them all.

Opposed Lugs Lance Point

I didn't like admitting I felt scared. We were out there, only beginning to learn each other. We'd have years to earn deceit and boredom, to repeat our stories as our marriage evolved. I knew Garrett felt determined to make it work. I felt better when we talked, putting me outside of my head. I told him about an Uskerton gas station where I once watched with horror as a mechanic told an elderly lady to go fuck herself because she was taking too much time at the pump.

My question remained. Is it the incompleteness of freedom that keeps us striving? How render what I'd learned? What was I determined to trap between the margins of a page? My pencil was barbed wire rendering lines across what the Japanese called Ukiyo, the floating world.

One Oklahoma waitress we met pronounced the city of Miami as Miameh. Her hands were swollen adobe-spackled mittens that had stretched more wire than I could name. Bull-necked, her flesh was white where it never got sun, her forehead and cheeks magenta. She had Indian blood, all right, though her hair was dyed blond.

A bit afraid of her, I smiled seeking a connection. She didn't smile back. When I mentioned this later to Garrett and how I thought her unfriendly, he gasped as if I were an imbecile, asking, "What do you expect? This is a hard life here. She's a real working woman."

He was right. I had to wake up. To really see.

We reached Indian Nation Turnpike, officially no longer in the Sooner State. A reservation. More barbed wire.

Now I was getting somewhere.

I couldn't change. My pastels didn't bring compassion to light. It didn't matter. I painted for myself, not for those who needed it. My question, like all the workings of my mind, was another luxurious distraction.

Pulling off the dark highway, my face caked with dried sweat, I told Garrett, "That's it. We're going back."

A trailer truck roared past and our whole car shuddered.

"But our dream," said Garrett.

"I don't even know where the hell we're going!"

I was in a panic. Burning. What on earth had I been thinking? This wasn't me. I should be home in my room painting night after night, probing the depths of my imagination. I should be painting for others. Outside of my skin and needs.

Garrett touched my neck. Nobody else had ever touched me there and in quite that way. He leaned over and kissed my cheek.

"Georgia O'Keefe," he said. "You like her flowers. We'll go there first. *Cheri*, you can't stop now."

"I think we made a mistake."

"You're tired. We'll find a hotel and we'll make love. We'll sleep. Don't you realize it? This isn't our honeymoon. This is so much bigger."

I shook my head no. I couldn't see anything.

He said, "This is something we'll never again be able to do. So let's make it happen now. We can't fail. There's no failure in this."

I'd never thought of it that way. I told him so.

He gave me time to think. I don't know how long we just sat there, stewing.

He kept repeating, "There's no failure here, not in this, no failure at all."

Jayne & Hill Locked Staples

In Groom, while most Texans were eating breakfast, I nearly gagged when I saw The Cross Of The High Plains. Garret pulled over, had to photograph it.

I said to him, "Americans. Everything so big." Craning my neck to study it, I reminded myself that St. Roch's had sponsored Mother and me. "It's not all bad. I mean, Christianity. When they really follow it."

"But this is propaganda," said Garrett.

He's so French, I thought. So *au contraire*. I loved him for it. He challenged me.

"Must stand a hundred feet tall," he said.

"More like 60 meters," I said.

"I wouldn't know."

"That's why I said it."

The sky looked cold, mineral-hard. "That closer to two hundred?"

I nodded, staring up. "They're brain-washed, these cowboys. Mind control."

"No church and you wouldn't even be here."

"Here in the USA. Yes, that's true, I guess."

"I'm glad we agree," he said. "You feeling better?"

"I am. But not because of this."

"I know it's a symbol."

"But I like to think of it as the forgiving soul of an adolescent nation."

"Please don't paint it," he said.

"Why not?"

"Paint your question," he said. "Did you forget it already?"

"Can I paint the answer?"

"If this is the answer, then you're a cliché. Dullsville."

I had to agree. But I was toying with him mostly. I was, indeed, feeling better.

He asked again.

"Yes, yes, I'm feeling better. Quit asking or it will wear off."

"It's just that I care."

"I know that," I said. "You don't have to tell me. Not in words anyway."

I told him I'd needed to fall apart. It was out of my system. Wouldn't happen again. Girls will be girls and all that, but what the hell, I didn't have to *justify* my behavior. Even he could admit this was a risky little trek we were on.

We rolled along, crossing the panhandle under blooms of light that reminded me of Turner explosions. Nothing ahead, nothing behind. Only massive light, blaring.

I remembered in McAlister that the only motion had been the soundless shadow of a hawk over Main Street. The vacuous panhandle was equally silent, disturbingly so. The rigidity in scripture, a controlling of freedom, made sense.

So did Conway Twitty on the radio crooning "It's Only Make Believe."

I saw my first armadillo. Dead but intact in the breakdown lane.

Sharply tabled dirt, much chrome yellow and everything manmade looked chintzy compared to the vastness.

"It makes for a bad feeling," I said. "Desolate."

No trees to speak of other than stunted, twisting dark-green shrubs, perhaps piñon or scotch pine (I didn't know) around low tiny houses. A lot of big-box buildings designed for storage. Everything square, off a game-board.

Outside of Claude, there was a massive billboard for Love's, a mega-sized truck stop. All must be gargantuan in Lone Star State. It's an unwritten law. This billboard advertised Sparkling Tiled Restrooms. I remarked to Garrett that this was my second ad for restrooms and I found it amazing. I'd never seen toilets promoted anywhere. This had me laughing as I told Garrett, playing up my coquettish streak that the word "sparkling" didn't quite fit. Not in Texas anyway.

"Like it's magic," I said.

"The magical Texas toilet." He laughed. "That's awesome."

Seizing on this moment of fresh levity, I told him about the Devil's Rope Museum, taking the brochure from my shirt pocket.

He read, "Just 75 miles east of Amarillo, off the heart of old Route 66."

"I'll think about it," he said.

I'd thought he'd be thrilled. I changed the subject, telling him in Texas he could buy gasoline with an 86 octane rating, which was impossible everywhere else.

He wasn't impressed or distracted. "No museum," he said. "Nope."

"It's not far. I really want to go." I pouted. "Why not?" I sounded hurt. "It'll help with my question."

We passed a steel windmill and a grazing herd of longhorn cattle, all Herefords with tawny coats grazing under a billboard that read: Don't Mess With Texas!

Garrett pointed toward the billboard. "That's why. Don't mess with Texas."

"At least they warn you first."

He waved the brochure in my face. "Besides, today is Sunday. Museum's closed. And tomorrow, too. Sorry, but I'm just not feeling it."

"But barbed wire. It means everything in America. It may mean freedom."

I sunk deeper into the front seat, sulky and flushed.

He kept shaking his head no as we kept rolling along.

Arrow Plate

The horizon west of Wichita Falls lay like an inner tube recently deflated that had started to leak soft blood along its edges. Torpor set in, dispensing any need to hurry. Acceptance of time and gravity pulled down my neck as if it were a limb weighted with iron fruit. Expanses sloped up like massive ramps dotted with lonely bushes and anemic trees. Umber walls of mini canyons, arroyos, wrinkles and folds in bundled leather terrain.

West Texas. Ten miles from the New Mexico border. At Glenrio the desert began, a cornbread hardpan, a ranch here and there to alter the horizon.

A trance state, this middle of vast Somewhere. It had a name: Dear Smith County. The sere, the desert.

"This is it," I said. "We'll never be the same."

Garrett looked a bit awestruck, whispering, "Man, it sure is big."

"So very big," I said. "Like we're one big dry wave on its way to a dry shore."

"Perfect," he said.

My question still gripped me as we approached the New Mexico border.

Mister Transparent

I'd just turned thirty and had left Kansas City to move into a drafty attic with my younger brother in Sling Hollow. He was smarting from a divorce that had cost him his house, his innocence, and his will to live. I assured him I held the cure for dissatisfaction. It was indifference.

For the past five years I'd been drifting about, detached and unconcerned between both coasts and odd jobs and adventures. I'd rejected the idea of settling down or participating sqaurely, since, in my opinion, life was a comedy of errors and nobody really knew what was going down.

My brother, amused, admitted to needing the company. "But get a job first," he told me. "I know how you are. No freeloading."

I landed a temp gig at General Mills, Gate 6, where I reported to the security guard that I was a hire from the Focus Temp Agency assigned to the fourth-floor Quality Control Lab. Situated on Lake Erie, the General Mills complex was a sprawling pigeon-colored citadel from the coal-fired hardhat and gut-bucket era. Its intersecting lines fascinated me, crossing between silage chutes, storage buildings, fences, ducts and smokestacks suggesting a monochromatic heyday that had passed its prime.

As a peon in QC, I knew enough to keep my mouth shut and my hairnet on. I was all smiles when I met co-worker, Benjamin Corot. Haitian on his mother's side, he was, surprisingly, the only black worker I'd met at the plant. When I called him Benny, his nostrils flared a little and then as if cooling himself off, he said quietly, "Not Benny. It's not Ben. But Benjamin. Always was. Always will be."

We were the same age. We didn't discuss it, but I gathered we were also of the same political bent, meaning sick to death of feeling like we were getting screwed. When Corot asked what I was doing there, I told him I could help build the bombs or drop them, or take what I found for work. I assumed he knew what I meant, just as I assumed that as two outsiders looking in we shared an unspoken solidarity that ran against the grain.

The whole of General Mills, its enormity, remained an enigma that out of fear and awe I figured I'd wait a while to dare try to comprehend. The QC lab was staffed with paunchy middle-aged men in white lab coats and hairnets, many of whom walked around with clipboards, snacking on junk food bought from vending machines.

Herbie Kraska stood a little over five feet tall, with thick eyeglass lenses and his lab coat down to his ankles. His stomach gave him the look of an egg as he puttered in and out all day with an orange box of Kix under one arm. Sometimes, he'd carry a bowl of Kix with milk and spoon in it, munching from it as he walked. Whenever anyone asked him how the Kix tasted, he'd remark in Brooklynese, his mouth leaking milk, "Yeah, I dunno, kinda brown, a little brown today, I'm thinkin'."

Herbie got paid to eat Kix all day and this astonished me. He had nothing on svelte Maureen, one of the top chemists who ranked higher up on the chain. Maureen told Benjamin and me during our orientation that she didn't hold a degree in chemistry, but in food processing management. She explained this was a growing and much more specialized discipline and kept her on the cutting edge.

Even with her neutralizing lab coat buttoned, Maureen's figure obsessed me. She'd graduated from a college in Minnesota, native home of General Mills. She told us if we were interested in a solid career, we should check out food processing management.

"You mean you can earn a degree in making this stuff?"

"Don't criticize what you don't know," she replied. "This is the future. It pays."

I shut my mouth and kept it shut, contrite at my station as I learned how to do my job. With latex gloves on, Corot and I had a table to ourselves. We were in the QC lab but off to one side, away from the action of the test tubes and computerized graphs and regular impromptu meetings Maureen held with her staff. Our job was for the lower Neanderthals; we had to count the marshmallows in each box of Lucky Charms.

We did this by emptying the contents of one box of Lucky Charms from a case of twelve. The cases, at least fifty of them, were stacked to form walls behind us. It was expected we'd test one box from every case before quitting time. We had to act fast but without sacrificing accuracy.

A quick study, accustomed to temping, I got the gist right away. I learned Corot had also come as a temp via the Focus Agency. I believed we were cut from the same cloth with the same world view: too cool for school, so to speak. I never asked Corot about this.

After all, I was just as alienated, as much a street poet and a brawler and we stood shoulder to shoulder together, our stainless steel table connected to a tubular metal chute that curved like a contraption out of a Doctor Seuss drawing.

From my box, I emptied all contents into a sieve. I shook the sieve until a fine oat dust known as "the shake" — what you find at the bottom of many cereal boxes — sparkled sugar-coated on the stainless steel in front of me.

I swept that shake into the hole built into the table connected to the chute. Then I pushed a button which started a vacuum that sucked the shake down to ovens on a lower floor to be cooked back into the oat mix. It made me think of the dwarf employees in the Willie Wonka story. Any minute Gene Wilder would appear in full purple regalia.

With the shake out, I weighed the mound of Lucky Charms, recorded that weight, and then removed by hand every single marshmallow — the hearts, moons, shooting stars, balloons, rainbows, pots o' gold, and clovers. They were all dyed in various pastels. They stuck to the tips of my rubber gloves. To amuse myself, I started singing the Wonka dwarfs' song, "Oompah, oompah...oohbitty do... "

I then weighed this sticky pile of confections. Using a calculator, I subtracted the marshmallows' weight from the weight of the entire batch. I jotted down all weights before I dumped the remaining Lucky Charms into the chute hole and then hit the button.

It was imperative that I keep my rubber gloves on and resist the temptation to nibble. Supervisor Ball from one of the manufacturing departments showed me how to calculate a percentage between the marshmallows and what he called the "oats" in each box. He explained that one box gave a near enough measurement of the percentage in each of the twelve in every case. Once a box was done, I should write a check mark on the case. Speed meant everything.

Stanislaus Pylon, an old-timer known as Stash, stopped by to check us out. We were new on the block. With bad breath and bloodshot eyes, Stash Pylon picked at nose hairs and assured us in his rough cranky voice that he knew amateurs when he saw them. I took offense at the way he condescended to us. I assumed Benjamin Corot felt just as insulted. I scowled, head down, pretending to listen as Pylon boasted he'd worked the plant thirty years, had seen my type come and go like the seasons.

I wanted to tell Pylon that no one from my generation would expect to work anywhere thirty years, so what in the hell was he trying to say? I had Benjamin Corot at my side to back me up. Surely, Corot saw things the way I did. The old American industrial system was getting dismantled. Globalization, a creepy form of corporate fascism was on the rise. The notion of a factory worker earning a living wage to feed a family for a lifetime had become a figment of the past.

But I didn't speak. I aped Corot. I stayed silent. We were a mountain of defiance and skepticism.

Still, the banter I heard between old-schoolers like Pylon, Ball and Kraska made my skin crawl. They were gung-ho on more war against Muslim terrorists. Why wasn't I over there? They spoke openly, sharing their hard-line pespective. It seemed to me these men lived in a haze of denial, with a nostalgia for America's mid-century years. Again believing Corot and I shared the same convictions, I avoided talking politics. Corot certainly knew these men had no idea what it was like for a young worker coming up. There wasn't any security left to fight for. Worst of all, there weren't jobs.

I wouldn't dare tell these men I'd been to college, and so had my brother and neither of us had anything but student loan debt to show for it. No matter how hard Corot and I worked, we didn't stand a prayer of getting into their good graces. We'd reached the best we could hope for — counting marshmallows. It was disheartening; maybe we'd stick it out and maybe not. The key remained indifference. Corot, my man, was with me.

***** ******

At 7:00 A.M. sharp on Wednesday, fleshy garrulous Stash Pylon stopped by to study a mound of Lucky Charms that I'd just dumped out of their box.

The mound lay in front of me. Did this really pass for food?

Pylon barked out, "Forty percent."

"How do you know?" I asked.

"I can tell just by looking at 'em. Go on, Slim, figure it out. When I started, we didn't have them calculatin' things."

Using my calculator, I saw that the marshmallow count came to 38 percent. I remained quiet, thinking that Pylon's estimate was impressive, but I wouldn't tell him. He had a big enough ego already.

Leering at me, Pylon whacked his paunch. "Off by two points. See, Slim, you ain't needed."

Yeah, you're telling me. I get that each time I visit the unemployment office.

"Yes I am," I said.

"Not here you're not. You know, my nephew was in Falluja, back during the Iraq thing. Where'd you serve? Oh, let me guess, you *didn't*."

Why was he bothering me?

"You know, Slim, I could stand here all day and size these up just by looking at 'em. Living proof there's no better teacher than experience."

I was about to speak, but as if he knew this he walked away, adding a snort of disgust to punctuate the end of my lesson for the morning. I'd been categorized as useless and I was back in high school hating the bullies. I felt comfortable assuming Pylon had been in the military, earned a union wage with health and dental insurance and lots of vacation time and possibly stock options, and hadn't looked for a job in three decades.

As I watched him drift off to pester someone else, I muttered a few curses under my breath. So what if he had a nephew who'd signed up for Iraq. At the time, I had thought Bush's war a stupid waste of lives and I took no solace in seeing how time was showing that it hadn't proved or changed much. Now we were in Afghanistan just like the Russians and Brits before us, determined to prove we weren't any more visionary than they'd been. It was painful to hold in my smoldering rage and frustration, but I had no choice.

Benjamin Corot had seen everything. He stopped working and faced me. "Why you talk that way?"

"What way? It's Pylon. I'm just happy to see him go."

"But I ain't," said Corot. "I need this job, man. I want to learn from him. I want his approval."

"Did you say *approval*?"

"Don't you?"

This wasn't my Corot. This was a stranger. Lips dry, I faced him. The best I could muster was a smarmy, "Who peed in your Lucky Charms this morning?"

Corot didn't smile. He scowled at me and for the rest of the morning we didn't talk, didn't even look at each other until it was lunch time. We sat together in the employee cafeteria. It was a busy place. Workers converged there from all the floors. I felt sorry for him. There were so few black employees having lunch. I'd counted two, both of them women.

I broke the ice. "Why you love Pylon so much? He's a jerk-off. How come I never see him do any real work?"

"He's got it made," said Corot. "You got to get in good with him. He's in with the union reps. He's been here forever."

"I can't stand guys like that."

"It's your funeral."

"No it ain't."

Corot sighed once before he stood, looked around and moved to another table. When I moved to follow him, he held up both his hands as if to stop traffic, making it clear he didn't want my company.

After that awkward lunch-time disagreement, I felt an increasing amount of tension from Corot. He didn't smile when I joked with him. I followed his lead and tried to pay better attention, but I despised the work and by three each afternoon I felt sluggish, limp and surly.

I sought refuge in fantasies of making love to Maureen. Gawking at her, I'd slow down, my back stiff, my vision starting to blur. She wore her red hair pinned up inside a black net to expose the milky radiance of her neck. She always had a smile for us, tinged with sympathy, and it made me glow inside.

Addressing her various listeners, Maureen would lift a bowl of raisins and proclaim, "Now pay attention, all of you. This is what we're after, folks. Just look at their color. Plump, juicy, and dark. Our Sunmaid rep is here today and we'll be meeting with him later this afternoon."

I didn't have to wonder if those serious listeners, mostly men such as Pylon, lusted for Maureen the way I did. But sexually charged comments were not heard. There was in Maureen toughness to the extreme that I found easy to admire.

I also doubted if any of these men thought of the obesity epidemic among American kids and how this "food" factory was one culprit. So many of them favored more military action against Muslims, and many openly disliked Obama. I'd hear them grousing each day at lunch time. A few had sons over there; they were the quiet ones.

I remained fixed on Maureen. On one occasion, she flashed me a smile. I smiled back expecting our silent communiqué to evolve, but that fantasy ended once she held up a Raisin Bran flake with a pair of tweezers while an assistant behind her drew a large version of that flake on a chalk board.

She wasn't smiling at me. She was smiling about Raisin Bran. In her practiced professional manner, she explained, "This is the kind of flake we're after. A beauty. That's why I'm smiling so much. You boys are really doing a good job."

This brought a few light-hearted comments from her male listeners. She held the flake up to the light. "Don't you just love these edges? Take a good look. Six total, all the same length and thickness, and not burnt."

The assistant drew arrows on the board, writing in big letters: EDGES. The listeners looked impressed. I thought the act beyond absurd, but I had to remember this was the QC lab. Big business. A billion flakes a day generated, maybe more.

I looked at Corot, but he ignored me. This had become habit. Head down, plucking and counting chartreuse clovers and dusty-rose moons, he hummed lyrics to "Just My Imagination".

I moistened my lips and held back urges to get lost in more fantasies of Maureen and me naked on a beach in Tahiti. I'd sweep her away from all this *Soylent Green.*

"But this flake, my God." She had changed her tone, scolding a new flake as she held it up with tweezers. "Burnt. Too brown. Our customers won't like it. And look at these edges. Not even. Too rough. Bumpy. No consistency. Keep this in mind, boys. Smooth and not too burnt. We want that golden look."

I assumed Corot's humming soothed him as he labored and kept his mind off the distractions around him. With each day, he kicked his tunnel-vision into a higher gear, counting those lavender horseshoes and cyan stars, making his calculations and pushing the man-handled oats down the chute. I did my best to keep up, but my heart wasn't in it. I tried to talk to Corot, mentioning sports, music, women, anything I thought would grab his attention. He continued to politely ignore me.

At lunch on a Thursday, after not saying a word to me all morning, Corot confessed, "Man, I'll never eat cereal in the same way again."

I sat across from him in the cafeteria feeling both shock and relief. "Me neither." We were back on track to being soul brothers. Things were cool again. "But at least we can look at Maureen."

"No. Don't look at her like that. She's married." He sounded upset. "Four kids."

"Four? But she looks so fine. No way."

Corot nodded with pride. "She goes to my church."

"You're Catholic?"

He made a sour face. "What's wrong with you? Her husband's a brother."

A black guy? I was shaken. I collected myself. "Well, that's cool."

Smirking, Benjamin Corot poked around in his lunch pail and took out a pamphlet and laid it on the table in front of me and asked if I'd been saved.

First he tells me my dream girl Maureen is married with four kids, and now he's asking if I've found Jesus. What planet is he from?

I looked at Corot, eyes wide, keeping my voice low. "Saved? You mean, Jesus stuff?"

He reached across the lunch table, picked up the pamphlet and slid it into my shirt pocket. "You need this. Read it tonight. Think about the love of Jesus, instead of getting all worked up about Maureen."

"But Corot," I said.

"Benjamin to you."

"But Benjamin." I stopped. I wanted to ask if Jesus approved of our manufacturing of toxic loaves and fishes. This wasn't my Corot, my man, my brother.

"But what?" he said. "You don't *approve*? You think I *like* counting marshmallows? You think this is *easy* for me? Like I *deserve* to be here?"

"No. Now wait a minute. Hold on. I didn't say any of that."

"Just zip it, all right? Read the brochure."

"But I thought we were cool."

"C'mon, like I don't have Maureen fantasies? Is that what you think? Let me tell you something, I pray every night this will all change and I know it will and I know I'm blessed. You may think you're better than this place, but you're not. Neither am I, but at least I got the courage to know it and get some help. So you think what you want, but I'll be praying real hard for you."

I wilted as he glared at me. He put down his sandwich.

"Corot, I mean, Benjamin, look, I'm not a bad person."

"You got way too much nerve to think you know me. How much you really know, not just about Brothers, but about Pylon, Maureen, Kraska? Worst of it is we all know you better than you know yourself."

I didn't defend myself. I'd been hearing similar complaints, of late, from my brother.

"You know what you are?" Corot asked. "You're the leprechaun on these cereal boxes. But you ain't got no charms. That's you. Mister Transparent. You're nothin'."

That was all he said to me that day. And the next. The anger in his voice wouldn't leave me. It gave me chills that kept me up at night.

A week later on a Friday afternoon at quitting time, Supervisor Ball pulled Corot and me aside and told us we'd done adequate work. He said he'd forgive my lack of speed because I was a beginner. Then he dropped the axe. Corot would stay on, but I wouldn't be needed until the next batch of Charms was ready in another month.

I stood there sulking in front of both of them.

Ball must have felt sorry for me. Clearing his throat, he added that because of my regular attendance, he'd do me the favor of phoning the Focus Agency to ask specifically for me next month, if I was still available. He had meant this as a compliment, a little gift, but I didn't take it as one.

After Ball had said his piece and walked away, Corot turned to me. "I'm sorry," he said. "Just how it is, sometimes."

This was serious business to him. I took comfort in knowing that at least I hadn't been fired. "Yeah, whatever. At least they're keeping you on. I'm happy for you."

Corot smiled then, genuinely so, showing he cared. He knew I'd never read his pamphlet. He most likely thought of me as one more sinner on a road crowded with them. "Why you think I read those pamphlets?" he asked. "Why you think I testify? I got kids, man. Problems of my own."

"You have kids?" I sounded stunned. "But you're as young as I am."

"Maybe younger. But maybe not as stupid."

Each Bumpy Spiral In Its Cone

Barefoot in only red swim trunks, having forgotten his metal clam basket and digging spade, Rollo walks the beach parking lot. He holds Dad's car keys in hand, arms spread, his twelve-year-old flesh pelted by rising winds. It's going to rain. He can smell it coming. The sky is the grey of an old stone, and as each gust rises he hears it snap, flap and flutter, shredding a kite lodged between two phone lines that hang low over the road fronting the lot. What he wouldn't give to fly such a kite.

Looking across the street, Rollo sees a cluster of stunted pine trees. He sees pools of sand filling recesses in the driveway to the Windjammer Hotel. With its A-framed front, mirror-like panes of glass and swimming pool, the Windjammer reminds Rollo he's in a much different and ritzy place, nothing like home.

The asphalt doesn't burn his feet, and this pleases him. The lot isn't crowded. People don't go to the beach on such a day. Not the Shea family. They're on vacation. Unless it's pouring at breakfast time, they swim every morning at this little beach where for one week a year Dad has a sticker that allows him to park there. Their little rental cabin isn't too far away, a walk to the beach, but Mom won't allow it. When you're older, she's told him. Not until then.

No point in gawking at a busted kite, a few parked cars and a hotel with a funny name. With clam basket and spade, he hurries back to the sand. He hears his name shouted. It's not a common name, and it's mostly his brothers and cousins in the water, so they must be shouting for him. He hurries into the cold water, letting waves splash into his face. He sees brothers Philly and Stewart waving their arms, calling for him. He sees his brother Pete up to his shoulders in the dimpled and roiling surf. Pete's holding what looks like a large rock with two hands over his head.

The keys! Rollo stumbles out of the water and lumbers through sand to his parents, returning them to Dad. He leaves him the basket and spade, too. They can wait, he tells Dad. He wants to see what Pete found. His mother tells him he should spend time with his Aunt Agatha and Uncle Massimo who are visiting from a place where there are no beaches. This is the first time Rollo has met them. Uncle Massimo is Mom's oldest brother. He grins at the man. His uncle grins back. His mother tells Rollo to apologize and to sit tight. He has done wrong. The adults were talking and he rudely interrupted.

Assuming that if he obeys his mother, she won't punish him long and let him join his brothers, Rollo drops into a crouch, his bottom hitting sand. Sulking a little, he listens to his mother's all too familiar voice as she remarks to Uncle Massimo how surprised she was to see so many new hotels going up. Rollo hears his father lament that he can hardly afford the rates for a rental cottage any longer, and that Dennisport is booming, and Hyannis isn't what it used to be.

Uncle Massimo listens. Rollo, watching him, thinks the man looks funny in his rumpled white shirt, white cotton hat, matching white shorts, and triangle of white cream on his nose. He pokes a stubby cigar in his mouth and asks Rollo if he's having a good time and did he enjoy the Kennedy memorial yesterday. Rollo tells him yes, he liked it all. His Aunt Agatha smiles at him as if she approves. She says to his mother, "These kids, they grow up so fast."

Off you go, cries his father. Rollo, beaming, bolts across sand that isn't as hot as it was yesterday. He caroms into waves toward his brother Pete, who is closer to shore now, in up to his chest and still holding the object with both hands over his head.

Rollo sees that Pete's skin is a slick nut-brown after only a couple of days at the beach, and he wonders if his own skin has browned in the same way. He sees that Pete's eyes are blazing full of the sea's green waves and all the life that stirs in Pete's blood. Rollo knows that same life stirs in his own blood, because Pete is his Irish twin, born only ten months after he was. Each summer for two months they are the same age. Many people, including their mother, can't tell them apart from a distance. They stand at the same height, with the same stocky build, and dark hair.

Seeing Rollo, Pete shouts, "It's still alive."

"What is that thing?"

"It's a big snail. Biggest I've ever seen," says Pete. He shouts for his parents to look — look at what he found on the bottom.

The Shea parents, shading their eyes, acknowledge Pete. Rollo sees his uncle swat away a horsefly as he barks, "What's he got there?"

"Petey, what are you up to now?" asks Cousin Judy, seated in front of the adults with little Ginnie, baby sister of family Shea.

Mom says, "They're always digging up trouble."

Pete charges out of the water with the big snail. Rollo, along with his brothers and his cousins Matt and Eddie, both of whom he's getting to know for the first time, joins him. They gather around Cousin Judy, who is older and Rollo thinks very pretty. She explains that Pete has found a conch.

"Conch," asks Rollo, "Like getting conked out?"

Judy, looking pleased, says that's right. That it's also called a whelk, and there are different kinds.

Rollo, impressed by his cousin's knowledge, beams at her. Pete, also beaming, steps between them and says, "I stepped on it and I thought it was a rock, but when I reached down it moved, so I grabbed it."

He puts the snail on the sand. Their mother shouts, "Keep it away from the baby."

"It's okay, Connie," cries Cousin Judy. "The baby's fine."

The boys start to shout and laugh as they watch Judy tease the big snail, and she says, "Watch now, it's coming out of its house."

Emerging from its shell — tubular, charcoal grey, soft yet solid — Rollo thinks of it as a connecting muscle behind a tongue, a controlled blob of spit and sand worming its fat soft-turd essence out of a spiraling bone-like shell. A beautiful shell, but an ugly snail inside.

"Stinks like crazy," says Stewart.

"Shut up," says Philly. "Who asked you?"

"Quit arguing, you two," says Rollo. "All you do all day is argue."

"Look!" says Pete, gasping.

The gray tube of snail life retreats into its shell, laboriously so, its stench growing higher. It pulls a brown cap at its end, the color and texture of horn. Rollo thinks of it as a disc of dried varnish. He watches until the disc has fitted snugly into its housing, and he remarks, "Like a trap door."

"Can we take it home?" says Pete. "I want to take it home."

"But it stinks," says Cousin Eddie.

"No, don't take it home," says Stewart.

"Ask Rollo," says Judy. "He's the oldest."

Pete turns to Rollo, who hates this part of being oldest. Rollo looks up to the sky. The sun hasn't been out all day. He looks to the horizon. The ocean has darkened. Breezes feel colder now, his flesh is pimply, and he hears shouts down the beach: "Rain...rain...it's gonna rain...."

He doesn't care. Neither do his brothers and cousins. Gathered in a circle, heads down, little wet hands on little wet knees, they surround the snail on wet sand, and wait for it to move again. It doesn't. It sits like a rock, and it stinks. Rollo thinks of it as treasure, to be sure, but what can you do with it? Just another body. Like each of them, tender and muscular, and in need of a house.

"You put that thing back," cries their mother from her chaise.

That answers that, thinks Rollo.

"Yeah put it back," says Eddie. "Before it rains."

"Shea family let's go," from their father, his voice booming.

Rollo looks disappointed. He'd wanted to make the decision on his own. He stares at the adults and sees moving toward him short, stout Uncle Massimo in his white beach outfit with cigar in his mouth. Like a marshmallow, thinks Rollo. Pudgy with his shorts riding high up his big waist, and waddling through the sand, uncomfortable in it, and one hand on his hat to keep it from blowing off. The sight of his uncle strikes Rollo as cartoonish. He wants to laugh at the man, but he knows better. Uncle Massimo seems easy, friendly, and different. He seems a lot like this snail — soft inside a lumpy body.

"But I don't want anyone to step on it again like I did," says Pete.

Now that's Pete, thinks Rollo. Always concerned for the well-being of others.

"Can you eat it?" asks Philly.

"No, Stupid," says Stewart.

"Don't worry, it sinks," says Uncle Massimo. He's with them now, bulky, and he smells of suntan oil, cigar smoke and after shave. He breathes louder than any of them. Rollo sees that his cousins look glad that he has joined in — they look comfortable around him, and Judy takes his arm.

"Look, you kids, it's going to pour any minute," he says. "We need to go. So, c'mon."

"Can we take it?" pleads Pete. "Please, please, Uncle Massimo."

"No," says Uncle Massimo, and with a swift scoop of his hand he lifts the snail, waddles it toward the shoreline and flings it into the sea. Rollo and the others follow him, watching, shocked, as the snail sinks, and the rising tide swells and retreats. The waves sound their thunder, splashing up foam and sucking down sand. One hissing wave after another, each one a little larger than the one before.

"Did you hurt it?" asks Pete, glum now. Rollo knows this look from his brother. It means he's about to cry.

Uncle Massimo must know this look, too. "Don't you worry, Petey. I didn't hurt it," he says.

Rollo hears his father crowing, "Let's go, let's go!"

The others start to run toward him. Pete doesn't run. He looks as if he wants the rain to fall on him until he's soaked. Rollo stands next to Pete, and thinks he knows how his brother feels. Together, they watch their feet sink with each wave that rides up their legs and leaves a residue of foam and sand. They wiggle their toes to dig in deeper where the sand is colder. Rollo feels as if he's sunk about half an inch. Yet neither he nor Pete has tumbled down into the undertow like some of the stones and broken bits of shell, and he wonders why.

Uncle Massimo joins them. He has big feet, yet the waves and sand envelop them, just the same.

"Like heavy cement," says Rollo.

"It's what cement is mostly made of," says Uncle Massimo.

Rollo says, "I didn't know that."

"Now you do," says his uncle.

Rollo looks at his brother. He holds in memory an image of Pete gleaming and brown with the big snail over his head for all to see. Such a beautiful shell it was, large and shaped like a tower in a fantasy castle, like a series of wizard's caps, like a tiny mountaintop at one end, each bumpy spiral in its cone a line of miniature icebergs gleaming in Pete's wet hands.

"I'm glad you let him put it back," says Rollo. "Away from the people. So it can live."

Uncle Massimo steps between the boys. A wide man with thick legs, his eyebrows are the bushiest Rollo has ever seen. Rollo warms to something like a twinkle in his eyes. "Don't worry," he tells the boys, "We did right."

Pete has begun to cry. He sniffles and whimpers. "But I found it. I could bring it home and take care of it."

Waves rise, crash, and slide down the beach. The three of them sink a little deeper. After looking at Pete for a long time, Uncle Massimo puts his arm around him, and he pulls him close, gently so. "But it has a home, Petey." He points toward the horizon. "Right out there in Davy Jones Locker."

Rollo, watching his brother, works up a smile for him. He says, "You know, just cuz you find it, doesn't mean you get to take it home."

"Couldn't have said it better myself," says Uncle Massimo. "Can't keep everything you find."

"You can't?" asks Pete.

"Nope," says Uncle Massimo. "I'm afraid not."

Trusting by suppertime that Pete will get over his disappointment, Rollo looks out to the sea. He likes this name: Davy Jones Locker. He likes thinking of cement made of sand, and of Pete's hugely glorious whelk-snail, and all those mysterious creatures out there under such a deep dark beyond.

Geezerville Without A Cadillac

When did I become obsessed with age? I can't stop thinking about it.

I seldom feel old when I'm alone. A feeling of age, not of decrepitude or staleness, but of ripeness, comes over me in public settings such as this Myrtle Beach parking lot. I'm here to celebrate my parent's fiftieth wedding anniversary. My four brothers, my sister, and all their spouses and children are also here.

My parents are old in such a setting, are they not? Certainly, they don't care to tan in Speedos or bikinis. Dad plays a little golf, but at 74 he's been battling a minor hernia. No green fees on this trip. Yet on the beach earlier today, I saw men who looked older than Dad who were not only in Speedos but were earnestly jogging as if in training for a competition.

If I feel old, how does Dad feel up there on the 18th floor of his hotel room? It's his naptime. How does Mom feel, having survived two minor strokes during the past four years?

When did a stroke become minor?

And me, will I be like Lear, old before I'm wise? I ask myself this when I spot in a parking lot a shirtless freshly crimsoned frat-boy-type in chrome wrap-around sunglasses, rubber sandals, and an oversized pair of flowery trunks still wet enough to hug his hairy legs. Early twenties, muscular, hair wind-blown, his arms are tattooed wrist-to-shoulder to look as if dipped in kaleidoscopic melted candle wax.

His phone remains glued to his ear in that distinctly 21st-century pose that makes me think we've all rushed to sign up for our own 4-G key cards to the tower of pretense. Does Frat Boy really need to be on the horn? Is he CIA or FBI? He looks like a cross between Tom Selleck and Frankie Avalon. Extra-aware of his sex appeal, he leans against the grill of a white SUV with gold trim, and then jumps away having scalded his back.

My eyes sharpen when I hear him bark in a distinctly non-Southern accent, "Fuck that ho, man, I mean..."

The editorial bleep is mine. You see, I must be old; I rather like polite speech.

The air carries traces of coconut lotion mixed with motor oil under heated car hoods. I hear my conscience let out a stage whisper: *Just ignore him.*

I don't like this young man. Will he address me as Dude? Or as Sir? Likely the former. I don't understand him. At his age, I addressed all older men as Sir. The best ride I could afford was a silver Chevy bought for $300, with a blue driver's side door, and a white hood. We called it the Three-Tone. Did all repairs myself, didn't own a mobile phone, and I worked two jobs. True enough, I hated every minute of them, but I had no choice. I had to pay for a room in a house shared with three other young guys. Two were Navy vets. We worked all the time, and our idea of a party was a lot of cheap beer and striking out at bars that featured live music.

Was he really a frat boy? He looked so well heeled, groomed, with perfect teeth. Yet his act was gangster, with his profanity, exorbitant tattoos, his dope-dealer's posture and ride.

Was there a day or an hour during the nineties when an entire generation decided to grow up posing as gangsters? Am I old, downright senile to think that the feral sexist racist lyrics found in rap music haven't generated anything like decency among the young? What are white kids so pissed off about, anyway? There's no draft. They have cars, phones, stylish clothes, and even the poorest among them have a safety net that's never been bigger and better funded.

Granted, unemployment is high these days, but it was during Carter's, Reagan's, and Daddy Bush's eras, as well. I see the wealth such young men flaunt everywhere I go. Chrome wheels, techno gadgets: hyper-individuality overstated with an urban veneer — he, like all members of his posse, superstar special. Born to kill.

I'm forty-nine, young by most accounts, but one glance at Frat Boy turns me into a fossil.

Conscience smirks, asking if I listen to myself. Maybe turning inward is what makes me feel old, wanting to listen rather than rant, trusting I lack any new macaroni worth flinging at the public arena's walls.

I see a car parked next to the SUV, a faded Ford *Taurus*, the kind of rig a dutiful middle manager might own. As if hiding behind the sedan, a woman and two boys and two girls, wipe sand off their feet. They share a ratty towel and slip into worn sneakers and dry shirts. The mother of this quartet looks nervous. She, too, has heard the foul language.

I want to tell Frat Boy this planet is more than his stage. My old-man voice steps in to say that I know better. One day, someone will tell Frat Boy when he needs to hear it most. When it hurts the most. He won't like it. Until then, I'm wallpaper to him, like everyone else.

There's a clicking sound. SUV doors pop open. Frat Boy's ride is an *Escalade*. Squinting, he lands one paw against his crotch to hike up his package, crowing, "Yo, Homey, whassup?"

I cringe. He's trying so hard to sound menacing and black-ghetto, like he's an underworld force to be feared. Have all 20-somethings sounded so ridiculous and venal to their elders? Perhaps so. My old-man voice assures me of this, too.

I sneak a glance at the mother near her *Taurus*. Is she wondering if it's possible to protect her children from such influences? I remember my Mom's threats to wash out my mouth with soap. They seem tame and silly. My Dad, like Mister Rogers in his cardigan, cooked pancakes on Sunday mornings. As punishment for curses I'd used during the week, he'd send me outdoors to burn trash in a steel barrel. Mom kept a list for him. Dad would sit my brothers and me down every Sunday after church, and word by word he'd go through his list. Our choices of profanity were lame by today's standards, but Dad would ask, "Do you know what these words really mean? Do you know how they can hurt people?"

I seldom did. My father would enlighten me. He liked to say I was better than such filth, that I had imagination.

Who lectures the Frat Boy? Does he even have a father? Why do I care?

I have to. I'm old. I see that we're sharing this space. I fear he may be carrying a weapon.

The mature thinker in me takes over. I begin to wonder if we, as a society, have grown too permissive. I don't want to judge. I'm not this lad's parent, but I am a citizen. I suspect others have these moments, too, when they feel an ethos of consideration and public respect has died. That the simmering violence beneath our public surfaces has gotten out of hand.

On the other hand, have we ever really been a peaceful nation?

If my wife were with me, she'd say the young have always been brash. She wouldn't remind me that I'm getting old. I'd remind myself. She'd say I'm growing up. There's a difference.

So to be old is to be worked up over every loud monkey in the woodwork? Is it to know loss and humiliation, and to find it easier to be compassionate? To have these fearful puzzled moments when you're outside looking in? I feel sympathy for Mom hiding behind her *Taurus*. Looks as if she gets sun maybe twice a year and is making an effort to spend quality time with her brood. Perhaps she finds it pathetic that she lives near the ocean and never sails, dives, or goes fishing. Never walks the shore at sunset. Is there a husband in the picture? If so, judging by Mom's figure, I doubt there's much voltage in the bedroom. I imagine her kids, cooped-up on rainy days, screaming through the house.

This mother wants her kids to be well adjusted. So do I.

Perhaps in the eyes of older men — those who fought in Vietnam, Korea, and WW2 — I came across the same way when younger. I wore an earring, tight jeans, my hair short but always a mess. I was a fan of Johnny Rotten, but I never dealt drugs, carried a gun, or a phone. Tattoos were earned by Navy men and prisoners. One of my friends peddled baggies of weed, and he learned the legal system the hard way.

I hear a gull caw overhead. I look up. I'm blinded a moment, can't see it. When I look down, I see Frat Boy getting into his big ride.

I see Mom shoving her kiddies in. The task of getting them home looms, a nagging presence, like the bills. Mom lifts her left leg and wipes sand from a scar there, an unsightly glob of shining pink that's the size and texture of a jellyfish. This jellyfish has exploded and stayed put, flesh blown from flesh and stitched in place, sloppily so, never to be removed.

This is Mom's tramp-stamp and pledge of solidarity with the unique. Does it represent a life-threatening injury, or a long-gone wildcat past? I suspect that Mom can't afford laser surgery to have it removed.

I just can't stop staring. Mom gets in. The kids are hungry. She must stop for dinner; she promised. It will be cheap, the food unhealthy, and for a crew of four that means another swipe of the plastic. She isn't sure which one she'll use. They're all nearly maxed out.

Never easy for a parent. Never enough time. With the Internet at our fingertips, each moment holds the expectation of arrival. Nobody dies in cyberspace. Google isn't seen as a private company, or a Soviet-like version of a Ministry Of Information. Google is our portable memory telling us we all get old overnight. No time for gravity, long books, sullen rumination.

Frat Boy starts his ride. As he rolls away, music comes up, a bass line like an overstated pulse meant to cannibalize every tender vibration the terns, gulls, sandpipers and salty air have to offer. Does this affect the four children? Yes, but they don't know it. Such a pulse is normal for them. It's cool.

I know I'm an antique when I happily admit to disliking anything deemed cool.

I watch the power struggle between Mom and her kids until the little ones relent and start locking seat belts. Handheld electronic devices appear. A girl with wet brown hair, the oldest, sits next to Mom in front. Sun-parched, frowning, she plugs in ear buds.

What's a mother to do? Has she a ready outfit for work tomorrow? She isn't sure what she'll make for the kid's lunches. Where should they eat dinner? This choice can be tricky. Two have food allergies and all four have prickly tastes.

I can't stop feeling pity for that mother. Maybe it's the scar. Looks like her doctor used a butter knife and trowel. The kids in the back seat, each in their own orbits, run thumbs over tiny keypads. Mom behind the wheel has often worried this keypad obsession may cause Carpal Tunnel. The kids didn't enjoy the beach as she'd hoped they would. Not the way they're enjoying their gadgets. Her oldest didn't swim. Sat on a blanket and sulked the whole time.

What happened to family togetherness? Maybe it was never there. Maybe it's a myth.

I hear the mother try to sound perky, asking "All set?"

Her oldest keens her eyes through the window and sees me gawking from across the lot.

"Mom," she whines, drawing it out. "That stupid dork is staring at us."

"No he's not. And don't call him a dork."

I could be a pervert. They're everywhere, Mom's worst nightmare. Just to be sure, Mom glances my way. I'm a step ahead of her. I look up at a shoreline horizon lined with chalk-white hotels. Even for all its over-development, Myrtle Beach retains a honky-tonk charm. It may look like Florida's glitzier eastern coast, but it's not.

The moment is a tight one, and when I look down, I see Mom's hardened features. I want to tell her that I know her pain, that I saw her scar, that some of her frustrations are my own.

The moment ends when a red Mini-Cooper, music loud through open windows, screeches around a corner and nearly blindsides me. Its driver, a young girl with a cellphone wedged against one ear, shoots me a malicious scowl. I hear the kids in the car shriek with laughter.

Now I've become a museum piece. I'm cracked leather in swim trunks, limp flesh with rolled towel, white hairs on chest, sagging nipples. I want to roar and pound my chest, howling *out vile jelly* like Lear when he gouged his eyes from their sockets.

I blush, head down, and shove myself along toward the beach. Have I learned anything about tolerance, patience and adult behavior? I'm the one, not Frat Boy, the mother, or the girl, who must be better.

Over the murmur of surf, I hear a voice from the beach shouting, "Ice cream, Mommy. Ice cream."

The struggle is everywhere. My mother would have grinned and reassured me some other time. She wouldn't have promised a thing. She never promised. It was one of her rules.

I look back hoping to see the *Taurus* rolling away. I don't. What promises must that mother never make? Do we live by choices or fate? Do we control anything? My conscience, with a shrug, says we don't.

I argue back that we do. The ride, the phone, a concealed weapon, tattoos — these are all choices.

Conscience reminds me that anger is convenient, and faith is difficult. A sneaky smile plays on my lips. So that's it. No crime to feel old. I blow a sigh of relief, but I can't say why.

I walk along to the beach in my sandals. The sand is hot, the fumes of seaweed strong.

Who doesn't love the beach at this time of day? Sunlight soft and sherbet hues settling in. High saw-grass blades that bend under small erratic breezes.

If I'm of sound mind, I can trust my worst hours will bring lessons. I'll never again feel that mix of dread and elation that comes with events that mark earned passage. Old? Perhaps. Wise? Getting there. The cloying racket of the day-to-day won't go away. I need to remember this, along with my mother's patience and my father's disciplined mind.

It's their fiftieth, by God — I should talk to them about these things. How would Dad respond to my remarking that filth, like anger, is popular because it's easy?

My face lights up as I scan the horizon. Am I not blessed to have any family, let alone my dear old parents, still around, still together, still in love? Tonight is gonna be one heck of a dinner for them.

The surf throws down a soft boom, each wave rising from a dark mutable source we never know completely but must endure. Time slows. I look again to the sky. Low cirrus blazes flamingo pink. Gulls hover, tilting in flight to remind me we are not young, and we are not old. We are forever in motion.

Albino Elephants

Kozart in sunglasses in a dark room, shades drawn, mused in silence by his window. He was ready. Tightened a rubber cord around his bicep. Pumped his fist until a vein rose in the back of his hand. His veins were slow to rise, and soon he'd have to start shooting into his calves. He dragged a wooden Ohio blue tip against the thigh of his dungarees. Heated his skag in a spoon.

Bell bottoms were out. So were peace signs. The new slogan under Reagan was Peace Through Strength, and Kozart didn't like it, but he'd deal. He'd keep on wearing tight dungarees and muscle T-shirts, but he wouldn't shave off his sideburns. They matched the gold hoops that pierced both his ear lobes, as well as the tattoo of a serpent coiling up his chest.

A serpent was a guide. Serpent dreams meant wisdom slithered from within. He'd learned that in prison, surviving on two rules. Trust a man who carries a blade. Never trust anyone who didn't respect serpents.

Others were going soft. Not him. Prone to violence when he saw contradictions that limited his notions of freedom, he had to keep that violence under a lid, and stay on guard.

Maybe he should stop a while. Get well.

So many had weak minds and big egos convinced as they were of knowing right from wrong. Nobody knew. Celebrity serial killers proved it; their violence revealed a pathological individualism that like the serpent coiled inside everyone.

He found a vein. Pierced the flower that kissed him into oblivion.

* * * * *　* * * * * *

Did the leather-assed salts at StemCo Frozen Foods know about his habit? He was lying to himself. Sure they knew. They just didn't give a rat's ass. Put up with him because he'd deck a newbie who gave anyone lip. He laughed at the bad jokes Dubois, his foreman, liked to tell. Laughed at the right time, never offered his opinion on anything, and wasn't resentful of pushing himself to the limit. It was idiot work, a dead end. Crummy pay, no union, no bennies. Welcome to hell, they told newbies. Dante had it wrong. It ain't no fiery inferno.

With their neck aches and sore shoulders, the leather-asses had every right to their bitterness. They loved watching a newbie try to make it through his first day. If back strain didn't get them, the blue in their fingers would, even with gloves on. Nobody worked as a team. You unloaded. You humped. You stacked. Each box of food weighed at least fifty pounds inside frigid cardboard shrink-wrapped in plastic. Those boxes slipped off your apron, or out of your rubber gloves. With three pairs of socks on, your toes never got warm in required steel-toed boots.

Beat the hell out of his body, but Kozart shut down his mind and saw the job as a gym work-out. Kept focused on needs. His latest was a car. He'd bought a *Valiant* with a 225 horsepower slant-six engine. Like its cousin the *Duster*, the *Valiant* was a model Kozart had owned in the past. He didn't like to rely on things, but he swore by Mopar products. Couldn't kill a slant-six with a sledge hammer, and the price was right. Four-hundred cash. A week's take-home after taxes. The buyer had been asking six. Money talks, bullshit walks.

No Japanese eggbeater for him. The car allowed him the mobility he'd dreamt of in prison. On moonlight drives in the city, he'd poach for hookers. For a while, tilting beers at McNulty's, he bragged about his ride. Didn't care who he offended.

McNulty's was a sewer, but he shopped for skag there. Nobody gave a damn about the drug traffic because McNulty's family was related by blood to the town mayor. Wrapped in this knowledge, Kozart felt immune. It paid to be out of the city, got boring sometimes, too, and he'd dream of heading west to California as if he was seventeen again. No need. He had a square gig in a kind of no-name town where he could hide. Lived walking distance from all the skag his misery allowed.

So shrewd his seedy ways. How many jokers came out ahead when they bought a car? Why waste hard-earned take-home on a slick ride, showing it off like a pimp begging for cops to start tracing him? Not his style. He kept it simple. No *Camaro* or *Trans Am* for him, even if it meant less pussy. Didn't matter. Babes he liked didn't care what a man drove. Only bimbos cared for that. Made him sick to think of what some guys paid to maintain a bimbo and a flashy ride.

Not like the skag. When that powder gripped him sideways it

was endless purgatory. He'd puke green snot in shiny strings until his ribcage was hot and aching like he'd been pummeled by a gorilla in a death-cage match. Couldn't eat for days. All sorts of vertigo. Just coffee and cigarettes and he'd clean up a little until he'd start jonesing. At StemCo they'd say nothing, but they knew.

Then he'd meet a woman. Off the skag and getting laid for a while, in a regular way, he'd go to movies and get used to regular meals, and the smell of purses and lipstick. Massages after dark. Soothing quiet talk and he'd vow never to return to skag. He was skilled that way, could clean up, go cold turkey if left alone.

He'd feel himself going soft. He and his lady would suffer one argument too many. She'd want something from him. Something he couldn't define. He'd end it. Swear off pussy and nights out. Hit the skag hard. Hit the booze harder.

* * * * *　* * * * * *

A year had passed. He told Crick, who drove for ChemLine, "Having problems with my Dodge. Ain't a lemon, always starts, even on cold mornings, but the front fenders, and rear quarter panels, I dunno."

"Rotting," said Crick, who knew.

"Been almost a year since I brought the thing home," said Kozart. "The quarter panels are shot along their bottom edges. Front fenders black with rot under the hood where they're bolted to the frame. Both fenders are soft, and the other day I jabbed at them with a screwdriver. They were ice cream."

"A lot of snow this winter," said Crick. "The salt ain't helped."

"Maybe I been taken," said Kozart.

"We've all been taken," said Crick, amused.

"No, I mean maybe the car's been in a flood."

Crick shook his head no. "American cars ain't what they used to be."

"What the hell is," said Kozart. "Gets me to work each day."

"There you go."

Crick sipped his beer. They watched hockey on the TV. Kozart made a show of buying another. Then he left for the night. He disliked Crick, with his porcupine crew-cut and his ChemLine job, but Crick was the only one who talked to him.

***** ******

Kozart got rid of his cowboy boots and surplus Army coat. They were out, too. Splurged on a tattoo of a serpent across the back of his neck. He bought new tawny leather shit-kickers. Had to roll with the times, but he refused to cut his hair or buy another car. Parts were getting harder to find, but he replaced them when needed. New fuel filter. Cheap. No problem. New starter. A dirty job on his back, but he'd bought one second-hand for forty bucks. So what if others jeered at his ride. Guys like Crick drove pick-ups they'd taken out big loans for. Most had debt up to their ears. Some were still living at home. Not him. He had about $1,600 in the bank, and he could afford his room, his skag, and the occasional tattoo.

Still, he was starting to worry. Nancy. Eileen before her. Cora was his last one. They all took a piece of him. Left a piece of their souls buried inside. The *Valiant's* rusting body he could live with, but his own hurt was another story. Wasn't like he was stupid. He knew a good woman was worth seeking out. A lady friend helped with more than the soreness he felt in every tendon and joint. She helped with the silences, and his fear that he'd reached his peak.

The skag helped, too, fire-bombing him out of a bazooka to strafe a cosmic no-man's-land within. Still, there were days when he couldn't stop thinking about women. Turned his flesh the yellow of one of those glue strips that hang in restaurants. Days when his zits were like so many trapped dead flies in those strips.

What a body he had. Proverbial six-pack. Deltoids. Pecs. No fat, and he had stamina; he ran the newbies ragged. Dubois had promoted him to forklift detail, and he got to drive two days a week as part of the rotation. That meant only three days of humping frigid boxes. Dubois liked him. He, too, had done time.

Mongrel dog, that's what he was. He had some French like Dubois, some Irish like loud-mouth Ferry, some English like Crick, and enough Polish to give him his father's name. Man, that fuckhead father of his, whoever he was. Didn't need no father. Didn't need pussy. Those other mongrels didn't burn like he did. They didn't change a room just by entering it.

So leave him alone.

He kept his kit and his room clean and in order. Window shades always drawn. He'd learned to enjoy reading while in prison. Didn't own a television. Couldn't be bothered. Owned a boom box. Preferred music.

One of the leather-asses at StemCo, a pencil-dick named Fitzpatrick had called him Pipecleaner. The name had stuck. That's how skinny he'd gotten. Called him Kozart The Pipecleaner. He didn't care until he heard Fitzpatrick use it on him at McNulty's. In the StemCo freezer was one thing, but in public was another. He swung at Fitzpatrick, who dodged the roundhouse. Kozart was reaching for his blade when Crick wrapped him from behind and bent him over. A wrestler in high school, Crick matched Kozart's strength. Go home, sleep it off, he told Kozart. Before you get yourself killed.

No, Crick. I'd rather be a dead man.

* * * * *   * * * * * *

It was his *Valiant* that saved him. Unable to sleep, jonesing, wanting to keep clean for a while, he drove into the city at night, up and down her wide avenues. He'd nurse endless cups of coffee in the all-night diners. The city was peppered with them, and he knew where they were — this was his territory, after all, where he'd found all his trouble before prison. Before town life and a room. Before his felony convictions. Before a freezer warehouse meant the best living he could find.

Like his mind, he thought, his car continued to rust. The rear quarter panels flaked like dried once sun-burnt skin. He'd wrapped duct tape over the frayed bottom edges. Looked stupid, but there was no point in restoring such an old beater. No point in buying another. The engine ran fine. Kept him out of his room. Maybe he'd buy sheet metal and Bondo to patch those quarter panels.

Why bother? He'd stay clean. Drive all night. Listen to something trippy. It was better to be a night owl. Easier to stay clean and out of fights.

* * * * *   * * * * * *

"Wild Horses" was playing on his boom box when his phone rang. Comfortably sober, he expected a telemarketer. Instead, he got his mother's friend — his friend —Helena Liberato. Helena still lived in the same building with Ma. Same city, same old neighborhood. Helena had raised him. She was from Italy, a childless widow who didn't dance anymore. When younger, she loved to dance.

He shut off the music. He was kind to Helena. Growing up, she'd kept him fed when his mother was on a toot. Helena had visited him in prison. Not his mother — no son of hers was prison scum.

His father, Helena told Kozart in her Italian accent. Cancer. Kozart should be a good boy, go to Memorial Hospital. He'd find his mother there. She was too upset to call.

His father? Was this a joke? No way, he said.

Helena paused before pleading with him, for his mother's sake. Helena knew their history, but hadn't his mother tried her best?

"I say a rosary for you," said Helena. "Please, you go see your father. Do it for Helena. For your soul."

He said he'd think about it. It was Helena, after all.

He told Dubois at work. Dubois said take a few days. He'd still have his job when he got back. Not like anyone else wanted it.

His father had left when Kozart was ten, and his brother fifteen. A few years later his brother shipped off to Vietnam. Came back in a bag. Some years after that, Kozart got iced for attempted manslaughter. Too many priors: grand theft, larceny, arson. The judge said ridiculous. Enough already. He needed to cool off.

When he'd really needed a father — nobody was around.

Sipping coffee over the wheel, Kozart drove to Memorial Hospital. He thought about his Ma. She was the one who needed him. At seventeen, she'd married a loser. How could she have known? How does anyone know?

Now and then, his mother dried out and worked for a cleaning service, in a laundry room, at a hotel, at various restaurants. When she worked, she did any job she could find, but never stayed long before her spirit flagged and she succumbed to drink. How many times had Kozart found her alone in the dark, staring at the television, saying nothing to him as if he wasn't even there? Helena had saved him. She'd appear from her unit upstairs. She'd make him a spaghetti dinner. Helena had no one but him, and she needed someone to care for. He finished school for her. That was the joke of it. For all his criminal stupidity, and his time in lock-ups, he'd managed a GED. He even owned a library card.

Helena always said she and Ma missed him, but growing up he'd done both women a big favor by staying away. Found all the friends and hangouts he needed in the city. Sold coke, crack, weed, anything. Fenced stereos. Boosted cars. Money any way he could steal it. Into and out of court, and county cells until an appliance warehouse job — a security guard knocked him out from behind with a length of chain. Hadn't ratted to the prosecutor, kept his two friends clean, both of whom were later shot dead in a dope bust that made the evening news. Dumb-asses.

Mother and father? They were spirits floating through skag dreams. Mealy white presences with pink eyes. Albino elephants. He chucked spears at them.

* * * * *   * * * * * *

The man, his so-called father, sat in a smock at the edge of a bed. Grizzled sack of bones with bare feet. Unshaven. Hair falling out. Coughing in front of Kozart and his mother, who was bawling. She turned away. The man stopped coughing long enough to chew her out, disgusted by her squeamishness.

His mother was so soft, so gentle, so insane. She kept shying away. Helena at his mother's side. The man glaring at both of them.

No love there. Hardened and shriveled, he cursed in a busted, out-of-date slang.

What am I doing here? thought Kozart. *Who are these people?*

The man spouted in his thin voice: You shut up before I slug you.

Enough already, Kozart shouted back. Don't talk to her that way.

Little punk, who are you, anyways? said the man.

Your son, shouted Kozart's Ma. He came for you.

My son is dead, shouted the man. Dead in that war.

Your other son, the one you never did nothing for, shouted his mother.

The shouting made Kozart's sweat run cold. Late night brawls in the kitchen, igniting darkness with rage. The whack of his open hand against her cheek.

Was he supposed to like or make sense of this?

You are dead to me said the man's eyes. Not an ounce of mercy in them.

He started to cough again, struggled to keep from keeling over.

Sobs from Kozart's mother who continued to look away, Helena still close to her side. Kozart didn't look at them. Didn't want this. Least of all this stranger he was supposed to care about. He wanted the son of a bitch to croak in agony.

* * * * *   * * * * * *

Having gotten the call from Helena, he'd walked to McNulty's and scored. The kit waited on his bed. He wanted to cry. *What is the matter with you?* No crying. Not this time. Not ever. They'd find him in his car on the edge of this rotten town. Needle in his leg. Drowning like a rock star in his own vomit.

His phone rang. He watched it ring five times. Then he picked it up. He felt relieved to place attention away from the kit. Nothing worse than jonesing alone.

It was his mother. She sounded sloshed, rambling on about how she loved him. She knew his father was a bastard. She was sorry for all of it.

Would he go to his funeral? For her, in a nice suit, to show respect?

He didn't own a suit. No funeral. No way in hell.

Don't make me beg, she said.

He waited, expecting her to rant on and on. She didn't. The silence held him still. His head throbbed. He twitched.

Helena on the phone broke the silence. Kozart heard his mother's sobs in the background. Helena had a knack for taking over. She said, We all know about you and the drugs. You no fool nobody. He was bad man, but your mother, she loves you, why you break her heart?

He wanted to say he didn't care. That he needed to hurt them both in a bad way, with authority. He needed his blade, his serpent, his wisdom.

So much that he needed to slay his albino elephants.

Impermanence Dazzles

When I first laid eyes on lanky ginger-haired Phoenix Strauss, I knew. A sanguine half-baked genius eccentric, he was more than my type. He was my crazy-girl dream of love at first sight. As time passed, I learned I was only partly right about the half-baked part. His father, a Stanford graduate, worked in administration at Cedars-Sinai. His mother had an MS in Psychology from UC Berkeley and she lectured at Pepperdine. As an only son, Phoenix was born into a degree of privilege, yet he chose to drive a banged-up Ford *Escort* and lived alone in a two-room apartment on a less than desirable fringe of Santa Monica.

A Buddhist, he'd grown up in Westwood, earned a Master's in Human Factors from USC and on more than one occasion had to explain to me what Human Factors meant as a course of study. I vaguely understood it as an arty Jung-inspired system for counseling factory workers and management to help them cope with emotional problems on the job.

Two years after Phoenix graduated, USC cut the program. Having failed to land a job in this chosen profession, he earned an ESL teaching certificate. He began teaching English to refugees and immigrants. The pay, usually grant-funded, was low. He loved the work.

This was how we met. We were teaching in a summer program at UCLA, preparing foreign-born high school grads for college-level English. I didn't hide my affection for Phoenix and in order to get past my shyness and talk to him, I occasionally asked him about pedagogy. I tended to ask questions I already knew the answers to. In this way, I might come across as erudite and I could keep our conversation going. I never doubted he had answers. He always did. I couldn't keep my eyes off him. He was kind, sexy, smart, gentle and earnest.

I was thirty-two years old and looking for a husband. It was that simple. I wanted kids. A home. I'd gotten over the likes of Luis, Duane, and Kyle during the past decade, and I'd sworn off men for the past two years in the hopes I'd get them out of my system.

No such luck. I was back in the hunt. When I first saw Phoenix, I felt that we shared something non-physical, timeless. We'd met perhaps in another life. He was part of that rare species: a native Californian. One of few I'd met. I considered myself lucky, at last. When I told all this to my roommate Katie, who was also my older sister, she told me to be careful. Katie was in grad school at USC and had also sworn off men for a while. She reminded me that I had a tendency to leap into the flames, and that maybe this time I should go slowly, cautiously.

I took her advice. But it was so easy with Phoenix! Along with his curly blond hair, crystal-blue eyes and long aquiline frame, he came acroos as a lonely misunderstood sort. He was more than a Buddhist. He was an iconoclast. Just brilliant. We were not only a suitable physical match (just the right height), we were also educated in the same field.

To top it all off, we shared a passion for nature. I learned he was a docent at Topanga Canyon and had worked summers as a volunteer assisting park rangers at Yellowstone. He was an avid backpacker. So was I.

Everything was falling into place. Katie kept reminding me it didn't hurt to act shy, and not to come across as too hungry. So I didn't, but when Phoenix told me he liked to take weekend hikes in the mountains around Los Angeles, I nearly threw myself at him saying that sounded like something I'd love to do. He said in his self-possessed way, "Then we should do it, then."

I ran this by Katie. "Then go, Eileen," she said. "Get to know him."

I was thrilled to have plans for a change, and to get out of our two-room apartment in a South Central neighborhood, providing Katie needed weekend time alone to study. She was working toward her Master's in Physical Therapy, and hoped after that to get her DPT. We'd been in Los Angeles together about ten years. Katie had her bachelor's from Ohio State, and I had mine from Kent State. For a couple of long-legged plain-jane girls from Salem, Ohio, we weren't doing too badly in sunny LA.

Nearly every Sunday, Phoenix and I began to take hikes. He'd pick me up early in the morning, usually around five, so that we could hike at least ten miles before temperatures climbed and the heat became unbearable. I encouraged him to share all he knew about local history, geology, botany and Buddhism. I loved that we never talked pop culture. Nearly everyone in LA was obsessed with such mindless stuff. Admittedly, I had been, too, but only for a while. Not only was it vapid, but I couldn't keep up.

We tried different trails until we realized our favorite was the Mishe Mokwa in the Santa Monica Mountains, just a short drive up Highway One north through Malibu. Named after an extinct Pacific seacoast tribe and roughly ten miles long, the trail was easy for Phoenix. Not so easy for me at first, but I was determined to improve. I did. He liked this about me. As I said, I had long legs and what my father called spunk. I was also athletic, had been on the swim team at Kent State. Phoenix had about nine years on me. He'd been fit all his life, tended to eat vegetarian, didn't smoke or drink, took care of his body and looked closer to thirty than forty. I loved all this about him.

We'd sputter along in his battered Ford *Escort* and turn right at Neptune's Net while heading North on Highway One to snake our way up steep narrow precarious Yerba Buena Road, fearful the *Escort* would expire. It never let us down. We'd arrive to our trailhead at sunrise between five and six a.m.

One morning, I jumped at the sight of a roadrunner. Grinning, Phoenix said he was happy for me. Roadrunners were difficult to spot.

I took it as a sign. Phoenix laughed, asking how I thought the roadrunner might take it.

"We have to get inside the mind of the animal spirits," he said. "To see as they see. Have you ever read Casteneda? I think you'd like him."

Nobody had ever spoken to me in such a way. Such soft calm intoxicating power in his voice. Such a hold he had on me, and he was so honest, so innocent, I thought he didn't even know it.

We finished hiking by noon before the trail became intolerable. Parched, sucking down bottled water that had turned warm in the car, we rolled back down Yerba Buena to Zuma Beach for a swim.

My legs throbbed and I molted off layers of skin that washed away in the cold Pacific surf.

Phoenix said he wasn't lonely. He had the mountains. He had Buddha consciousness. I saw peacefulness in his sun-bleached eyebrows and the ruddy crag lines of his forehead. He had learned from me that I was losing patience with all the difficulties I had living in a sometimes dangerous and seedy LA neighborhood, often unable to sleep due to the *ghetto bird* helicopters that flew so low over my apartment that their searchlights crossed my bed and glared into my eyes. He assured me that weekend hiking trips would give me a much different view of what LA living had to offer.

He was right. This was the LA I'd been looking for. In awe of him, I said little, which was rare for me. I was usually the blabbermouth at the party. He had a quieting effect on me. He could talk as much as he wanted. I believed I was in love. I trusted it this time. I saw my future unfolding the way I'd thought it should. At last, at last....

Phoenix and I didn't teach in the same program any longer. He was teaching out of Santa Monica in classes sponsored by a private school called English Language Services. I was teaching English full-time days at a private language school off Wilshire owned by a corporation based in Korea. I also taught part-time weeknights to Korean adults, earning enough to pay my share of rent. My sister and I often jokingly agreed that if LA was teaching us anything, it was how naïve we were about the cost of living in California. Not to mention just how white we were.

As time went on, Katie and I saw less each other. I needed someone to talk to about Phoenix. Was I going too fast or not fast enough? Katie was just too busy. If she wasn't in classes, she was working part-time in the Doheny Library or meeting required hours of observation at a hospital. I'd arrive home from teaching around four p.m., change my clothes, wolf down a Power Bar and head back out to teach a three-hour night class that started at six.

When Katie and I did see each other we were exhausted, but our nights were seldom restful or quiet. There were gun shots to punctuate the helicopter fly-overs. We lived about a mile from the Staples Center. It was basketball season. Whenever the Lakers won, there were parties along Vermont and Hoover that never seemed to end. It wasn't unusual to learn someone's car had been lit on fire. Car alarms erupted constantly into squawking blips and monotonous sound loops.

With Phoenix, however, all was peaceful waters. Money was no object. His Buddhism rubbed off on me and I remembered why Southern California had held such an appeal during my years of shoveling snow in Ohio. His mellow vibe and his knack for showing me he understood the stress I was coping with, allowed me to lighten up and become as whimsical as a sea breeze. I'll never forget the flock of grouse we stirred one morning, about fifty of them flapping off at once in every direction. I froze on the spot and marveled at their escape. I felt like I was thirteen again. Oh my God, the way Phoenix smiled at me. The way I felt smiling back at him. It was true. Love was really the most sublimely exhilarating experience I could have ever wished for.

Bees pollinating Mariposa lily flowers were one of countless details he stopped to observe. We experienced small moments with nature on intimate terms, reverently. We hiked for hours without a word. A cyan hue blushed over burnt sienna and crimson ridges along one part of the trail. Khaki sand wastes came to life, their olive-drab undulations deepening. The sun rose an inch higher and the shadow across our boots slid upward toward our knees. The copper cliffs ahead of us brightened. A fence lizard watched us stoically, changing its color to blend in with the igneous stone it was perched on.

Sheared crimson mountain walls offered sheets and tabletops of cooling shade. Each cleft and crevice became for a moment no longer weather-forged scars but squinting eyes and bleeding seams in a blood-orange clay cheek. The mountains were real. They were breathing. One moment they were all of a purplish vaporous quality. The next moment they grew dense, fiery, with sharp orangeade inflections.

All of it quietly dazzled me — and to think that without traffic it was less than an hour's drive away from my so-called stressful *'hood*. None of it felt explainable.

"It's all one," Phoenix liked to say. "You're part of it. So what is there to explain?"

I struggled with this. How justify my goals and purpose? How get to the romantic part, the violins, the physical communion, and wedding vows?

I had to be patient. Katie hadn't given me this advice. I'd given it to myself. I was on my own with this one. My man stood in front of me. I shouldn't look too ready or eager. I should remember all that was good happened in its own time.

Phoenix said explanations and justifications for what happened in life simply weren't needed. "Look at the wholeness of life," he remarked. "It's given to you. Pay attention. Receive. Don't judge. If you see Buddha on the road, kill him."

Kill him? I didn't understand. Did I have to? My breathing changed on that trail. It deepened and slowed. Steam rose off my shoulders as my body cooled in Zuma's waves after so many hours of unrelenting sun. Nature was so much larger than I was: a vibration for me to fold into as I disappeared.

Another grant had come through and Phoenix had left ELS in Santa Monica and was earning a better salary teaching immigrants and new refugees in a program housed in a school near Echo Park. Unlike my own work, his teaching put him in contact with some of the poorest residents in the city. He liked to remark casually that these poor students didn't see themselves as poor because they'd brought with them cultural beliefs that prized family togetherness and learning as true wealth.

I adored him for this. Such children we would have. I never tired of talking to him. What wealth we had alone in these mountains — all to ourselves! We seldom met other hikers on the trail. We spoke of cabbages and kings, as it were, and I grew fonder of him and began to send out signals that it was okay for him to touch me. A little kiss, for starters, would be okay. But just a little one. I liked our slow pace. It felt like courtship.

We hiked under skies sometimes air-brushed as blue as a gas flame. Skies that ferried cirrus clouds stained along their fringes with magenta and small smears of lilac and other wispy pastels that brought to mind the dream-like color palette of a Monet. In my mirrored sunglasses and wide-brimmed hat, I'd pause and stare upwards, catching my breath. I loved my hiking partner's sere good looks, his stamina, his smile, his legs. I told him I wanted to change myself, to keep getting into better shape, but most of all to deepen my spiritual life, perhaps become a Buddhist like he was. Did I have the discipline? Could I actually kill the Buddha?

Phoenix said time would tell. "Not all religions are guided by zeal and a missionary spirit. This is what you're used to. I'm not even sure Buddhism is a religion."

"Should it be?" I asked.

"Not if it means rules and regulations."

I saw in his shale-blue eyes that he revered our time together. I learned that every day, three times a day, he chanted and prayed alone at an altar of candles and incense burners inside his apartment. He'd shown me this altar, though briefly when I'd stepped into his apartment to use his toilet. Everything about his living space was modest, spare and clean, just as he was. He went to his official temple near Long Beach one evening a week. He liked telling me about other worshippers at his temple, but he never suggested I join him.

On our mountain trail I sensed he felt comfortable nurturing our growing bond. I heard the jump in his voice whenever I phoned to ask, "Are we on for a hike this Sunday?"

No, he didn't have a girlfriend. When I asked him why, he didn't answer.

"What do you want from life?" I asked him.

He didn't want anything. He said he already had everything he needed.

This was my first bit of troubling news. Did it have to do with my inability to grasp what it meant to kill the Buddha? When I asked him this, he simply chuckled.

"Eileen," he said. "I really enjoy your company, you know that?"

Of course I knew. I wanted him to say more. He didn't. He grew strangely quiet, more quiet than I'd ever seen him.

We hiked on and he paused, delighted by creosote fumes from chemise bushes. I smelled them, too, and had always wondered where they came from. He explained that creosote helped the chemise burst into flames during long hot stretches. They were the cause of many a devastating brush fire. As they exploded into fireballs, helped by winds, they scorched all in their path. Was this a problem? He didn't think so. The problem was those who built homes where they shouldn't be, and who insisted on permanence.

This was a second bit of news that I found disturbing. A home meant permanence. So did a marriage. Was the illusion of permanence, if nurtured lovingly, such a bad thing? I didn't think so. But I didn't discuss it with him. I was starting to fear that certain topics — certain leaps of faith into the future — might scare him away. It wasn't as if I'd scared off my share of eligible men in the past.

But I was a girl on a mission and we got around to speaking of permanence and homes and nature. This led Phoenix to recommend an essay by Aldous Huxley titled, *Wordsworth In The Tropics*. We had both read *Brave New World*. During one hike, he told me Huxley had lived in California and befriended Bertrand Russell and Christopher Isherwood. For years, Phoenix had been curious about Huxley the erudite Englishman with a house in Pacific Palisades, contending with the zaniness and greed of Hollywood.

Phoenix had read *The Doors of Perception*, knew about Huxley's drug experimentation and interest in Eastern religions. When I'd first met him, Phoenix was reading a biography, *Huxley in Hollywood*. He told me that after devouring all 300-plus pages of what he called Dunaway's terrific book, he felt he was finally getting closer to understanding Huxley the man. The key, he was learning, was to attempt an impossible balance between work-a-day demands and feeding his higher cerebral, spiritual and emotional instincts. He felt Aldous Huxley understood and lived this balance.

With my sister's help at USC's Doheny Library, I found a copy of the essay Phoenix had recommended. As I read it and came across the following passage, I felt a glimmer of understanding what Phoenix had intimated when he'd said we can't expect permanence.

Huxley wrote: "The Wordsworthian adoration of Nature has two principal defects. The first is that it is only possible in a country where Nature has been nearly or quite enslaved to man. The second is that it is only possible for those who are prepared to falsify their immediate intuitions of Nature."

For all my thirty-two years, had I been wrong about nature and myself? Had I been enslaving and falsifying everything? No rules and no delusions of permanence or sainthood made man in the image of God. Nor did mountains, religion, a job, children, a swing set and a manicured lawn.

It was all very confusing. I took needed comfort each Sunday as Phoenix and I continued our hikes. He was so dang smart. Whenever possible, I steered him toward talking about books. Upon his recommendations, I read John Muir, Edward Abbey, and Suzuki's *Zen Mind, Beginner's Mind.*

In my apartment late at night, with my sister trying to study and the *ghetto birds* whirring overhead, I sat with eyes closed. I waited for calm. Suzuki's book on Zen sat open on my lap. Once satisfied that I felt calm, I drilled my finger into a page. Opening my eyes, I read the first sentence that I saw, which was usually illuminated — ironically enough — by a helicopter spot-light beam that lanced up and down my apartment walls.

The sentence was neither what I had wanted nor thought I needed to experience. It puzzled me. Yet it soothed. As Phoenix had suggested, it encouraged thoughts of another door, a different set of windows, the many exits and entrances I hadn't yet made or even imagined. Most importantly, it showed me where I stood and that I had nothing to fear.

It led me to remember when we'd pause on the trail and Phoenix would tell me to inhale the dryness of windblown desert sand rubbing against the marine layer, its cooling brine always to our west. A breeze shuddered through rock-cropped shadows and holly-bush shoulders. Sweat ran cold in the roots of my hair. Within seconds that sweat became arid. Everything I saw appeared as if washed clean — all because I'd paused a moment to look at where I was.

How my thoughts on the trail sprinted, cooled, and heated again — temperamental and impermanent. They wove their tapestries through aberrations and verges that led from one question to the next, each without a ready answer.

One Sunday while Phoenix and I cooled off at Zuma Beach, I managed to swim with a wave that brought me to his side. Together, as if in harmony, we stepped out of the frigid water, both of us shivering as we hurried to our towels on the sand.

It was all too perfect. To gain traction was to release one's hold on gravity —any seasoned hiker knew that. So I let go of gravity.

I reached with both hands for his damp glistening shoulders. My lips were salty and not yet dry, but they were hot and ready. I thought for a moment I might even close my eyes.

I pulled him closer to me and I held on. When our lips touched, his felt like a cold hard surface. Like a concrete wall. Those lips were sealed. His body was a cold wet slab. It was too cold. Too rigid. Maybe even dead.

This was not what I'd expected.

Worst of all, he was pushing me away. "What are you doing?" His voice jumped, nearing hysteria. "You crazy?"

Perhaps I was. I felt my face growing hot, flushed, turning scarlet. "I'm kissing you, what do you think I'm doing?"

"Don't. No. Never."

Never?

I couldn't swallow. Couldn't move. I had to laugh to ease my nerves, but I couldn't laugh. This wasn't funny. This hurt. I felt weightless a moment and knew it was fear. Okay, so I'd caught him by surprise. I'd made him appear weak in front of me. Men didn't like this, especially the sensitive ones — my type, Phoenix — so I shouldn't be impatient with him.

But he'd said never. He'd been like ice. Like death.

He turned away from me as if disgusted. "Eileen, I thought I could trust you. You ruined it. I thought you knew."

Ruined it? "What do you mean?" I asked.

"What do you think I mean?"

Oh. Oh God. Oh no. Was he talking West Hollywood? Was he gay?

I was thirty-two years old and Katie was right. We'd both die shriveled up and lonely. A couple of old maids.

Walking alone to his car, unable to face him, disgusted as much by him as my own ignorance, I remembered something Phoenix had told me earlier that day. He'd said there's always just enough silence to drive you mad if you let it.

ALL WE HAVE

Diana Jara wasn't one to tell her father not to cry. In a quiet respectful way, she said it thrilled her to say this time it was for good. No more deployments. In six months, she'd be a civilian in college on the GI Bill. She didn't say she knew her parents were proud of her and glad she was home. She didn't have to.

She helped Lindsay, her mother, wipe away tears. She wanted to tell Lindsay that arriving home was the easy part. That she'd been through hell — more than most women her age — but she didn't. A show of pride would be ridiculous. All of her sisters had been through hell over there. Silence was best. She even kept her phone turned off and in her pocket.

Diana's father, Eduardo, trusted his daughter understood it wasn't sadness that made her mother weep. It was a releasing of the helplessness they, as parents, had been living through. So many had returned maimed or dead. Eduardo had followed the news closely, reading all of Diana's online postings, learning as much as possible about the war. Statistics, like politicians, often lied cleverly. How many limbs blown off? How many families torn apart? Who counted such things?

He could now say his daughter had seen mankind at its worst and best, and she'd survived a test of her inner fortitude. There wasn't a father he knew who wanted his child in war, especially a daughter. Yet if that daughter had to serve — would make no other choice — then let her return home braver and wiser. No medals on her chest. That didn't matter.

It wasn't wrong, he thought, to be idealistic. Yet stupid, Eduardo thought, all these wars. Still, he supported his daughter and his country. Having done her part, at last his Diana would begin a peaceful life.

He had no word for the giddiness he felt. He couldn't stop beaming at Diana, letting her grip his arm as they walked the airport concourse, feeling such a sublime happiness. *She's home — my baby girl is home.*

Once outdoors, when Eduardo's tears came, he couldn't control them. He felt such overwhelming gratitude to all forces in the universe that had brought her back. A small man with a slender waist and rounded shoulders, he felt puny next to Diana in her camouflage pants, jacket and camel-colored boots. He didn't care. He let the tears flow, bawling the way Lindsay had, and the way of his Mama during his childhood whenever she shared tales about her life in Mexico. The tears shook Eduardo and he felt for a moment as if he'd collapse.

This was not how it was supposed to be. Not how he'd imagined the homecoming, or how he'd planned to reveal himself as a grateful steadfast father.

But that didn't matter, either.

* * * * *   * * * * * *

In the basement of Saint Andrew's Catholic Church, Lindsay McElmore Jara sat in front of young Father Donlan, a beefy tattooed red-haired ex-Marine who was far too grizzled to be Hollywood's version of a kindly priest. Lindsay was a regular in a loyal Tuesday evening group of Saint Andrew's parents who had children in uniform overseas. Eduardo often worked late and seldom made the meetings, but Lindsay hadn't missed one. About twelve parents in all, each in turn spoke of fears about their children. Some remarked this war in Afghanistan, like the ones in Iraq — and for some like Vietnam — was unnecessary. One parent called it a "racket" and another said it was "sanctioned bloodshed." Lindsay agreed with both points of view, but she was shrewd enough to know political opinions wouldn't hasten Diana's safe return home.

When it was Lindsay's turn to speak, she put aside the big picture. She thought about her neighborhood's residents — many of whom she knew and liked well enough — and said it disturbed her that so few others without skin in the game, so to speak, seemed to care about what was happening over there. She'd thought they cared, but they really didn't. Why should they? It didn't affect them directly.

Lindsay struck an impassioned note. A high-school drama teacher, she knew about reaching an audience. "These are our blessed children," she said. "They are not abstractions to *us*."

"Well put, Lindsay. But remember, faith will pull you through," said Father Donlan. "Your faith is more real, more powerful than anything else."

Maybe, thought Lindsay. She liked these meetings for many reasons, not the least of them was that her skepticism and her philosophical streak got a thorough workout. "Faith can't stop an I-E-D if Diana happens to step on one."

"It sure can't," remarked one of the parents, a divorced caterer named Brenda Craft whose son was a Marine deployed near Kabul.

"But your son can be sharp enough to avoid that IED," said Father Donlan.

"Why is that?" asked Brenda.

"Why?" asked Father Donlan. He turned from Brenda to face Lindsay. He smiled at her. "Because he has faith in himself, his training, his brothers, his experience."

Lindsay sounded a snort. She hoped her sarcasm was obvious. "We'll see."

"God sees," said Father Donlan. "God shows the way."

Does he? Lindsay wouldn't dare express this thought, but she hoped Father Donlan could read her face and the doubt, anger and frustration there.

When the meeting ended, Lindsay approached Father Donlan and moved him into one corner of the room where she could apologize in private.

"I'm a mess," she said. "Sometimes my sarcasm gets out of control."

"It wasn't directed at me," said Father Donlan. "Why should I be offended?"

Lindsay thought it the perfect answer and was reminded why she admired this sometimes truculent yet optimistic priest.

"But there's nothing we can do," she said.

"You can pray," said Father Donlan.

"No," said Lindsay. She held back an urge to burst open and scream. "Praying is like begging. I want to *do* something."

Father Donlan grew silent. He studied her face a moment. Lindsay believed the man was trying to help her. She wanted to look into his eyes. She couldn't.

"When I was in Mosul, in Iraq," he said. "I was pretty scared. I thought about a lot of things. My mind racing all the time. So to slow it down, I kept thinking about how little it takes to breathe. How little it takes to stop. You know, just seal yourself off. Clam up. Try it some time. Stop breathing until everything gets dark and you drop out."

Someone shouted Father Donlan's name and the priest raised his hand and shouted wearily: "Over here, I'm coming."

Excusing himself, he started to lumber across the room.

Lindsay, intrigued, followed him. "Really?" She was puzzled. Was he advocating suicide? "But I don't get it."

"Neither did I" said Father Donlan, throwing his words over his shoulder. "And I didn't like it, so you know what I did?"

"What?"

"I started thinking about something else."

* * * * *   * * * * * *

They sat in the living room in the dark and Eduardo held Lindsay in his arms on the couch. Lindsay had been sobbing for the past hour. Finally, she was spent. She felt an eerie lack of gravity. Eduardo asked if she'd like some ice cream. He'd stopped at the market on the way home and picked up her favorite, Cherry Garcia. Lindsay didn't want any. She asked Eduardo if he'd pray with her, for their health, for Diana.

Eduardo said later, not now. He touched Lindsay's face. He then kissed each place he'd touched. *This is all I can do and it isn't much.* He held his wife. He said they should pray in their bedroom under the crucifix for all the mothers who would never see their children again. For the children who'd died, lost a limb or a parent. They should pray for love to flourish and for wars to end forever.

"Because we're all we have," said Eduardo. "Just each other."

Lindsay knew she was an intelligent and emotionally complex woman. After twenty years of marriage, Eduardo still sometimes felt incapable of understanding her *gringa* ways. Not this time. He had broken through. Perhaps it was his simplicity. Nothing seemed to ruffle him.

"And you know how much I love you," he said.

What would I do without him? thought Lindsay. "I love you, too." She paused a moment, fearing she'd sounded automatic. "Father Donlan knows how to make me think better, but you know how to make me feel better."

"Not that you can't do those things on your own."

"That's right," she said. "I'm more than capable."

Eduardo hugged her and within that hug much of Lindsay's anguish dissolved for a while.

All these nights, they're all like this, Lindsay thought. The anguish would return. The waiting would continue. She had her job, routines, her weekly meetings, and Eduardo — but they were still not enough.

They'd have to be. It was that simple.

* * * * * * * * * * *

Walking to the car across the vast airport parking lot, Diana kept her head erect. She struck an aloof toughened tone with her father. "I'm no hero, Daddy. I just did my job. I'm glad to be out of that hell in one piece."

"Really bad, wasn't it," said Eduardo. He carried Diana's duffel bag for her, surprised by how light it felt.

"No, not really," said Diana. "I'm just tired, that's all."

Lindsay stepped up between them. "We prayed for you the whole time," she said. "We really, really missed you."

"I know you did," said Diana. "I prayed for myself. All of us did, in our own ways. Funny thing is that the hardest parts were when we had free time. There was nothing to do. Had to keep busy. Keep my mind off. Sometimes, I'd just do stupid stuff like holding my breath to see how long I could last without blacking out. I read this cool book, *Ask The Dust*."

"No," said Lindsay. "Don't go back there." Lindsay sounded peeved, recalling her conversation with Father Donlan. "You're home now, Sweetie. It's time to look ahead."

"But I'll always go back," said Diana. She shrugged. "In a way, I'm still there. I'll always be there."

"No! You're here now," said Lindsay. Her voice had jumped and it held a firm edge. "It's *safe* here. We're all together. A family again."

We were always a family, thought Eduardo. He looked at Lindsay as if to scold her. She should let Diana have her say, no matter how illogical. *Madre de Dios, my little girl is fresh off the plane from a war zone.*

"Say that again," said Diana. "Please. Just say it."

"Say what?" asked Lindsay. "That we're a family?"

Eduardo stepped in. *The girl obviously needs to hear this.* "We're a family," he said. "As my grandfather used to say, the family is the first and last government."

Diana paused a moment, her high forehead brown in the sun. A guarded and pregnant smile spread slowly across her face. A faraway look brightened her round eyes as if she were remembering a difficult yet inspiring moment. She snapped out of it by giggling and landing a playful slap against her father's shoulder. "All I know is that I don't care if I ever see a fucking desert again."

Eduardo stiffened. "*Madre de Dios*, don't swear like that," he said. "Especially in front of your mother."

Looking at her parents, everything about Diana softened. There was a gleam of recognition in her eyes, as if she were seeing them and her whereabouts for the first time. She apologized. Taking her mother by the shoulders, she held her and kissed her on the cheek. She let out a small sigh.

Holding on, tears began to well in Lindsay's eyes. She didn't care if pedestrians were looking. She slapped her arms around Diana and held on and she cried, hugging her for what seemed an hour.

When she let go, her first thought was that she'd never held Diana quite long enough.

Apron And Shawl And Housedress

I was a burden. Had nothing to offer. I'd been sleeping in the same clothes for three weeks, sweating through fever dreams and the realization there wasn't a quick fix to improving my health. I'd started in September as a guest professor in Bălţi, a Moldovan city that had never hosted an American resident. I'd been warmly received, yet in my third month on the job I'd come down with double pneumonia.

I fumbled my way to Elena's kitchen. Hard afternoon light heated her small table. When there was electricity, Elena liked to make *plov*, a mixture of rice, cubed beef and carrots. I found her seated and thumbing through a beat-up copy of *Time* I'd given her.

It was one of the days everyone under her roof had to speak English, rather than Russian or Romanian. I began to speak but stopped when tinny music came from the speaker of the state radio system wired throughout the building. The electricity was on. Usually, the state played Moldovan folk music. This afternoon was no different.

"I must hurry," said Elena. Her manner was polite, her English tinged with a gentle BBC-approved accent. "I will make a dinner. We shall have tea."

I offered to help. She said I must rest. I didn't argue; I dropped into a chair near a window that overlooked a courtyard three stories below walled in by dirtied limestone block buildings of the same height. An iced-over walking path divided frozen hardpan into quadrants; each one looked like stippled dough that had failed to rise.

A pair of dogs snarled over a bone. This made me think about the political talk I'd heard in Chisinau where I'd spent the summer before moving north to Bălți. There had been excitement and anxiety about Moldova's declaration of independence from Russia, officially passed in August of 1991. The year was 1993 and Moldova was simmering in the aftermath of a civil war over its Trans-Dniester region — a war few in the West had heard about. East of the Dniester River, the city of Tiraspol had held its status as capital of an autonomous Soviet state the U.S. government refused to acknowledge. This state was off-limits to the handful of Yanks residing in Moldova. I couldn't wait to sneak a visit.

I doubted Elena cared to talk politics. I told myself to heed her advice, shouldn't pull her away from precious time with electricity. I watched her hurry to the balcony where she kept a pot of *plov* among root vegetables and eggs. This was her fridge. She rushed the pot inside, placing it atop one coil of a double hot plate. A slight hum as voltage turned the coils orange. On one coil she boiled tea water in a pot coated with white porcelain-like enamel. Flowers were painted on the pot's side. I told her the word for such a pot in Romanian, then Russian. Correct on both counts. Despite illness, my language skills were improving.

Much of Elena's kitchen ware, furniture and clothing weren't part of a process of throwing out the old and replacing it with the trendy. Like her husband, she respected one of everything, including a pair of shoes expected to last many years. Things needing repair were not discarded. If unable to repurpose them herself, she brought them to her mother's village about an hour away by a slow diesel-powered train. Her mother, brother or sister-in-law would repair and use them. In return, Elena got onions, potatoes, wine and jars of fruit compote from the dirt cellar of her mother's house. These monthly trips kept Elena's family larder at subsistence level. Vova, her husband, spent weeks at a time each spring and fall helping Elena's mother in her garden.

It was never a guarantee a train would show up. Sometimes, Elena waited three hours in the cold. Other times, no train arrived and she'd resort to bus routes that connected her from Bălţi to any northern village remotely close to Mom's. She'd walk the difference along mud roads, sometimes twelve miles.

When Elena shared these difficulties, she didn't show self-pity. She hastily reminded me that all over the former USSR it was a battle to survive. By bus or train, seldom a seat, she had to fight her way on, hold her place and keep an eye on her goods, fearing they'd be stolen.

"When I see how we live now," she told me. "I can't believe it. I ask how is this possible. We are good people. Why did we allow this to happen?"

The trill in her voice proved her fatigue and frustration. Perhaps by sharing, she helped herself feel better. I seldom felt she expected a clever response that would comfort her.

A voice on state radio announced in Russian they were going to present Rimsky-Korsakov's *Scheherazade*. Elena, sighing, grinned enough to show me gold-rimmed molars along one side of her mouth. Like our fellow teacher Gabriella, Elena had a pleasantly disarming smile. Her teeth had been well cared for. Most could not say this; they smiled reluctantly, if at all. All the wayward and gold bicuspids I'd seen — in some cases full jackets, top row and bottom — explained why.

She sighed dreamily. "It's like old days when I was a student with Vova in Saint Petersburg. We loved the classic music."

Neither of us said it, but we worried the electricity wouldn't stay on long enough for the *plov* to cook and for us to get through Rimsky-Korsakov's masterpiece. All we could do was wait. Looking relieved, Elena removed her apron with its splashy floral prints. She draped a gray shawl over her shoulders. At home, she always wore this apron and shawl over her housedress. The same combination each afternoon. The same wool skirt and sweater for work.

As she sat across from me, I asked about the housedress. She explained that in Russian it was called *khalat*, pronounced with a soft k. In Romanian, *halat*, no k. The word dated back to Persia and later the Turks. It meant any robe worn open in the front. In Russian, a doctor's lab-coat was called a white *khalat*.

We soaked in winter sun as it bleached lace-like doilies of frost seized to windows. As it inched lower, the apartment grew colder and a *khalat* made much sense. So did rabbit-fur hats. We lost ourselves in *Scheherazade*, getting about halfway through when all went quiet. I assumed it was nearly five p.m.

Silence bloomed. We sat over empty tea cups. Elena said nothing. Did she feel disappointed? I did. The tea water was hot enough, but not her *plov* — the evening's meal. She grimaced as she slipped her apron on, leaving it untied. She stepped out to the balcony. A blast of air whistled in that made me quake and sniffle.

I was still weak, hating myself over it. She poured tea. No lemon but some sugar. I stayed far from windows, wishing I could turn back time to the moment when Elena's face was placidly radiant, her cobalt eyes lit with the serenity she must have felt while listening to Rimsky-Korsakov.

Beyond sunshine, a protracted joy had passed between us. I knew one thing. I'd never forget the word for housedress.

Her son and daughter were due home soon. After them, Vova would return from a factory that still wasn't operating. If he didn't go to work each day, he'd lose his job. It had been months since he or Elena had been paid.

Maybe Vova would find bread. Maybe not. Once again, Elena hadn't been able to prepare her family a hot dinner.

"You see this?" She broke into rare stridency as she removed her apron and tossed it aside. She drew her shawl tighter around her neck. "How we live?"

I thought she might weep. This wasn't an inconvenience. This was her life.

No bread that night — just leftover beet salad by candlelight. Our breath visible as we sat close to each other, sharing bodily warmth.

✳ ✳ ✳ ✳ ✳ ✳ ✳ ✳ ✳ ✳ ✳

Gabriella and other university teachers continued their hunt to find me an apartment while I remained a shut-in, recuperating with Elena's family. I continued to sleep fully dressed. Two months had passed since my only pair of jeans had been washed, but I was still too weak to launder clothes. Elena insisted on helping. Together, when we had electricity long enough (or so we hoped), she boiled water Vova had brought from a city well. She filled a wide plastic pail and soaked my jeans, underwear and shirts. On her knees, Elena scrubbed my shirts by hand, using her knuckles and a dung-colored brick of soap that left no suds. She hung them dripping to dry on her balcony. Three days later they were frozen stiff when she brought them in.

I told Elena I had to get stronger, to test myself. Elena thought this very American of me. I washed my jeans, but the task sent me to bed wiped out. At least I'd done it. They needed a week to dry. In the meantime, I wore pajamas under sweatpants that smelled as mealy as I did.

We talked books whenever possible and this helped me fend off a creeping depression. I could bury myself in a coat and brave an evening walk outdoors with Vova, but I'd suffer a relapse if I rushed back to work. I needed to heal completely and that meant time and patience.

We seldom had water or electricity for more than an hour. The blackouts came unannounced, yet Elena managed to prepare for classes. I never saw her reading student work. I think she awakened at dark and read by window-light as dawn arose. I was asleep during those hours when the apartment and the city were silent as a tomb.

With our schedule of alternating language days, Elena was pleased to see her children acquire some English. These were hard times, but she expressed hope there would be choices for her children she hadn't imagined possible. After all, her father had disappeared on one of Stalin's trains. Rode off and was never heard from again. Vova had lost his parents in a similar way.

Like many Moldovan intellectuals I'd met, Elena was realistic. Everything she'd believed in had betrayed her. Hope was what she had and yet hope was for dreamers. Work kept her mind off her struggles. She'd been teaching English for fifteen years at Alecu Russo State University. Before me, she'd met only one native speaker, a missionary from North Carolina. Raised as an atheist, as all teachers were during Soviet times, she'd listened to this man for an hour before finding his sales pitch tiresome. She told me she was saving her patience for breadlines not miracles. She didn't need a preacher to show her evidence of man's sinful ways and God's fury.

Throughout her decades as a professor, she'd had access to only Soviet-approved textbooks that featured such droll essays as *Lenin In London*. The American novelists she'd read — Jack London, Theodore Dreiser — she knew well. She wanted to know others.

"Of what value," she asked, "is a professor who is not learning all the time? These were our ideals as Soviets. Yes, our government gave us problems. But our intellectual class, our teachers and scientists, they never stopped learning. It was expected of them."

She brought out the best in me, as good teachers tend to do. By listening well, I allowed her to refine her already sophisticated English. She asked if I knew Eugene O'Neill. I did. I'd seen Richard Jenkins play Hickey on stage in *The Iceman Cometh*. I assured her that seeing the play was a different experience than reading it. She reminded me that with Chekov and Gorky it was much the same.

"He's a better playwright than given credit for," she said.

"Chekov, you mean."

"No," she said. "Gorky. I see that you're reading *My Universities*."

She was right. During periods of clarity, I'd been enjoying a Soviet *Raduga* translation that Gabriella had borrowed for me from the university library. Gabriella was tutoring me in Russian. I hadn't seen her in a month and found myself thinking about her constantly.

"Many people forget his plays made his reputation," said Elena.

"I saw *The Lower Depths* once," I said. "A student production."

Elena shrugged. "I prefer Chekov."

"I've never seen his work on stage."

"You must. But in Russian. It's like not seeing Shakespeare in English. I'm sure Gabriella told you."

It was my turn to shrug. "The last couple of months, they're a blur."

"I saw Gabriella today between classes. She sends a big hello."

"I miss her."

Elena's face lit up. She shared a knowing smile. "I think she misses you, too."

If I had a crush on Gabriella, I was likely the only one in the city who didn't know it.

One night, I took from my duffel a paperback essential works of Stephen Crane, and selected poems by Robert Frost, who Elena had sampled while a student. I gave both books to her the next afternoon. As she pored over the pages, delighted by my gift, she struck a note of despair, saying that books, like everything else that was good in Moldova, had become impossible to find. She held the Frost edition against her breast and proudly recited a line from *Fire and Ice*.

She begged me to read the poem aloud to her. She wanted to hear a native speaker's intonations. So in my pajamas and smelling like a meal worm, I read Frost aloud by candlelight as the sun went down and the kitchen grew frigid.

I saw in Elena's eyes just how unforgettable a moment it was.

* * * * *   * * * * * *

I told Elena how impressed I was with her knowledge of American literature, especially since so many western writers had been taboo.

I agreed with her that in regards to education, the Soviets hadn't been as close-minded as Americans had been led to believe.

"We had such a system. First class," she said. "I think, for older generations, this is our disappointment now. We had good teachers. If they were so behind, they didn't know. But still we learned from them. They were dedicated. Always. This, I think, Americans don't appreciate."

I was amazed by how quickly she read in English. Four days after I'd given her the Crane collection, she'd finished *Red Badge Of Courage* and said it reminded her of the Ukrainian, Ostrovsky, and his *How The Steel Was Tempered*. She'd been forced to read Ostrovsky's novel. Like Crane's, she saw it as a crafty show of patriotic political philosophy rather than an account of what had happened.

I'm paraphrasing much of what we shared. Gleanings often came between lines, through gesture and facial expression, especially on days when I spoke in her native languages. Like all her colleagues, she'd been trained to pursue intellectual discourse. Under the Soviet system, intellectuals were not second-class citizens. What they earned as salaries didn't define their cultural value. They were respected.

Therefore, I never felt freakish — as I sometimes did in the States — when I rambled on passionately about the importance of literature. I knew I was a disaster in broken Russian, trying to explain Dostoevsky's genius, but Elena listened. She corrected my grammar. She cared.

I was stunned by her ability to explain in English why Crane's novel hadn't moved her. Conversely, I was thrilled to learn she'd enjoyed *Maggie A Girl Of The Streets*. She thought Maggie a powerfully believable woman. Rendered by a man, no less. An honest picture of poverty and despair that spoke to her in the same way *Sister Carrie* had.

In the same way, I asked her, that Tolstoy had taught me about Moscow under the czars?

Exactly. Crane's realism, like Tolstoy's, was, to a degree, doomed to fail. Such big ambitions were impossible to achieve. Yet that was the genius and the charm of Tolstoy.

"When you feel a language," she said. "That's when you know a pure joy. How do we help our students to *feel* it? That's what we must do. Show them it's their own, that they'll always have it, and it takes them places in its own way, anywhere they want to go."

My mouth went dry. I stared at Elena. Each day, she had shown me a different facet of herself. She hadn't been paid in over six months. Nor had her husband. Her family barely had enough to eat. Still, her passion for her work glowed from within and she continued to abide by unselfish concerns for those she'd been entrusted to mentor.

"This is why we're here," she said. "Because we love to learn and we want to share."

Face to face with her in the silence of that kitchen, I was unable to muster a response. I was nothing. I didn't deserve to be there. Due to my monstrous ego, I had expected to change lives in Bălţi. What naïve delusions I had been living under: the worst one of all that I had something to offer and just had to find it. These thoughts loomed, making me feel preposterous, unprepared and useless.

Yet for the first time in weeks, I felt a spark of health. I breathed easily. I had connected with another — of a different gender, culture and generation — who shared a similar interest. Learning the terrain of what were once alien shores had to lead, in the long run, to enlightenment rather than fear. Naïve I'd been, no doubt about it, but the bright heat in Elena's eyes told me to trust any philanthropic motives behind my desire to be in Bălţi at that time.

To listen, to learn, to inspire. If I was a burden, it was to myself. That much, at least, I could change.

You Remind Me Of A Naughty Springtime Cuckoo

Rollo, you're named after my Pa, Roland Myles, once known in Beantown burlesque halls as Bones O'Shea. Like many Irish new to America, he eventually dropped the O. He danced buck, wing, waltz, eccentric, clog, tap and soft shoe, and he liked to say you could always judge a hoofer by following his left foot. He and Tweet Sullivan and Ray Bolger grew up together in Dorchester. Tweet married a Jewish girl, which was unheard of in those times, and changed his name to Fred Allen. Ray broke through big as the scarecrow in the *Wizard of Oz*, but long before that he and Pa worked twelve-hour days as ushers at the Metropolitan.

In that era, movies ran 'round the clock, no less than five times a day. For a nickel, you could watch a cartoon, a serial, and a picture. Pa and Ray would show up at ten a.m. and clock out at midnight. Ray often slept on a couch in the back room of a Chinese restaurant. It took Pa an hour to get home. He'd stay up smoking cigarettes as he listened to the radio. He'd sleep in his favorite chair and then pop up, skip breakfast, and catch the trolley to work. Thursday was his day off.

He and Ray, fair-skinned slender dandies with gangly legs, both stood over six feet. They weren't rich, but sure dressed that way. Pa never went without wing-tips to match his dark suits and ties — if not a flower in his lapel, then a silk hanky folded into the top pocket of his jacket.

Between each showing at the Metropolitan, they'd rush down to the large tiled foyer dividing the men's from the ladies room. There they'd dance the routines they'd just watched on screen. Those tiles provided the right surface and acoustics for them to perfect their slides and rat-a-tap-taps. As ushers already in suits, they'd study how to look dapper in front of big mirrors. They'd change their shoes, run back upstairs and get their flashlights to seat the new patrons. Watching the pictures again, they'd try to memorize each routine before hurrying back down to practice. In this way, they developed their talent. Bolger was unique. Watch him in *Stage Door Canteen*. Pa thought he, Donald O'Connor, The Ritz Brothers, and Sammy Davis Jr. were underrated dancers. He'd met Sammy when Sammy danced with the Will Mastin Trio. Pa and Will had worked vaudeville together on the Keith Circuit.

Ray moved west. Pa wanted to join him, but chose not to, making a decision that changed his life for good. He stayed on the Keith Circuit because he'd fallen for Lilly Paradise, your Nana. They formed a duo. Nana sang and played piano and mandolin while Pa danced his routines. For ten years, they traveled by train, three shows a day in every Keith theatre from Maine to Atlantic City.

As a solo hoofer, Pa never caught his big break. Lew Walters became his agent. You know Lew's daughter, Barbara, from TV.

Try as he might, Lew couldn't help. Tastes kept changing. Live theatre gave way to movies and radio, and Pa just kept getting older. He had no formal education, having been raised by his half-sister, Irene, a redhead whose mother was a Cooney right off the boat.

It got tough for him. At one time, he and Bolger had been debonair princes of Scollay Square, with plenty of work in the burlesque halls there, especially the Old Howard Theatre, which had once been a church and used to pack in the sailors every night. In its heyday, the Old Howard took in 15,000 patrons per week. For vaudeville and burlesque in Beantown, it was the place.

Nana, on the other hand, modeled herself after a Ziegfeld girl. She wore long dresses with frills and tassels, silk gloves and picture hats, and her solo career took off. She got her break on Broadway, with George M. Cohan in *The O'Brien Girl* at the New Victory Theatre, which is still there off Forty-Second Street. She even had a song written for her, called "Just For You, Dear." She's pictured on the sheet music, and if I do say so myself my mother was a lovely gal with flowing yellow locks and green eyes brighter than the sea. Some called her a flapper, but she paid no mind. On the surface, she came across as a sweet Catholic girl, and she certainly was, but she took no guff from show-biz frauds. Nor did she take her talent for granted. She practiced constantly.

Her family? Stuck on themselves, in my book. Never came to see us in Roxbury. Nana would do anything for them, but they made no effort to support her. We had to go to them in Southie. As I got older, I came to resent this. I saw that family for what it was, her mother being the worst. She had, you could say, delusions of grandeur. Not one of Nana's six sisters ever saw her perform. Her father had passed early, and even with Nana's Broadway success, her mother insisted a girl who worked the stage was a tramp. When Nana got sick in New York, her oldest sister Tillie brought her home on the train. Her career had reached its end. She'd taken sick because she was pregnant with me.

That was in '29, year of The Crash, and same year Pa's dancing school at The Strand on Columbia Ave in Dorchester went belly up. He'd quit the Keith Circuit to raise me and start his school, and his timing couldn't have been worse. Like a lot of Americans, he struggled to find a job. For a while he worked for A. Stowell and Company at 24 Winter Street, just down the hill from the State House. It was a jewelry store owned by the Cooks, but I'm not sure what he did there.

What I am sure of is that he loved the Boston theatres. He went back to Loew's Company and begged for his old Metropolitan job. It was taken. They offered him a manager's position, part-time. He still had Thursdays off, but from Somerville to Roxbury to Roslindale, he went where Loews needed him. The live theatre culture had dried up since his Scollay Square days with Bolger; it was mostly cinema but steady pay.

When America joined the war effort, everybody's father, it seemed, was shipped overseas. Pa tried to enlist, but he had liver problems and was too old. Secretly, Nana was relieved. It would have killed her to raise two kids alone. See, my sister Fay had come along. Pa loved us kids but needed dough. He found a full-time job with the Office of Price Administration, an agency that FDR cooked up to keep Americans off the dole.

Problem was, Pa had to type. One night, he lugged home an Underwood with a platen about three feet long. You could have sunk a ship with that machine. He planted it on the kitchen table and there it stayed. This drove Nana bonkers, but Pa insisted on staying up late, hunched over that keyboard, pecking with one finger *ka-tunk…ka-tunk…ka-tunk*. Kept me and Fay awake, but it paid off; he learned enough typing to keep that job for two years. Eventually, it was offered to a returning serviceman. All the jobs were.

As I got older, I'd ride the T with him out to Carson Beach and Kelly's Landing for whole-bellied clams. He loved baseball, and together we saw the Boston Braves, the Red Sox, and the House of David team, which was all Jewish men who wore beards. Once, he took me to see his favorite pitcher, Satchel Paige, who starred in the Negro Leagues. Most of Boston was segregated then, but Pa insisted on crossing color lines. It made him unpopular in fanatical Hibernian circles, but he didn't waver.

We'd walk everywhere, even when we needed the trackless trolley, which only cost a nickel. We'd stop now and then at corner taps and he'd have himself one shot, no more, and then we'd carry on. Always the niftiest of dressers, he wore his collars starched, a long wool coat in winter, a silk smoking jacket at home, a blazer in summer, and he never went anywhere without his soft Stetson hat.

He took pride in staying fit. He'd walk his grocery errands for Nana, and dance for Fay in the living room. He wasn't New York City, or lace curtain, or *Mayflower* English, but in those corner taps full of Boston Irish he found fraternity. Many a working stiff remembered seeing him at the Old Howard, and he'd stand at the bar and suffer the cry, "If it ain't Bones O'Shea, the *hoof-ah* from Scollay Square."

This was often followed by a free drink and questions about Ray Bolger. After Ray left, Pa seldom discussed their friendship. Ray hadn't kept in touch, and I think Pa resented this. Walking home from those corner taps, I'd want him to explain what it had been like on those stages with sailors cheering, and women throwing garters. I wanted him to talk about Ray, and tap dancing, and Fred Allen's success in radio. He never would. I don't think he knew how to burrow under his own disappointment and confusion and accept how things had changed. He'd become one of the hats in the audience, and he lacked the prestige and income his youth had promised. His dance school had folded, and he read with remorse Ernie Pyle's columns from the front. He listened to FDR's fireside chats, and he watched countless newsreels of Europe and Japan getting bombed.

He loved his Trilby. This was another hat, of course, but it was also Beantown slang for a hamburger on toast served with a fat slice of onion on top. He'd wash it down with a boilermaker, dumping his whiskey, shot glass and all, inside his beer mug. Scollay Square days weren't coming back. His Trilby, boilermaker and long walks helped him cope. Not to mention Mass every Sunday.

I wasn't much help. I'd turned fourteen and I had no direction. Scrappy Monahan and his brother Gig went to Commerce High, so I went there, too. Scrappy became a miler, and his locker was next to mine during gym class. He was part of a championship track meet in our conference, but I never followed it and this hurt our friendship. Doc Fleming was always after me, "Go out for football, go out for football." He'd seen me play in the street, where we also played stickball, but my sports career ended when I went out for a pass, slipped and landed on a curbstone, snapping eight of my fingers.

All sorts of characters patrolled the halls at Commerce. Donkey Walsh kept a key tied to a string wrapped around his fist. Not just any key. This was a skeleton about eight inches long. If you weren't buried in your textbook, he'd sneak up from behind and swing that key and knock you on the skull with it. I had a dozen welts from that thing.

In the past, Pa hadn't minded that I'd done so poorly in school, because I'd done my part to keep the household going. But as my grades kept dropping, I think he worried I might not have much of a future. When Loews promoted him to full-time manager of The Capitol at Winter Hill in Somerville, I pleaded with him to get me a job there as an usher. This led to one of our first arguments, which ended with him shouting, "Don't even dare think about going into show business."

I'll never forget the way he barked that out, since he took pride in being the stoic nimble expert in the soft shoe. "I could only hire you on Sundays," he explained. "Why would you want that? You should be with your friends on Sunday. You should do your school work during the week."

"I hate school. You never went. Why should I?"

"You want to clean toilets all your life, is that it?"

Your Nana intervened and calmed us down, assuring me Pa would discuss it with her. Pa promptly sent me away to spend a weekend in Orient Heights with my Auntie Irene, who spoiled me first by giving me a dollar, which I blew on 20 candy bars, wolfing down each one in a sitting. After that, she bought me a red bicycle with big balloon tires and a foot brake. Man, I had to pump those pedals to get up a head of steam, but braking was even tougher. For years I rode that bike all over the city, losing all my baby fat.

Nana's talk with Pa must have gotten to him. He spoke to his higher-ups at Loews. He explained to me how little money a theatre manager earned. In his case: $40 a week. They'd pay me 40 cents an hour on a Sunday. I'd gross $2.00. Each penny helped.

I started as a pick-up boy with pan and broom. I wore a maroon usher's jacket, not a full uniform. I swept up wrappers and popcorn, and emptied the round cans full of butts that stood outside the doors. I didn't clean toilets. I had to be there at noon, but got paid to work from one until six. Pa never said it, but I sensed he liked having me there.

It wasn't long before he made me a full usher. Thousands were dying in the war, and I felt guilty for getting the flashlight and pay raise I'd wanted. I no longer had to pull butt ends out of the sand. I broke at six for dinner, and this was when Pa and I would walk together and I'd bring up movies like *Sergeant York*, and *Destination Tokyo*, sharing with him my growing enthusiasm for the Air Force. He frowned when hearing this, and in his oblique way explained that movies were not reality, war was a grave matter, altogether different, and I should never take it lightly.

On the main drag through Somerville, the Capitol Theatre was no shoebox. It was a gem, with dressing rooms and a backstage area from its days of live shows. I got there by bus and trackless trolley. Dinner was usually a sandwich and cup of soup that set me back fifty cents. I spent what I earned just to feed myself on the job. Pa agreed to let me work any day, and as many hours as I wanted, but only if I kept up my grades. I rekindled my friendship with Scrappy Monahan, and he tutored me.

I started working from 7 to 11 every night. Theatre owners never let a movie run beyond 11, even if it hadn't finished yet. They didn't want to pay the projectionist overtime, since he was union. I decided that until I joined the Air Force, this was what I would be. I studied and got my projectionist's license.

My first interview sealed my fate. The projectionist said, "Doesn't matter, Mikey, if you have a license. Next job that comes up will go to the son of a dead or retiring projectionist. You'll never get a job. Ask your father. He'll back me up."

My dream had been crushed, but I stayed on as an usher. I liked being part of a team, spending time with Pa, and seeing every movie that came to town. At 11 sharp, I started putting up seats. While patrons filed out, I swept the aisles and emptied the trash. This took no less than forty-five minutes for which no usher was paid. We understood and didn't mind. We were proud of our false fronts, also called dickeys, and our bow ties and short night jackets and striped pants. Nana kept those black pants cleaned and mended. Pa taught me how to take care of the required black shoes he'd bought for me. I wore my uniform on the T with pride, and no one poked fun.

Home remained a small dark room in Roxbury, cold each winter, even with the heat on and *Terry And The Pirates* to read about. There were no driveways or parking lots in my life. Movies were a relief from the war. I went to Mass, which helped my grades in Latin. Having a job to help my family would put me in good graces with God. It wasn't enough to believe this, I had to live it. Too many were dying in the war. I wanted to sign up, and to fight, but I was too young.

The owners of The Capitol also owned The Ball Square Theatre in Medford, and they paid twelve dollars to screen an A-run. They'd tell Pa to start the movie in Somerville with its second reel. They'd send a taxi to Ball Square with the first reel. Once it got there, they'd call Pa saying he could open the doors. They'd screen the first reel in Ball Square while screening its second at The Capitol. When one reel ended, they'd taxi it back to the other theatre, and vice versa. This was called back-timing the film. It meant paying for only one copy.

It didn't always work. I remember when a taxi carrying a second reel got a flat. The screen went black. No second reel in one theatre. No first in the other. It was a Saturday, the theatre jammed and the kids going berserk. Pa decided against showing cartoons. He told the projectionist to rewind the reel and play it again. The kids didn't care. They'd paid their nickel to make a lot of noise and get in from the cold. They could stay as long as they wanted.

I learned to smoke, but all ushers had to do so outside. I watched how Pa would handle the unruly kids. How he'd hold open the door for patrons, politely pay refunds, and put at ease angry customers. He may not have been as famous as Ray Bolger, but he was a gentleman, always stately, never forgetting he'd had a taste of fame.

Decades later, I formed an understanding of how wounded he'd been by fate and ambition. After his passing and the failure of some of my own ambitions, I grasped how it must have stung him to learn that Fred Allen had become as popular as Alice Faye and Jack Benny doing the Lux Radio theatre. How it irked him to see a dancer with a weak left foot get so much applause on the Ed Sullivan show, a program he watched each Sunday night. It stood for the vaudeville he once knew, but it was still television. It marked the end of an era, and his career as a theatre manager.

He and Nana never owned a car or property. As rents went up, they moved from one apartment to another, each one cheaper and smaller than the last. Not once had he heard from Bolger or Allen. The hopes of his past were sometimes a curse that refused to die within. To his credit, he never took to drinking, but on bad days he'd only leave his room to mope while eating supper. In a futile effort to cheer him up, Nana would chirp about her workday, but he'd keep moping. During his darkest days, I think he even envied Nana's Broadway past.

I prefer to remember him on the bright days, when even in winter the sun through our living room windows held a loony quality that made me forget my comic books and smile. Pa in his silk robe would fill that room, cozying up to Nana and coaxing her to sing "You Remind Me Of A Naughty Springtime Cuckoo." She'd give in, put down her sewing, and croon away, ever the dulcet soprano. While he'd ad-lib through a routine with an umbrella, a banana and a ball of yarn, his arms spread out and tilting as he leaned and swayed and his big light slippers glided across glowing floorboards.

The Flora Sandwich

You know what Tod means in German? Death.

Maybe Flora knows that, just as she knows I'm on the rebound, even though I never told her. Delaney knew. My sweet, gone Delaney.

Flora keeps glancing away, looking fearful. Makes me nervous. She wasn't that way on the bus down Vermont Ave. Did she think I wouldn't show up? I'm a man of my word, but I don't want to come off as harassing. I order a tuna sandwich and she starts making it. I ask the skinny Korean kid who works there if her name is Flora. The kid won't answer. A Mexican guy, paternal-like, who runs the cash register, gives me the hairy eyeball. He must know what's going on. He and Flora don't say a word. I smile, try to be friendly-like. Flora finishes my sandwich, wraps it to go. I hadn't asked for that. It's her way of telling me to get back into the LA sunshine.

When I walk out — I mean steam out, talking to myself — I hate the city for what it does to people. What it does to me. Hate the walls between light skin and dark. I start thinking maybe Flora has a baby and no husband. Maybe she's in a bad marriage. Maybe while riding the bus she doubted her good looks and flirted with me because she wanted to see if she was still attractive. I'm one of few gringos who live in this part of LA. Probably look like a sucker, like I've been played before.

Window down, riding home with my sandwich, the air clings like a yellow sleaze. I drive as if watching a movie of all the strange Angelinos behind their wheels. When I get to my hole, my cell, my earth-ship, I pass Whiffle's room. I don't know his real name. He told me call him Whiffle. He's the hippie surfer brother I never had, an AA grad with a ponytail who once tried to convert me to Jesus. His latest kick has been the sci-fi fiction of L. Ron Hubbard. I feel like talking to him. I often feel this way when I get back to the boarding house. I knock a few times, get no answer, but that doesn't mean he isn't in.

Whiffle's no stranger to my life story. I think he likes having a place to parcel out his earned wisdom, so I leave my door unlocked. Once in my room, I try to forget Flora. To forget Delaney. I need to move on. I feel consumed by loneliness and the ironing board incident with Delaney. She's blue-eyed, cinnamon-haired, rents in Glendale, originally from Iowa. Like so many others, out here for movies. I'd had too many beers and in a fit of rage knocked over that board and sent a pair of cherished ceramic candlesticks crashing to her wood floor. They'd been a gift from her grandmother. She started ranting, calling me cheap and irresponsible. I argued it was an accident. I'd raised my fist to her, but I'd never brought it down. She'd threatened to call the cops. I talked her out of it. Bolted from Glendale, and then phoned her night after night trying to make amends. I took her to the Bowl for a classical concert, and then a dinner afterwards, but it wasn't the same. She hadn't even kissed me goodnight.

So after keeping to myself a while, questioning my choices and daily m-o, I got back into the mix. When I sat next to Flora on the bus, she started the conversation, not me. I joked with her about how I was wrestling an illusion of self-control back into my life. You know how it is. You have to let off steam somehow, and when I met Flora, I thought it was happening again, that I could be with someone, so I opened up to her.

On the edge of my bed, I drop chin into hands and let my fan blow cruddy air into my face. The landlord still hasn't fixed my AC unit. I feel weak inside, unsure of myself. I remember my car accident — man, when it rains it pours — how that collision set me back, got me to doubting myself in a way I'd never doubted before. Cops yanked my license because I had past fines due. Had to phone my mother in PuertoVallarta and beg her to cover a lawyer's fees so I could get my license back. She sent the money, but did it to spite my old man, who's still in Detroit. If I'd asked my old man, he'd have said suck it up. Next time I phone, just to piss him off, I'll tell him Mom helped me out of a jam.

Hard to live in LA without wheels and a license. I should be happy I have a ride, at all. Whiffle doesn't. He says that LA's public transport gets a bad rap. Can't say I disagree. Living downtown, it makes a difference, puts you in touch with the common folk, the good hard-working girls like Flora.

Mom had wanted to know when I was flying down to see her. Always a room there for me in Mexico. Didn't Flora see what she was missing? We could work at Mom's hotel. My Spanish was already decent. Maybe I'd learn hotel management. It's nice down there. Mexicans are the sweetest people on the planet.

I chew my sandwich, and replay my LA dramas. Is there a screenplay idea in any of them? How out of place and sawed-off

I feel downtown. For a while, I was getting calls to substitute at LA High. I had the most fun teaching city kids mathematics — a language I understand. When I was earning my BS at Wayne State, I learned that its logic would never let me down.

Cannot finish this Flora sandwich. Sapped, dehydrated, I wander to my bureau, open the top drawer and take out my Glock. I'm not sure it's loaded. Only one way to find out.

God, somebody save me. I put the Glock to my temple and stare at myself in the pitted glass of a mirror. Delaney, then Flora, and so many before them — all these women, these dreams driving me mad.

I'm about to squeeze the trigger, finish it all in a blaze of glorious self-pity when Whiffle swings open my door and crows, "Hey, Zen Master Todd, it was unlocked."

Whiffle. He's not a person. He's an experience. In a triple extra-large tie-dye shirt he stands there part kaleidoscope and part Humpty Dumpty fresh off the wall in sandals and over-sized cargo shorts, his legs so skinny they make him look a children's toy.

"Dude, I've done nothing but sleep for the past twenty years. I mean, it's all there. Drones, clones, and safety zones. I'm telling you, man, there's a lot to be said for the paranoia of the 50's sci-fi writers." He sees the Glock. Does a double-take. "Dude, just what are you doing?"

I slip the Glock back in the drawer. Why explain?

With two hands, Whiffle yanks up his shorts. He smells like peanut brittle and sour cream. "Know the feeling," he says. "Hey, I got an idea. Venice Beach. That's what you moved for, isn't it? You want the first-rate pussy we got here, not like in that Missouri hellhole you're from."

"Detroit," I say. "Hockeytown."

"Whatever," he says. "I need a freak-show right now. A little people-watching while I munch a fish taco for breakfast, even though it's dinnertime. Way I see it, that ain't asking too much of *la vida loca*."

He has a point. "But no drinking, and no weed," I say. "That's our deal."

"Betty Crocker, c'mon, you're killing me."

"You'll thank me one day."

"So out with it," he says. "You're playing with guns again. She got a name?"

"Flora."

"I thought Delaney was the one."

I shrug. I don't know a damn thing.

Whiffle sees my sandwich. "Gonna finish that?"

I hand it to him, still in its wrapper. He stuffs it into a deep wide pocket. Then he yanks the car keys out of my hand. "I'll drive. You're dangerous, and I need to feel like I'm in control."

On our way to my car, looking around at all the bars on all the windows, I start laughing. I want to stop, but I can't. The laughter pours out of me in hysterical surges.

Whiffle just smiles and mumbles something about heat, lunacy and hanging around too much indoors.

Wanderer Overlooking The Sea Of Fog

Christmas was a week away when Tillman Grossklag found Claudia Ruden face down in vomit on the floor of her Manhattan apartment. Tillman was the only person Claudia had entrusted with a key.

Tillman removed the emptied Ambien bottle from Claudia's hand. He turned off the CD of Dvorak's *New World Symphony* that was skipping on her stereo. Then he phoned an ambulance.

Five weeks later, he reminded Claudia that if he'd arrived an hour later, her suicide attempt would have succeeded.

"But it didn't," she said.

"So it's fate," he said. "You're supposed to be here."

Claudia said no. She believed in challenges, and free will. Not fate. Tillman said prove it.

"Pay for my ticket to Germany," she countered. "I'm off to Berlin for the film festival. Afterwards, I want to see Hamburg. You've told me so much about it."

"Okay, but no cell phones," said Tillman. "Just you and the city. *My* city. That's challenge enough in winter."

Tillman had work to finish in Manhattan, but he'd screen and inventory Claudia's calls. Claudia could stay in his Hamburg apartment. "Until you lose your need to need," he said.

"So you're my gatekeeper?"

He nodded. "I'll see you in Hamburg in about a month."

***** ******

Hamburg's streetlights cast a roseate sheen over Isestrasse as Claudia walked from the Eppendorfer Baum train station. She had reached a bridge where, like Dvorak in Manhattan, she could watch trains. Outlandish, mercurial, she and Dvorak were alike. She could jump, too, and blame her deathwish on her mother. Poor Mom. The woman had lived in boxes that fitted within each other like Russian nesting dolls.

Better to blame her unhappiness on Elaine for dumping her. Claudia could blame Barbara, as well, who'd run off with Monica to Seattle. Those two had married. Barbara wore flannel shirts and prepared stews. Monica trained security analysts.

At least she'd made it to this year's Berlinale Festival. Charlotte Rampling, whom she adored, had headed its international jury. The year before, a documentary about Moroccan women — one of six Claudia had helped produce during the past twelve years — had earned her pats on the back and polite applause after a Q and A, but nothing more, least of all funding offers for new projects. When she'd left last year's festival, she'd felt empty, neglected, and it had set the tone for the year. She'd had savings to live on frugally, but no forward momentum or a project to believe in.

"It's not where I want to be," she'd told Tillman.

He'd said, "Then it's where you should be."

She'd hoped to feel discovery in Berlin, where alone in tiny screening rooms she'd surrendered to bouts of sobbing. Her favorites had been classics from a retrospective called Dream Girls: Film Stars Of The Fifties. Perched in CinemaxX 8, she'd marveled over Crawford in *Johnny Guitar*, a gem she'd once prized on VHS when managing a Kim's Video store. She'd seen Rossellini's *Viaggio In Italia* for the first time — falling in love again with Ingrid Bergman.

Some of the newer films had been incredible, and should have inspired her. They hadn't. She'd felt unrelenting dread. Movie attendance was still plummeting. Few beyond an esoteric circle knew the work of the German genius, Jürgen Böttcher. Earnest, unheralded artists made courageous films all over the globe, yet who saw them? To worsen matters, it was Mozart's 250th birthday, and she disliked Mozart for the same reason she disliked reggae. Too damn optimistic.

Berlin had felt forced, a necessity. Hamburg, on the other hand, was surprising her. Quiet, easy to walk, she'd met the ghost of her great-grandfather Herman, a pediatrician who had hanged himself.

Herman told her: *You're right, Claudia. There is no fate. So risk changing yourself.*

* * * * * * * * * * *

No phones. Winter silence. Recuperation. Her therapist had thought it wise, but she'd warned Claudia that suicidal impulses would return.

Embrace them, said her therapist. *Then walk them off.*

* * * * * * * * * * *

A union lighting tech based in Brooklyn, Tillman had been

raised in the Grindelberg neighborhood of Hamburg. He recharged between pressured show-biz gigs by visiting the flat he owned in his mother's building off narrow Brahmsallee. His was on the fifth floor. Mom's on the eighth. They lived close to Hamburg's Abaton neighborhood and the State University, an area bombed by Americans during the Gomorrah campaign of World War II.

Saying goodbye at JFK airport, Till had given Claudia a daybook. Inside it, he had paraphrased Nietzsche: *If you have a what-for in life, you can stand almost every why.*

Under Hitler, Till's Mom had lost all her remaining family. Till meant something darkly unique whenever he remarked, "It's just Mom, me, and everyone else."

Claudia wished Tillman had come with her. Wished she could phone him. She glanced behind her. Followed? No. This was her habitual Manhattan paranoia. She told herself she didn't need Tillman. Didn't need a cigarette, either. Still, she lit one up.

In her wool cap, shoulders bunched, she watched her breath. At 41, she was nearly halfway to the end, older than her mother when she'd died. Weak arteries: another Ruden curse. Her father died at sixty. Ruden men had been mariners and doctors. The women: teachers.

Why fear death in a city with a nightclub like Fabrik, where Oma Hans was on the bill? Where a blues club featured Alvin Lee, and Mitch Ryder — both all but forgotten in the States. She liked thinking that Germans revered old-school rock music more than Americans did.

No need to phone Till. She could be more than another lonely itinerant without innocence on her breath. She had ghosts. She had bridges. She had trains to watch.

* * * * *   * * * * * *

How she rode those city trains. Per her therapist's suggestion, she kept a journal, using the daybook Tillman had given her. On the U1 line, the white cars with TV monitors and pink and lavender upholstery reminded her of Hong Kong trains. German trains seldom ran late. Announced clearly, each stop was shown on monitors. She liked best the striated aluminum trains with red doors headed for places with names like Bambek.

She wrote: *Covered in flames I make my way from the prisons of mind through chambers and tunnels into quiet places I deny as home. What's the point? I don't know. Who does?*

She wrote a description of the stone steeple tower of the Haupt-Banhof with its lit clock and tower that resembled a smaller version of the lighthouse she'd seen on the harbor. These places had survived American bombs, but much around them — from the Saturn dealership to the Karstadt department store to the Budnikowsky shop — appeared shockingly new.

She bought herself two pairs of leotards at Fitness Company. In such wet cold, she'd wear one pair to bed, and the other beneath slacks or jeans. She hadn't packed well.

Loitering in one neighborhood, she watched Turkish cab drivers seated at the wheels of Mercedes Benzes and yellow mini-vans. One night, she walked past a Renault dealership and saw slides projected in a timed rotation against a building next door. She liked the different bicycles, especially the *Prince* models. Discovery — perhaps an overrated objective — could bring satisfaction. Learning that one city region was named Bezirksamt Eimsbüttel, she thought it was Turkish. She was wrong. She liked being wrong, just as she liked dressing in layers.

She splurged on sweaters at a clothing store, Wormland, on the Alster shopping mall. She bought fur-lined leather gloves. She watched new Metronom double-decker trains. She spotted one train, the Berlin Warsaw line that she'd seen for the first time in Berlin's ZooBanhof. She found new bridges. She lingered when crossing them.

At night, she chain-smoked, read novels, and scribbled in her journal while steadily downing a cheap bottle of Riesling. On more than one drunken afternoon, she wobbled through the Deichtorhallen to view contemporary photography, or else the Kunsthalle with its famous collection of oils by Runge, and her discovery: Caspar David Friedrich's *Wanderer Overlooking The Sea Of Fog*. The loneliness in Friedrich's masterpiece held her in thrall, capturing both what she was, and couldn't be. Lost, wanting, gently heroic. Not tragic or dramatic but poignant. She bought a postcard of the painting and taped it inside her journal.

Along with art and train stations there was the TOB bus depot, a modern structure of curvilinear silver tubes and lightly tinted glass sheets. One day, she saw the ghost of her father there — white-haired in a gray scarf and matching flat cap. He rode a kid-sized bicycle with pannier bags.

Roter steher: red light signal. *Grüner geher*: green. She devoured Tillman's books in English on film and German literature, learning that Brecht loved American detective novels and penned Fritz Lang's *Hangmen Also Die*. But Brecht meant Berlin. Claudia wanted Hamburg — eighth largest world port, allegedly home to more bridges than Venice. City of Brahms, canals, and BMWs speeding down cobblestone lanes. During the war, 80 percent of it was destroyed.

One morning a bicycle zipped by, grazing her leg. Lunging out of the way, she cursed until she realized she'd been walking in the bike lane. Steeling her nerve, she expected the cyclist to curse back at her. There was no such commentary.

It seemed the Germans of Hamburg walked and biked, but few appeared to be going anywhere. Claudia reveled in their aura of restraint — many were out to take the air, their destination irrelevant. Small groups mingled, waiting for lights to change. She never saw them jaywalk, and they often used a word that sounded like *tooz*. It had various levels of meaning as a way to show respect in public.

Claudia smoked where she pleased, bought coffee where she could drink from a ceramic mug to *remember* how her coffee tasted. She couldn't find peanut butter anywhere. On Sundays, the quiet was so complete it disarmed her; she found herself looking for people and commotion.

On weekdays, she visited the same bridge near the Eppendorfer Baum station, where she watched a woman panhandle for her cat and dog. Each pet sat in a box on the sidewalk. Attentive, disciplined, they looked as if trained to appear hungry. The woman held a sign that explained her plight. Euros fell into her basket on the ground.

At a different time of day, but on the same bridge, Claudia passed an old man cranking an organ grinder. She dropped a Euro into his cup. The man didn't even look at her.

Another old man panhandled in a comical way; he beamed at commuters, not daring to offend, and his smile revealed traces of lunacy. Some handed him a coin as if he were a friend. Amiable, grateful, a fixture, he appeared to get by. He lacked the menace Claudia had seen in Manhattan panhandlers: their broken bodies camped on a sidewalk, their toothless faces leering.

How clearly from a distance she saw the native trappings that had formed her.

* * * * *   * * * * * *

February would end. Claudia felt it. Sidewalks gleamed with snow pushed by volatile winds. Warmth meant everything, and so did trash receptacles. The white streets gleamed, spotless. The winds didn't blow any trash. They carved ripples in puddles where ice had thawed.

The torpor of deep winter was passing into suggestions of change. Even at night she saw a growing brightness in the sky. She felt this brightness in glimmers of resurgence that stirred within her limbs. With each day, she walked a little further from Tillman's apartment.

* * * * *   * * * * * *

On her way to Innocentia Park, she said hello in English to a Philippine woman pushing two state-of-the-art baby strollers that smacked of Park Avenue West. Bundled against cold, a milky-faced child sat in each one, but it was the Philippine servant woman that held Claudia's attention. Had she torn up her roots to work so far from home? No doubt, she had a story that needed telling.

The woman thought Claudia was English, maybe Australian. Flattered, Claudia told her New Zealand. Why be associated with those Yank tourists in Berlin at Checkpoint Charlie?

I know this woman. She nurtures hope in the wealthy children who will manage Germany's future. Who knows the darkness she faces, and the ghosts and heartbreak she has left behind? Who tells her story?

I do, thought Claudia. *The pain in her eyes shames me.*

* * * * *   * * * * * *

Hamburg *Sparkasse*: the word of a bank. *Reisburo* for travel agency. *Geldautomat* for ATM. Her allotted funds were running low, but she wasn't ready to return. She'd wait for Tillman. She'd keep herself busier, especially at night. Classical music was everywhere, with first-class concerts from the likes of Ian Bostridge, and Helene Grimaud. She chose an inexpensive concert at the St. Nikolai Cathedral, where she heard the Hamburg Camerata perform as part of an ongoing celebration of Mozart advertised on kiosk billboards as *Mensch!* She was grateful the program featured only one Mozart piece. The Bach went down like honey.

After the concert, she admired the tarnished copper of St Nikolai's green steeple. A new church, not a feature for tourists, it blended with the modesty of the park and its call to safety. She returned the following day, a Sunday, and found the park full of children.

Hearing their cries, she felt herself glowing inside.

* * * * * * * * * * *

Off she wandered at night, all senses primed and ready, getting lost, absorbing. Still, the bridges called to her. She went to them. She discovered another church, a small one. A clock in its steeple faced the street. Below the clock, and above a small narrow brick door, was the date: 1751. She studied it from a bridge in Haynes Park.

In another direction, down the river beyond the boathouse, lay a series of small arched bridges. Along the riverbank stood copses of naked birches, their branches black against silver air. Weeping willows fronds hung close to the river, brushing its surface, reminding her of Shakespeare's Ophelia.

Ghost Herman asked: *Why not drown?*

Lines of poplars planted as windbreaks ran between townhouses set back off the river. The steeple rose from the horizon but didn't pierce it.

Old steeple, old country and sky.
Old Claudia.

* * * * * * * * * * *

Snow started to melt as the temperature climbed a few degrees above freezing. The sidewalks were swept by men in orange jumpsuits. Using leaf blowers, three at a time they moved through residential neighborhoods.

Claudia walked Eppendorfer Strasse overwhelmed by echoes from the dead. Had she changed? She wanted to know why, this time, the dead annoyed her. She rested in a Turkish *Imbiss*, sipping coffee. With each puff on her cigarette, she felt thinner. *Why bother with suicide? Why not vanish and never return?*

She looked out the *Imbiss* window down a curving avenue with buildings on both sides at the same height. Red tiles covered many roofs. She hadn't expected this. The tiles seemed right for Florence, but reminded her how little she knew the city. Each day had brought new architectural treats. From steeply pitched narrow chalet fronts, to glass cube offices. She'd seen the gold memorial bricks mortared into sidewalks in front of houses where Jews had lived. Names, dates and professions of family members were etched into each brick with the date the house was blown up. In many cases, elegant houses had been built in their place.

In other holes in the city, she'd seen Bauhaus monstrosities erected next to fast food joints as if to say, sure, fire bombs had once wreaked havoc, but those days had passed. She thought these architectural vulgarities spoke a 21st century Esperanto that proved parts of the world were the same everywhere — a variation on a whore's greed.

The flow of the buildings, as Claudia followed them down the avenue, reminded her of Regent Street in London. Yes, she'd been places, but to what end? What scared her was the sudden gravity she felt. She saw the avenue in flames. She heard the whistling of bombs. Heavy furniture crashed through windows. Diesel fumes fouled the air. Massive plumes of smoke concealed ravaged faces.

Not long ago, this was rubble. She told herself to sink in. To play her miniscule part. She had time enough for ghosts. Let them feed her.

* * * * *   * * * * * *

Tillman's living room featured a window that opened like a door to a balcony. Too cold for that balcony, so she ate standing up in the kitchen. She stared at three identical buildings of the Grindelberg neighborhood complex, all of them dotted with chinks of light. Paths ran between them lit by big round lamps. By day, bikes were ridden there, and mothers pushed strollers. At night, with high winds, there was a closed-in feeling.

Dangerous or not, Claudia needed to walk. Otherwise, she'd get drunk again and pass out. After eating, she put on her hat, coat and gloves and found her Manhattan stride. Alert, bold, unwilling to stop, she belched up fumes of the prosecco, camembert and sunflower bread she'd bought earlier in the Aldi supermarket. When she reached the Grindelberg Cinema, she read the marquee: *Get Rich Or Die Tryin'*.

She paused a moment. The mainstream American message had never been subtle. So what? She was thinking movies again, and enjoying it. She could smoke and drink in the lobby, take a beer inside and place it in a holder of her arm rest. At this cinema, American movies were screened without subtitles. Many Germans grasped

English, and some spoke it better than Americans. Tillman was a perfect example.

As a woman over 40 in the show biz dance, was she a dinosaur? Was all of her angst about her *aging*? Was she really that banal?

Perhaps so.

Her insignificance was humbling, but she had to remember that the *choices* in the movie biz were made behind the scenes. She had to love something bigger than herself. She'd loved film since a ten-year-old, when Dad had given her his old video camera. She could remember how that camera smelled when it heated up. The weight of it in her hand.

In it for the long haul — a frigid trip, indeed. If there were compensations, she had to find them. Ghost Herman remarked: *You're a dreamer, Little One.*

✳ ✳ ✳ ✳ ✳   ✳ ✳ ✳ ✳ ✳ ✳

Wind blew in off the harbor and Claudia listened as it raced into gaps between buildings. The shine of the air, so opalescent, reminded her of sheared coal. It gleamed in snow-crusted walkways that wormed bluish and crystalline between Grindelberg's high narrow block buildings. Built of prefab concrete and without flair, they were home to small dramas lived behind curtained windows. She'd seen such windows all over the world. A few were still lit, perhaps still hopeful. Most were dark, with sleep as a blessing.

The complex was a government project carried out by British soldiers and funded by American money. It had been built for British officers, but according to Tillman the Brits hadn't stayed. They'd had their own country to rebuild. Where had she read that Brits lost 85 percent of one generation in that war?

Why wade in the past? What of the Padaung women of Myanmar, their elongated necks trapped within stacked rings, unable to flee to Thailand? What of the 10-year-old girls working 14-hour days without breaks in the sweatshops of Shenzhen, China? She'd visited Shenzhen. She'd seen those sweatshops.

It hurt to be informed, and to care. It didn't hurt to jump off a bridge.

You're a fool, said Herman.

At least she was starting to know it.

***** ******

Hers were cautious steps over black ice pooled in walkways between the block buildings of Grindelberg. Across the city in the Reepersbaum, night meant a carnal splurge for the young that would make Fassbinder smile. Not here, where angels wheezed through nightmares on sullen mattresses, and a blunt dawn came early with the seagulls. Here, Tillman's Mom lived with memories of her husband, killed in a U-Boat during Black May.

Tillman had said that Mom kept in a box the handful of photos, receipts and postcards that weren't destroyed. Claudia had never seen this box. She didn't want to. Every photo and hand-written card would only remind her that all wars remained an abomination. Still, she hoped Tillman's Mom guarded that box under the rafters of what defined her buried life. Claudia felt comfortable hoping this, because she kept her own box and thought it a morgue and a jewel. More than a reminder of who she'd been, it was a country to visit, and to flee from.

Once a traveler, always.

It was a bridge.

* * * * *　* * * * * *

How narrow the elevator in Tillman's building. Shaped like a domino, higher than wide, a box within a box, three big bodies would make the ride uncomfortable. So she didn't take that elevator. She seized the stairs two at a time, huffing into a smoker's cough.

* * * * *　* * * * * *

In a flat wool cap worn backwards, Claudia looked like a newsboy out of the 1940s as she loitered under the I-beams of Hamburg's U-Bahn railway between Dartmoor and Eppendorfer Baum. Every Tuesday and Friday, there was an outdoor market at this location, rain or shine. Market vendors had arrived at dawn to sell fruit, cheeses, herbs, fish and meat. The BMWs and Volkswagens usually parked under the railway had to be moved to make room for semi-trailers, vans, compact pick-ups and diner wagons lined up end to end up along both sides of the paved walkway under the U-Bahn tracks.

The food on display opened Claudia's eyes, and so did the cars that had been forced from their usual spaces. Here were Land Rovers and Porsches. In this neck of Hamburg it appeared Germans were living well.

She bumped along behind a middle-aged couple. The man wore leather shoes and a camel hair coat. His wife wore a fur with a cashmere scarf. They shopped as if they had nothing but time. Claudia envied the gravitas in the way the older man moved, his arms locked behind his back. In Manhattan, he'd get bowled over. Not here, where one could enjoy the smell of oranges so radiant in their neatly stacked pyramids. Their color was a comfort in the cold.

Fumes from fragrant pastries teased Claudia's appetite. Here, she could learn to eat again. Eating would help her sink in rather than vanish. Slabs of roseate fish fillets gleamed under portable lamps. Coiled links of sausage proved with their crimson skin that they were freshly ground. A sudden dose from an exotic cheese blended into the aromatic mix lingering in gelid air. It seized Claudia, dazzled her, and she felt invigorated. This, the European way — out in the open and without alacrity — allowed quality to take precedence.

A train rolled by overhead, and for a moment Claudia went joyfully deaf. Lips moved and gloved hands gestured. It was a Lillian Gish silent. Soon, the action would shift to a station. A train in black and white, shadowy and promising, would steam into the frame.

That era had passed, and so had the train. Claudia caught herself smiling and wondered if this was happiness. Market banter expanded around her. Aromas lingered as vendors measured grams over their scales. One old gent tipped his hat to an acquaintance. He sampled cheese conspicuously, in a mannered way. Claudia didn't see lumpy backs or cheeks with boils, or broken teeth. There were Turks, most of them seated in cabs. The shoppers looked fit, well-preserved, as much on display as the food.

She liked such a market for its pace and civility. The women vendors wore crisp aprons. Their hair bright blonde, eyes blue as cobalt. The men durable and tested in their bloodied aprons, their square-tipped fingers around big cleavers as they hacked at chunks of meat. This was a slice of Hamburg, and she revered how it moved — far too slowly to be American.

When had she last *wanted* to eat? But she wouldn't buy groceries here. She'd keep to her budget at the Aldi market in her neighborhood along Grindelallee. Everything was cheaper there. A less polished clientele crowded the place each Saturday morning, and she suspected most of them didn't care if their vinegar had been made from organic sherry.

Ironic, on the other hand, to think that without globalization and the EU, the Aldi market chain wouldn't have been possible. According to Tillman, two Italians had founded it. No one seemed to mind. Economics 101: affordable groceries won hearts and minds around the globe.

She was hungry, and thinking of food as more than necessity. Indeed, change had come.

* * * * *   * * * * * *

Tillman returned. If only, thought Claudia, to read the clockwork of his mind. He stood a few inches over six feet. Broad-shouldered, with a raw meatiness to his face, his ears stuck out in a charmingly impish way. He was half bruiser, half cherub. All there.

Claudia beamed upon their meeting, but no smile came from Tillman in return. No hug, no handshake. In the kitchen, he remained stoical, white-haired, his feet evenly apart, and he looked down on Claudia with skeptical slate-blue eyes. He had been all over: from Bali, to Thailand, and India. His favorite American city — and he'd seen many — remained San Antonio.

They were both travelers, thought Claudia. Brother and sister in some ways. She could tell him anything. It got bad when her Mom died, and Tillman had been there to listen, and to recommend a therapist.

Tillman had also chosen her as the one to share his early struggles with alcoholism, and his homosexuality. After AA, he'd begun reading Krishnamurti and practicing meditation. Written on scraps of paper tacked all over his Brooklyn apartment was the maxim: *All people suffer deeply.*

Tillman remarked, "When you get back, you will find your phone and a list of calls on the table. One of the calls I answered. It was from Juniper Resnick."

Claudia's face went flush. Her eyes bloomed. "Seriously?"

Tillman nodded. "She wants another meeting about the Myanmar project."

With a shriek, Claudia lunged for Tillman and hugged him. "We have to celebrate."

Tillman, ever phlegmatic, pulled himself away. "She thinks Susan Sarandon might come aboard if you let Tim Robbins narrate. She also said she hopes you like Hamburg."

"I'll always like Hamburg," said Claudia. "I really got to see it."

"It's fate," said Tillman.

"No," said Claudia. "I went after it. Look what happened?"

"What?" asked Tillman. "Tell me."

She said, "Don't I look hungry? I could eat a horse."

They didn't share a meal. Tillman, exhausted, needed time with his mother. He'd turn in early. Could Claudia wait until tomorrow?

She smacked a big kiss on his cheek. "I've waited this long. What's another night?"

* * * * *   * * * * * *

Tillman raised a glass of sparkling water, toasting travelers of the world, warm nights, cold lovers, and dreams of seahorses. Claudia raised her wine and toasted skipping gym class, and Daniela Vinge, her first crush.

Tillman stared at Claudia. He looked worried.

"I'm okay," said Claudia. "It's made a difference."

"I know it isn't easy," said Tillman.

Claudia, comfortable as philosopher in Tillman's presence, said the search for a home drove all lost souls and made her prone to self-pity just like any sojourner. She'd wanted less to die than to die publicly. That was why she was so thin. Someone had to see her wasting away.

Feeling herself letting go, Claudia laughed as she ordered another glass of wine. Tillman leaned over the table and told her that one paid and lost, and paid again. All were, to some degree, failures.

"Nothing is fixed," he said. "Travel is our natural state."

"How do you survive?" asked Claudia.

"I care about others more than I care about myself," he said. "And I do something about it."

***** ******

She had him to thank for being alive. She didn't want to leave — not Tillman, Hamburg, or her dark winter nights alone — they all meant something profound. She had her suitcase shaped like a box, but it was empty. She was leaving everything behind. She planned to return at least once a year. She had to walk those bridges in summer.

She'd made her first phone call. A therapist appointment for the day after her arrival.

Snow fell in fine pellets, not quite rain, swept along by uneven sea breezes. She heard seagulls, but she couldn't see them. Hunger pangs erupted as she walked past a Turkish-run eatery with squares of lasagna in its window.

She paused to envy one last time the hardiness of cyclists who pedaled in the proper lane. An earthen smell startled and comforted her, along with the sight of tulips, gladiolas, and other tall annuals put out for sale on the street in front of a shop. She saw hand tools, gloves, tin and copper planting boxes meant to hold flowers in place.

Spring would come to burst them open. Spring was a form of home. She wanted to share this thought with Tillman. With the world. But how? She'd have to produce another film. It was the best way she knew. It was why she'd survived.

They spent their last night at the Birdland jazz club on Gartnerstrasse 122 and listened to the Boris Netsvetaev Trio. With each pause in the music, whether disjointed or cerebral, Claudia felt pieces of herself expanding inside her body. She couldn't say she'd be able to use those pieces or even reassemble them. She could say she hungered now, and welcomed time pressure, neurosis, and talk for the sake of talking — as if she'd never seen a therapist in her life.

Her story, like many others, was one of motion, after all.

Fomite

A fomite is a medium capable of transmitting infectious organisms from one individual to another.

"The activity of art is based on the capacity of people to be infected by the feelings of others." Tolstoy, *What Is Art?*

Writing a review on Amazon, Good Reads, Shelfari, Library Thing or other social media sites for readers will help the progress of independent publishing. To submit a review, go to the book page on any of the sites and follow the links for reviews. Books from independent presses rely on reader to reader communications.

For more information or to order any of our books, visit
http://www.fomitepress.com/FOMITE/Our_Books.html

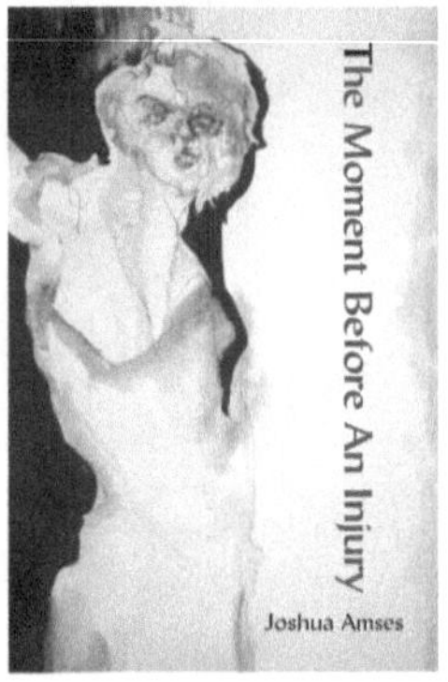

The Moment Before an Injury
Joshua Amses

Nothing Beside Remains
Jaysinh Birjépatil

*The Way None
of This Happened*
Mike Breiner

Victor Rand
David Brizer

*Summer on the
Cold War Planet*
Paula Closson Buck

Cycling in Plato's Cave
David Cavanagh

Fomite

Picking Up the Bodies
James F. Connolly

Unfinished Stories of Girls
Catherine Zobal Dent

Drawing on Life
Mason Drukman

Foreign Tales of Exemplum and Woe
J. C. Ellefson

Free Fall/Caída libre
Tina Escaja

Sinfonia Bulgarica
Zdravka Evtimova

Derail This Train Wreck
Daniel Forbes

Where There Are Two or More
Elizabeth Genovise

The Hundred Yard Dash Man
Barry Goldensohn

Fomite

*When You Remember
Deir Yassin*
R. L. Green

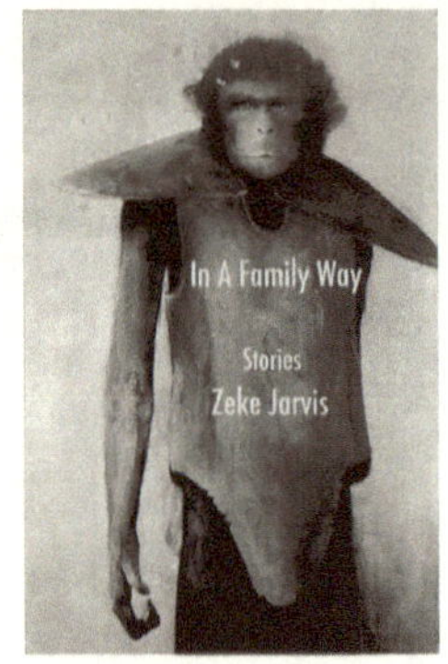

In A Family Way
Zeke Jarvis

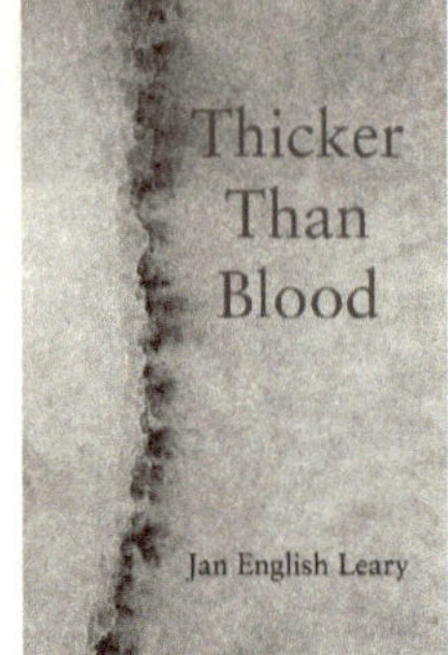

Thicker Than Blood
Jan English Leary

*A Guide
to the Western Slopes*
Roger Lebovitz

Confessions of a Carnivore
Diane Lefer

Museum of the Americas
Gary Lee Miller

My Father's Keeper
Andrew Potok

*The Hole That Runs
Through Utopia*
Joseph D. Reich

Companion Plants
Kathryn Roberts

Fomite

Rafi's World
Fred Russell

*My Murder
and Other Local News*
David Schein

Bread & Sentences
Peter Schumann

Principles of Navigation
Lynn Sloan

Among Angelic Orders
Susan Thoma

Everyone Lives Here
Sharon Webster

The Falkland Quartet
Tony Whedon

*The Return of
Jason Green*
Suzi Wizowaty

*The Inconveniece
of the Wings*
Silas Dent Zobal

Fomite

More Titles from Fomite...

Joshua Amses — *Raven or Crow*

Joshua Amses — *The Moment Before an Injury*

Jaysinh Birjepatil — *The Good Muslim of Jackson Heights*

Antonello Borra — *Alfabestiario*

Antonello Borra — *AlphaBetaBestiario*

Jay Boyer — *Flight*

Dan Chodorkoff — *Loisada*

Michael Cocchiarale — *Still Time*

Greg Delanty — *Loosestrife*

Zdravka Evtimova — *Carts and Other Stories*

Anna Faktorovich — *Improvisational Arguments*

Derek Furr — *Suite for Three Voices*

Stephen Goldberg — *Screwed*

Barry Goldensohn — *The Listener Aspires to the Condition of Music*

Greg Guma — *Dons of Time*

Andrei Guruianu — *Body of Work*

Ron Jacobs — *The Co-Conspirator's Tale*

Ron Jacobs — *Short Order Frame Up*

Ron Jacobs — *All the Sinners Saints*

Kate MaGill — *Roadworthy Creature, Roadworthy Craft*

Ilan Mochari — *Zinsky the Obscure*

Jennifer Moses — *Visiting Hours*

Sherry Olson — *Four-Way Stop*

Janice Miller Potter — *Meanwell*

Jack Pulaski — *Love's Labours*

Charles Rafferty — *Saturday Night at Magellan's*

Fomite